HIDDEN BY THE LEAVES

HIDDEN BY THE LEAVES

BOOK ONE OF THE HIDDEN TRILOGY

S D L CURRY

The Book Guild Ltd

First published in Great Britain in 2016 by
The Book Guild Ltd
9 Priory Business Park
Wistow Road, Kibworth
Leicestershire, LE8 0RX
Freephone: 0800 999 2982
www.bookguild.co.uk
Email: info@bookguild.co.uk
Twitter: @bookguild

All scripture quotes are taken from the Authorized
King James Version (KJV) of the Bible.
Used by permission. Public domain.

Maps used with permission from the Hubbard collection – London

This work is entirely fictitious and bears no resemblance to any persons living or dead.

Typeset in Aldine401 BT

Printed and bound in the UK by TJ International, Padstow, Cornwall

ISBN 978 1911320 173

British Library Cataloguing in Publication Data.
A catalogue record for this book is available from the British Library.

Between the years 1614 and 1643, nearly 5,000 Christian martyrs were executed under the rule of Japan's shogun and his regime.

At the broadest level, this book and the entire Hidden Trilogy are dedicated to all the courageous martyrs and missionaries of Japan, then and now.

On a more personal level, I would like to dedicate this book to the loving memory of Kimberley Ann Wilshire, who set me on a path of self-discovery and re-awakening.

Acknowledgments

In completing this novel, I would like to thank my entire family and circle of friends, who supported me on this long journey of bringing this story to life.

In particular, I would like to thank my father, David; my mother, Heather; my sister, Kristjana; and my grandmother Delores for their tireless support and for being the great listeners they are.

I would also like to extend a special thank you to Yana and Kristine for their inspiration, patience, and support in bringing this endeavor to fruition.

On the editorial side, I would like to thank my editors, Jerry, Jennifer, and Kathi, whose expertise, skill, and mentorship were vital in bringing this project to completion.

On the research side, I am extremely grateful to all the scholars, academics and historians whose work contributed to this story. Assisting with my research, I would like to thank the British Library in London and the New York Public Library, whose archives were invaluable and staff most helpful.

I would also like to express my gratitude to the Church, of all faiths, including Hillsong in London and New York for additional inspiration along with members of the Society of Jesus, who shared their research, insights and time with me.

Further acknowledgments must also be given to the 26 Martyrs Museum in Nagasaki, Japan, whose staff was most accommodating. Finally, I would like thank Jelena and my newborn son, Xavier, whose ongoing support has meant the world to me.

In sum, without all of you, this story would not have been possible, and for this, I am greatly indebted.

Foreword

Hidden by the Leaves was inspired by real history and real characters in history, including the Shogun of Japan and other members of his regime. Amongst others, these included his cabinet members, the Daimyo ("Warlord") of Arima, and the Governor and Deputy-Lieutenant of Nagasaki.

Not least, however, was this novel inspired by the real heroes of history, who are just, including all the brave missionaries of the Society along with their faithful converts.

As a forewarning, several chapters in this novel may be disturbing to some readers, including scenes of graphic torture and abuse.

For some readers, the brutality of these chapters may be too much to bear, or imagine, and as such, I recommend the more sensitive reader skip over them and move on to the next chapter— it will not inhibit your understanding of the story. Nor should these readers forget—there is light at the end of the tunnel.

For other readers, however, who wish to know the discomforting truth, these scenes and chapters are included because they are an accurate depiction of history—however brutal and horrific they may seem.

Remaining true to events of the past, I ask myself: Who am I to soften the edges of history to create a more pleasing story?

S D L

國鮮朝

釜山海
COREA.

TSUSIMA

IKI

NAGATO.
SOEWO.

IWAMI. IDSOEMO. FOKI
INBA
MIMA-
SACKA.
ARIN. I. P
BINGO. BITSIO. FARR
BISEEN

TSUCKU SEEN
PISEEN
BOESEEN

KIO E

TSUCKINGO. BOENGO

AMAXA.

MODERIO

SANNOKI

SIKOKF.

AWA.

FIGO.

TOSSA.

S I O E.

FIOF
GA.

SATSUMA
OSIMA
MI

M A R I S

LIQUEO.

VIRO PERII
JOHANNI PAVL
ABBATI S.Q
Potentiſſimo Gal
a conſiliis ſa
Academiarum
quibus cura ſcie
inſcriptionum
praeſi
literaturae Sinic
uti bonarum artium
omnium promo
hanc imperii Jaṕ
ſacram
RIANVS R

Te regina maris, quia prima citatos
Conſpicis a rubro purpurei Solis equos.
&c his triennas late diffuſa per oras.

Milliaria Germanica Communia

Particulam hunc quae ſinum exhibet: deſcriptus ex inedita magna quae penes me eſt in qua murorum aliquot populariū...

165   166   167   168   169   170

JEDSO.

NOTOTO.

SIIO.

DEWA.

OSIOE.

VACKASA

CAGA

JETSIOE   JETSIGO.

JETSISEN

FITA

SINANO

COOTSKE

JAPAN.

V I.

MINO

CAAY

SIMOOTS-KE.

FITATS.

OWARRI

Nagoia

MICAWA

TOTOMI

SOEROEGA

SAGAMI

MOESASZ.

Jedo

SMOSA.

ISJIE

CADSA.

IDSOE

SINVE

AWA.

PONICI   PARS

INSVLAE

Nangasacki Urbs

CONSPECTVS
VRBIS
NANGASACKI,
& Insulae ante illam sitae
in qua sedes est
Batavorum.

INSIGNIA GENTILITIA
NOBILIVM
JAPONENSIVM

OLSIOE

PARS.

Milliaria Germanica.

AMSTELODAMI Apud I. OTTENS.

fuerunt, et quicquid est insularum litorumque ab illa usque ad Nangasacki informaverint. Hinc liquet magnas Japonensium non esse adeo accuratas atque illae quae a nostris co... in magna imperii Japonici quod unica regio magnas Japonensium constituerint, quarum una erat praecipua, et hae ipsa quam dasius occupa major per virum ... in Asiatica, et magistro societatis Indicae orientalis, & profusio operae pretium est hoc distincte seu et sexaginta partes vastis illius imperii conspicari, ac vera ... inter se scribuntur, quod deprehendet quisquis hanc conferre cum aliis voluerit.

B. Ruyter Sculp.

Prologue

May 21, 1626
Arima Domain, Hizen Province, Japan

"Shigemasa is coming! Shigemasa is coming!" shouted a panick-stricken farmer into Father Joaquim's quarters.

Onaga birds abruptly ceased their calls and hastily scattered to the skies before the rattle of hardened-leather-and-metal armor and the clomping of hundreds of horses' hooves approaching down a well-worn path at a steady, military-like pace.

Had the village's early warning system—a child strategically situated on the forest's far edge whose waving arms could be seen by another child at the near edge—given the villagers enough notice?

The villagers had just minutes, so they mobilized quickly as they'd done numerous times before. Several lifted floor planks to expose secret spaces, some just large enough to hide forbidden items such as Bibles and crucifixes. Other hiding places had to be big enough to conceal their bigger secrets— foreign Christians, including Catechist Miguel, Catechist Tonia, and Father Joaquim. Already in a concealed room, the father was meticulously cleaning a small basin in which he would conduct a baptism. Alarmed, he quickly put it to the side, lifted up a muddied plank of wood, and hid himself underground. Powerless to do anything more, Father Joaquim closed his eyes, lay quiet, and prayed as fervently as possible that no one would discover them. Such concealment had become necessary when Japanese leaders' hostility toward Christianity had resulted in an official ban of the faith in Japan more than a decade before.

Arima was located in the old province of Hizen, situated on the island of Kyushu, Japan's southernmost island. All the villages in Arima feared Lord Shigemasa, but those in the village to which the *daimyo* and his samurai now rode had a special reason to fear him.

Daimyo Matsukura Shigemasa was a large man with a battle-scarred face. Adorned with a helmet that brandished menacing horn-like ornamentations, he wore traditional battledress armor, painted in his official colors of black and red. His body armor consisted of a metal breastplate lacquered to give a perfectly smooth finish, coupled with multiple layers of protective gear consisting of metal plates.

Having passed the rice paddies and now arrived at the upper edge of the village, Daimyo Shigemasa shouted sternly, "Where is Yamaguchi-san?"

"He is resting, Lord Shigemasa," one of the peasants, out of breath from running to pay homage, replied anxiously.

"Go get him." Shigemasa glared at the peasant bowing before him.

Instantly another peasant, no doubt grateful for the opportunity to escape the cruel lord's anger-filled whims, ran down a narrow path to fetch Master Yamaguchi.

As the nearest peasant raised his head from a humble bow and ventured a glance in Shigemasa's direction, the daimyo roared, "I have heard more reports of Christians hiding in Arima. Are you hiding any of the vermin here?"

"No, Lord Shigemasa; there are none here," another peasant answered. "We are a Buddhist community, Lord."

"So you say." Shigemasa scanned the peasants kneeling before him. "I will have the pleasure of torturing and killing any Christians found on my lands ... including any who aid or hide them."

"Yes, Lord, we understand."

"Do you? We will see." Shigemasa motioned for his samurai to search the village.

Quickly, several scowling, surly samurai dismounted from their horses, pushing villagers out of their way as they approached the dwellings.

In a sign of blatant disrespect, as the samurai entered the peasants' homes, none of them bowed, as was the custom. Worse yet, they plundered the homes ruthlessly as they overturned everything in sight.

Unable to find anything to validate the daimyo's suspicions, after sustained searching and ransacking, the samurai next converged on the village's Buddhist temple, where they scrutinized various Buddhist items of worship but again found no evidence of Christian observance. The lead samurai finally returned and bowed toward Daimyo Shigemasa, shaking his head to signal their failure at finding anything to substantiate his suspicions.

"As I mentioned, Lord Shigemasa," the nearest peasant ventured to speak again, not daring to look the daimyo in the eyes, "there are no Christians in this valley."

Aggravated, Daimyo Shigemasa glared menacingly at the villagers who stood before him. His silent gaze was interrupted by Master Yamaguchi's arrival on the scene.

"Lord Shigemasa, we are pleased to have you join us. Welcome," Master Yamaguchi said.

"You can dispense with the pleasantries, Yamaguchi-san," Daimyo Shigemasa sneered coldly. "I am here for your taxes."

"But Lord Shigemasa, we paid our taxes two weeks ago ... *and* on time," Master Yamaguchi responded confidently. "I believe our small community is the most reliable in all your lands."

"Your community *is* reliable, Yamaguchi-san—perhaps too reliable," the daimyo replied. "If you can pay your taxes so easily, I must not be charging you enough." He turned to look at the rice paddies, empty now of workers. "If the lot of you can be in your huts when I come down the mountain and not working in the fields, then I have been too lenient with you. Beginning today, I am doubling your taxes."

"But Lord Shigemasa, our community already pays more taxes than most! We cannot do it!" one of the peasants cried out in anguish.

"The next villager—man, woman, or child—who questions me will lose his tongue." Shigemasa slowly turned his head, assuring himself that his edict had been heard and understood.

"In one month I will return to collect your outstanding amount." Daimyo Shigemasa set his gaze onto the surrounding rice fields with a grin on his face, then continued. "Rice or a cash payment of five hundred silver coins. You may choose how to pay."

"May I speak, Lord?" Master Yamaguchi looked pleadingly at Shigemasa.

"What is it?"

"What if we need more time?"

Shigemasa scanned the villagers and placed his gaze, for a brief moment on each woman and child in the settlement before replying with volume sufficient to be heard by all. "If you fail to pay within one month, we will take all your women and children as hostages."

Master Yamaguchi heard a low gasp as parents throughout the village held, or moved closer to, their children.

Gesturing with his hand, the daimyo motioned for his samurai to prepare to depart. "Before I take leave," the daimyo added, first looking at Master Yamaguchi and then turning to focus on the villagers who appeared the weakest, "there is one other way for you to pay your taxes."

"What, Lord?" a villager cried out. "What other way?"

"Find Christians who are hiding and inform me of their whereabouts."

"But we are Buddhists, Lord. We do not know any Christians."

"Then let me motivate you," the daimyo replied. "Rewards for information leading to their capture are 300 silver coins for priests, 200 coins for brothers, and 100 coins for any other vile Christian!"

Daimyo Shigemasa turned his horse to face the mountains as his band of samurai attended to their mounts. "You would all be wise to help us root out any hidden Christians in Arima—and not *just* for the money."

"What do you mean, Lord," Master Yamaguchi asked.

"There are developments in the regime. The shogun has confirmed his appointment of Mizuno Kawachi as the new governor of Nagasaki. His first task will be to exterminate all Christian dogs from these lands. He arrives in June."

"We will cooperate in any way we can, Lord."

"See that you do," the daimyo answered sternly. "I can assure you that both the new governor and I will hunt down every last hidden Christian and annihilate them—all of them!"

No one dared reply.

As he turned his back on the village and signaled his flag-bearers up the mountain, the daimyo called out, "Have your taxes ready for me in one month."

One

For Confidential delivery to Father Andre Palmeiro
Visitor of Jesuit Province of Japan and Vice-Province of China
Mission of the Society of Jesus, Macao, China

May 22, 1626

Dear Father Andre,

I pray my letter arrives to you safely and finds you well.

  Please accept my first letter to you in your new role as Visitor of the Jesuit Province of Japan and Vice-Province of China. I am delighted to learn of your appointment, and am further encouraged that our Paternity in Rome remains responsive to our rapidly changing circumstances in the Japans and the Far East.

  As you are new to your role, I may now write more than is necessary, but because communication is all but shut off between Macao and Japan, I feel inclined to tell you all that I can.

  As I am sure you are aware, the Mission in Japan has become extremely dangerous as of late. Darkness has overshadowed our Society, as hundreds of Fathers, Brothers, and Catechists have been executed over the last few years. Without question, it is the most hostile environment I have ever witnessed for our Society since my arrival in Japan nearly twenty-five years ago.

1

Since Tokugawa Iemitsu became the third shogun of Japan in 1623, the number and severity of Christian persecutions and tortures have increased dramatically. Shogun Iemitsu is the most oppressive leader our Society has ever had to contend with, and we are in constant hiding from a militarized regime determined to exterminate us and all things foreign. The shogun feels his authority threatened by our teachings and the Word of God.

In Japanese society, the upper classes pay him homage, but many in the lower classes disobey him, a development the shogun finds inconceivable. He suspects that somehow the peasants are being seduced and supported by a foreign power. Regretably, he believes the Society is the channel for that foreign power—a suspicion that has led to our persecution and torture. As a result, I believe circumstances will only get worse for us before they get better.

On the southern island of Kyushu, our Mission has become even more perilous. Earlier this year, we heard news that Shogun Iemitsu appointed Mizuno Kawachi as the new governor of Nagasaki, to replace Hasegawa Gonroku, effective in June. And, while Gonroku routinely turned a blind eye to our movements and activities wherever possible, we understand the new governor's resolve is to the contrary. Under the express orders of the shogun, Kawachi has resolved to stamp out Christianity by all means necessary.

Thus, for the first time since the anti-Christian edicts of 1614, the shogun will now have one of his own appointed militants in Nagasaki. Regrettably, this adverse development is likely to spell extreme persecution for all Christians on the island of Kyushu, which includes the city of Nagasaki (our largest Christian foothold) and our neighboring community in Arima.

Following months of careful consideration, I will be coordinating an exodus of Christians from Arima to Yezo in the north, where, I understand, Christians can live our faith more freely and in less constant danger of death and persecution.

I, on the other hand, will return and stand steadfast where I am and act as anchor for our Mission and our Society in both Nagasaki *and the Arima domain. Rest assured, however, not in the least shall I abandon any Christian in these parts of Japan while I am alive. As always, I believe we will weather this storm like the great many storms our Society has withstood in the past. For, in the end, I know God will be with us, and His Word will take foundation in Japan. Through prayer, I also know that a great number of baptisms will take place, and a great number of souls will be saved. Yea, in the end, I believe the great Light of our Lord and Father Almighty will shine through the clouds, and the darkness hovering over Japan will yield to the Light.*

Now more than ever, I place all my trust in our Lord and Father.

Your most loving servant,
Father Joaquim Martinez, Society of Jesus

Releasing his pen, Father Joaquim meticulously re-read the letter. After a decisive nod, he folded up the letter, placed it into a camouflaged envelope, and sealed it. Pausing, he then drew a Buddhist insignia on the back of the envelope. *A necessity*, he thought. *Our activities must remain covert—at least for now.*

Startled by three slow knocks on the door, he hesitated for a moment before calling out, "Enter."

Following the sound of furniture being shifted, a creaking sound, and then the movement of some fabric draped from the ceiling, a young Portuguese man, mid-twenties, thin, of moderate height, and dressed in traditional Japanese attire appeared, revealing a secret doorway behind him. While clean, the young man's clothes were old and ragged.

"Catechist Miguel, enter. Good morning."

"Good morning, Father."

After a moment of hesitation, Miguel spoke:

"You wanted to see me, Father?"

"Yes, Miguel. I wanted to let you know I am taking a short trip to Nagasaki tomorrow. I am leaving at sunset."

"Tomorrow evening. That is sudden. Normally we make travel preparations weeks in advance. Can it not wait?"

"No, unfortunately it cannot," Father Joaquim replied. "As soon as possible, I need to visit our good friend Mateus da Costa and post an important letter to Macao."

"What? Why?"

Father Joaquim noted Miguel's look of concern. "You remember Mateus da Costa, do you not?"

"Of course I remember him, Father. He was one of the traders who helped smuggle me into Japan a year ago. What is happening? And why must you leave tomorrow?"

"Daimyo Shigemasa has increased our taxes exorbitantly. The village can neither produce enough rice nor gain enough silver to pay on time. I must seek Mateus' help immediately."

Miguel frowned and sighed.

"Our situation is quickly becoming more precarious."

Father Joaquim turned to look back at Catechist Miguel, who nodded in agreement even as he grew pale. As Father Joaquim turned his gaze upon the wooden cross above his bed, Catechist Miguel asked about the letter on the bed.

"It is to the Visitor, Andre Palmeiro, in Macao. Based on yesterday's developments, I have made some important decisions about our mission."

"What decisions?"

"I will let you know more tonight. First, I need to discuss it with Master Yamaguchi."

Father Joaquim saw anxiety cross Miguel's face. "Do not worry, Miguel. God will provide."

"Yes, Father, of course. I will wait to hear from you later. Master Yamaguchi informed me he is going to teach class this morning."

"That is good news," Father Joaquim exclaimed. "I always enjoy Master Yamaguchi's lessons. Shall we walk over together?"

"Yes, Father."

Father Joaquim took a moment to gather his *budo* training gear, which was carefully stored in the corner of his tiny, secret room. He had been under Master Yamaguchi's tutelage since his arrival in Japan when he was just seventeen. Since his training began, Father Joaquim had proved himself a gifted martial artist with great potential. Now, at the age of forty-two, the tall, athletic Portuguese priest was considered by many in the valley to be a master himself.

As Master Yamaguchi advised, Father Joaquim and all others who trained in the village kept their budo teachings a secret. After all, peasants were peasants, and samurai were samurai. Given that their only purpose was to produce rice and perform other manual labor for the upper classes, peasants were no longer permitted to carry weapons. So, as far as the government was concerned, there was no need for them to learn budo or receive any kind of martial training.

With training gear in hand, Father Joaquim and Catechist Miguel departed the hidden room. Behind them, they slid the secret door back in place, re-hung the covert Buddhist silk linen hanging from the wall, and moved back the furniture to conceal any trace of a secret room before exiting the hovel on their way to practice.

★ ★ ★

Outside the rundown hut, the two men were greeted by a strong, fierce-looking Japanese man, a guard, dressed in a tattered, gray-colored *dogi,* the traditional Japanese martial arts training uniform.

"Good morning, Father Joaquim." The young man bowed in formal respect.

"Good morning, Yamamoto-san." Father Joaquim bowed in return.

"Master Yamaguchi wishes to lead morning practice today," Yamamoto exclaimed eagerly.

"Yes, I heard." Father Joaquim smiled at the young man before taking in a deep breath of the crisp, fresh air as he gazed at the mist forming above the abundant green mountains. The village was surrounded by rice fields, which in turn were surrounded by forested hills and mountains, on which a light rain had begun to fall.

"Despite the rain, I feel energized. Shall we go?"

"Yes, please, Father," Yamamoto replied, leading the way.

Similar to other dwellings in the impoverished village, the exterior of the larger building where they headed was made of old, dilapidated, gray-colored wooden planks. The simple roof was made of thatched straw, and the building itself was of a very basic design.

Quickly approaching the end of the pathway, they arrived at the entrance to the *dojo*, the martial training hall. As they entered through the door, they bowed deeply and quickly removed their sandals. They were ready to begin their lesson.

Two

Father Joaquim, adorned in his black *gi*, glanced around the dojo at the nearly twenty other students, most wearing old, ragged, off-white gis, and stopped for a moment to focus on a young Portuguese woman, Catechist Tonia. Just twenty-two years old, the relatively tall and slender young woman was warming up next to him. Like the other students, a few of them women, Catechist Tonia was stretching as she prepared for the lesson Master Yamaguchi was soon to give.

Wondering for a moment what the morning's lesson would be about, he reflected on many of Master Yamaguchi's previous teachings, which were always more than just lessons in martial arts, but rather lessons in life and coping with its challenges. Meditating in silence, he began to whisper a prayer for his catechists and the survival of the village. The prayer was cut short as a senior student quickly clapped his hands three times in a distinct rhythm, announcing the arrival of their teacher, Master Yamaguchi, who entered through a private doorway at the rear of the dojo.

Instantly, all stretching activity ceased and the students quickly lined up in a kneeling position called *seiza*, in pre-defined rows, with the most senior students at the front and the newest in the back. Approaching the group from the front, Master Yamaguchi faced the martial artists from the center of the dojo and bowed. In response, each of the students, quickly and in unison, returned the bow, which they held for a few seconds, conveying great respect for their master teacher.

Signaling the start of a demonstration, Master Yamaguchi next bowed to Father Joaquim and invited him to the front of the dojo. Bowing in response, Father Joaquim arose and approached the front of the room.

"This morning we are going to learn about the power of soft versus hard," Master Yamaguchi announced as he handed a wooden practice knife to Father Joaquim. Employing body language, Master Yamaguchi next specified to Father Joaquim the type of attack he wished him to execute in order to perform his demonstration.

Father Joaquim bowed to Master Yamaguchi and followed his instructions, quickly attacking with a powerful side-swipe of the knife at Master Yamaguchi's throat.

Stepping back, Master Yamaguchi gracefully escaped the swooping action of the knife, allowing it to pass safely in front of him. Then, in almost the same motion, he grabbed Father Joaquim's wrist, and using his other hand with incredible speed, forced Father Joaquim to flip in the air and land on his side. Finally, standing above his vanquished protégé, Master Yamaguchi skillfully applied precision-like pressure to Father Joaquim's wrist, forcing him to release the knife.

Impressed and nodding approvingly in response, the entire room full of martial artists paused in an effort to absorb the masterfully executed technique.

"*Yokemenuchi koetegaeshi tanto-dori*," Master Yamaguchi stated as he bowed again to the dojo, inviting his students to practice the technique among themselves.

A short while later, however, Father Joaquim watched as Master Yamaguchi scrutinized the efforts of Chiba, one of the newer and more excitable students, who was clearly frustrated at his inability to disarm his training partner.

Finally, after multiple failed attempts, and grunting in irritation, Chiba lost patience and kicked his training partner in the side, forcing him to give up the knife.

Instantly, Master Yamaguchi clapped his hands, and all the students in the dojo ceased training, lowering themselves back into a seiza position.

"Chiba-san, Chiba-san, you seem to be having much difficulty removing Yamamoto-san's knife." Master Yamaguchi laughed playfully as he walked over to the pair of combatants. "Father Joaquim, perhaps you could provide Chiba-san with a demonstration."

"Yes, *Sensei*, if you wish," Father Joaquim replied humbly but confidently as he rose to his feet. Complying with Master Yamaguchi's instructions, Yamamoto attacked Father Joaquim in a forceful manner.

However, similar to Master Yamaguchi, Father Joaquim executed the defensive technique flawlessly and with tremendous speed, easily subduing Yamamoto and removing the knife from his hand.

All the students nodded in approval at Father Joaquim's impeccable performance.

"Solid execution, Father Joaquim!" Master Yamaguchi smiled as he commended his long-time student.

"Thank you, Sensei," Father Joaquim replied as he bowed humbly to his teacher.

Master Yamaguchi turned to address the dojo. "As you can see, one way to overcome great strength like that of Yamamoto-san is to execute solid technique with incredible speed. Father Joaquim has been training in budo for more than twenty years. As a result, his technique is very good. But what about those of you who have not trained for twenty years? Must you have even greater strength to overcome strength?"

Glancing at Chiba, Master Yamaguchi paused for few moments, allowing his students time to reflect on the question.

"So many of us feel the need to use hard to fight hard, to fight force with even greater force, but there is another way." Master Yamaguchi paused again.

Chiba looked perplexed as Master Yamaguchi stared out the window at the rain outside.

"Water is the softest substance in the world, yet it will wear down the strongest rock. The key to overcoming great strength ..." The teacher puffed out his chest, then exhaled and hunched slightly, looking almost feeble. "... is to use soft." He lowered his voice, nearly to a whisper. "Sometimes, soft is the only way to defeat hard. Hard cannot always overcome hard because there is always something harder."

To demonstrate his point, Master Yamaguchi invited Yamamoto to attack him with the training knife. Yamamoto stood and faced Master Yamaguchi. Next to the much smaller and frail teacher, Yamamoto looked enormous and powerful.

Waiting not a moment, Yamamoto attacked Master Yamaguchi with tremendous force. Master Yamaguchi quickly and deftly forced Yamamoto to swing through the air and land on his side. Then, seemingly effortlessly, Master Yamaguchi carefully found the proper pressure point with just one finger and delicately removed Yamamoto's knife.

Admiring their master's skill and wisdom, the students cheered in elation before nodding excitedly as they grasped their teacher's concept.

"As a *bushi* warrior, part of your skill must lie in your ability to detect hard and counter with soft. And when you truly understand this to be not only a budo principle but a life principle, then you are well on your way to mastery."

"*Hai.*" The students cheered before bowing.

"When we realize that one's true strength comes from the universe, then the soft water drop becomes as powerful as the ocean behind it."

Bowing their heads again, the students acknowledged their comprehension of the lesson. Bowing in return, Master Yamaguchi exited the dojo through the rear, leaving everyone the opportunity to train and absorb what they had learned.

Three

With the early afternoon sun warming them, a dozen or so of the village's younger children played with a few small broken wooden toys near the church building, with Catechist Tonia watching over them. The older children were in the rice paddies, working alongside the adults, trying desperately to produce enough rice to meet Lord Shigemasa's exorbitant demands.

"Who was that scary man on the big horse, Tonia-san?" a child asked the pretty, dark-haired young woman who was dressed in old, worn-out farm clothes.

"That was Daimyo Matsukura Shigemasa," Catechist Tonia answered. "He is warlord of Arima."

"He frightened me. I do not like him."

"Lord Shigemasa is a tyrant, and I do not like him either," Catechist Tonia replied quietly. "But you need not fear him, for the Lord our God is with us."

Most of the few foreign women in the country were married and lived with their businessmen husbands—nearly all of them Portuguese—in Nagasaki, the nation's center for international trade. Tonia's very presence in the Japans was unusual and risky, especially as a young, unmarried Christian woman involved in missionary work. She knew that, and so did the villagers, who respected her courage and determination. Fortunately, she had long black hair and her skin color was also dark, so she blended in with the Japanese from a distance.

She'd been born in Lagos, a coastal city in Portugal's Algarve Peninsula, nearly halfway around the world from Japan. Her father, a Portuguese merchant, had brought his only daughter on a commercial voyage to Asia after her mother died of a respiratory ailment.

Soon after their arrival in Asia, Tonia's father took ill and suddenly died while in Macao. Those familiar with the incident believed he was poisoned at the hands of jealous Dutch merchants who were envious of Portugal's dominant trading position in Asia. That was when the orphaned young woman chose to dedicate her life to serving God and missionary work.

Disguised as a Portuguese merchant's wife, she made her way from Macao to Nagasaki, where she met Father Joaquim, who sought to protect and shelter her in his small Arima village, some forty miles outside Nagasaki.

"Remember, Haruko-chan ..." Tonia spoke softly to the child. "... God will protect us from men like Daimyo Matsukura Shigemasa. No matter how big and scary the daimyo may seem, God is much, much stronger."

"Thank you," the child said as she gave Tonia a hug.

"Tonia-san?"

Tonia looked at Shiro, an inquisitive boy she knew to be about six years old, who was living temporarily with his uncle in Master Yamaguchi's village because life was too impoverished in his native village. Life had become hard in nearly all the villages, as warlords throughout the country continually escalated their demands on the peasant villagers who had no one to appeal to and no way to defend themselves.

Shiro asked, "Why is Daimyo Shigemasa raising our taxes? My uncle says it is impossible to make more rice."

"Daimyo Shigemasa needs the extra rice to feed all his new samurai," Catechist Tonia replied as she reached out her hand and placed it over the boy's smaller one. "The daimyo also needs extra taxes to build a larger castle."

"But there are already too many samurai in this domain. Why does the daimyo need so many warriors? Will he not use these extra samurai to hunt Christian families like us?"

"Do not worry, Shiro-kun. God will protect us."

"Are you sure, Tonia-san?"

"Yes, we are His children and He *will* look after us. I promise." Catechist Tonia gave young Shiro some time to think as she scanned the other children, all of whom had ceased their play to listen to the words of assurance. Her heart sank a bit as she considered the children's fears. Children should be free to play, unconcerned for their safety. But that was not the truth of the world they inhabited.

"Do you believe this to be true, Shiro-kun?" she asked.

"Yes. I pray for His protection every night."

"Good. Believing is the first step to receiving the Lord's help and blessings. And prayer is the best way to speak to Him."

Young Shiro nodded in agreement, narrowing his eyes and biting his lower lip firmly. For a young boy, Shiro had a very sharp mind and a developing faith.

"Come, let us all say a short prayer together," Catechist Tonia said, motioning for the children to gather around her.

In unison, the children echoed Tonia's lead.

"Angel of God, my Guardian dear;
To whom God's love commits me here;
Ever this day, be at my side;
To light and guard;
To rule and guide."

Four

May 22, 1626
Daimyo Matsukura Shigemasa's Castle, Hizen Province

To warlord Matsukura Shigemasa, even the strongest and most loyal samurai, while important for maintaining his status, were otherwise little more than chess pieces, employed to achieve his objectives. So as he passed hastily through the serpentine halls of his castle, accompanied by seven of his most loyal retainers, he never so much as acknowledged the mere presence of those standing guard at the myriad rooms and passageways of his ornate palace.

Equally inconsequential to the daimyo—unless one failed at his duties—were the hundreds of samurai outside, each wearing their Lord's official colors of red, white, and black, and who guarded the immaculately manicured grounds.

As Shigemasa continued the long walk through his castle, he passed numerous fine Chinese silk and satin embroideries, exceptional large-scale drawings, and various exotic ornaments and statues. This lavish evidence of his wealth also escaped his notice as he continued his resolute gait toward the castle's grand chamber.

As the daimyo entered the chamber, talk ceased, and all bowed and waited. Assuming a seiza position in front of the large audience of his retainers and samurai, who also were kneeling, Shigemasa asked, "Do you think our visits to the villages were effective?"

"Yes, Lord," replied a bald-headed senior retainer. "Although I would imagine the peasants are highly distraught with their new taxes."

"What is that to me? They are peasants," he stated matter-of-factly.

An adviser, still fairly new to his post, spoke up. "But after these new taxes, the peasants will have nothing."

Another more-seasoned retainer gave the younger man a careful look and furtive headshake.

Clearly losing patience, the daimyo declared, "Peasants should have just enough to eat and survive. The rest must be paid in taxes!"

"Yes, Lord," the young adviser answered sheepishly. "I am sure you will amass greater wealth."

Slowly scanning the retinue of retainers, Shigemasa asked, "What about hidden Christians? Do you think our forays to the villages are helping to uncover any of the remaining vermin?"

"I do not know, my Lord," another elder retainer replied. "The Christians are a very resilient group."

"If that is so, then we must put more pressure on them."

"It is wise to put pressure on them, Lord," the elder retainer said, nodding his head.

"Agreed. Sooner or later they will break and betray one another," the daimyo said, smiling.

"And what about our reward of silver coins? Do you think this tactic is effective?" He again scanned his followers.

"If I may be so bold, Lord," another of the retainers responded, "I am not sure if silver is effective in bribing Christians to betray one another. Over the years, this technique has generally met with limited success at best."

"I agree, Lord," another senior retainer spoke up. "These

hidden Christians are an incestuous group and strongly support one another."

"I also agree, Lord," another retainer joined in. "For them, Christianity is a way of life. It is akin to the way of the sword for the samurai."

Glaring, clearly impatient, Shigemasa growled, "Then give me alternatives. Do not tell me what will *not* work. Tell me what *will* work!"

Hosogawa, another longtime retainer, answered: "Perhaps it would be more effective if we concentrated our efforts on apostates."

"What do you mean?"

"Perhaps we should focus on those who have recanted Christianity. Apostates know who many of the Christians are, and they are much more amenable to bribes and enticements."

Shaking his head, the daimyo replied, "You tell me nothing new. We have exhausted our leads with the apostates; they have already informed on the Christians they knew, yet more Christians still infest my lands. What else can we do? It is critical we eliminate any remaining Christians in Arima before Governor Kawachi arrives."

"Yes, Lord," a few of the retainers dared to agree audibly.

"I will not lose my lands because of these vermin scum."

"Yes, Lord," an elder retainer answered. "If any Christians remain, we will find them."

"I must never again suffer an embarrassment such as I did when that filthy Father Navarro was discovered hiding on my lands."

Another retainer spoke up for the first time. "Yes, Lord. It was regrettable."

"Regrettable? Is that what you think it was—regrettable?" Eyebrows raised, nostrils flaring, the daimyo continued: "Regrettable is losing a dog in a boar hunt. Having the governor learn of Christians hiding in my lands is intolerable!"

"Yes, Lord," the retainer corrected himself. "It is intolerable. We will see to it that it never happens again."

"Yes, we will." The daimyo again slowly turned his head, scanning his senior retainers. "Let us not forget that the shogun bestowed these lands on me for distinguishing myself in battle at Osaka."

"We will never forget, Lord," several replied.

"I was selected as the daimyo of Arima to exterminate Christianity with an iron fist."

"Yes, Lord."

"It is for this duty that the shogun's regime has exempted me from all taxes and dues. I will not lose this status!"

"Yes, Lord."

"I will die before I lose my lands because of this putrid religion."

"It will not happen, Lord. We will exterminate Christianity long before that."

Flustered, the daimyo grunted, turned, and left the chamber.

Five

Huddled in a tiny, impoverished hut, with a small candle illuminating their surroundings and creating a peaceful atmosphere, Father Joaquim and Catechists Tonia and Miguel had important matters to discuss.

"The peace of the Lord Jesus Christ be upon you, my children. I have called you here tonight to tell you of some important decisions I have made about our mission," Father Joaquim stated.

"What have you decided, Father?" Miguel asked.

"I have discussed the matter with Master Yamaguchi, and together we have chosen to relocate our village to the north."

"Where in the north?" Tonia asked, looking startled.

"Yezo."

"But that is on the other side of the country, Father," Miguel exclaimed.

"Are you sure, Father?" Tonia asked.

"Yes. Tomorrow I am dispatching a letter to the new visitor of the Jesuit Province of Japan, Father Andre Palmeiro, in Macao."

For a moment, Miguel sat quiet in contemplation, staring at Tonia intently.

"I think I am relieved about this decision," Catechist Miguel stated as his tense posture appeared to relax just a bit.

Father Joaquim raised his eyebrows and watched the young man carefully. "Why do you *think* you are relieved?"

"Well, Father, the journey certainly will be difficult, but

recent developments here have been terrifying. I do not think we will last very long if we stay in Arima. Sooner or later, Lord Shigemasa will find us and kill us."

"Do not be terrified, Miguel," Father Joaquim replied. "Replace any fears you have with the presence of our Lord. When you do this, your fears will disappear. Jesus is the light that shines through the darkness."

"Yes, Father," Miguel answered, sounding less than certain.

I will need to discuss this notion further with Miguel at some point, Father Joaquim thought to himself.

"And how do you feel, Tonia?" Father Joaquim asked the quiet but contemplative young woman.

"I am not terrified, but I have concerns, Father. Every day, I pray to God for His support."

"That is good, Tonia. Only He can deliver us to the salvation of greener pastures."

"Father, this morning you mentioned borrowing silver bullion from Mateus."

"I hope to borrow silver bullion from Mateus da Costa to meet our new taxes."

"Do you think he can help, Father?" Tonia asked.

"I hope so."

"How can I help?" Miguel asked.

"It will not be necessary, but thank you for offering. The trip to Nagasaki could be very dangerous. I would prefer you stay here and keep an eye on the village."

"Yes, Father," Miguel answered, appearing somewhat relieved.

Because of the intensifying danger for Christians, Father Joaquim sensed that Miguel had become petrified at the thought of leaving the village.

"How will you repay the loan?" Tonia asked.

"The best Chinese silks imported into Japan arrive on Portuguese galliots."

"Yes, I know."

"I will offer to help Mateus sell this silk at prices above the fixed prices of the Pancado system."

"But the shogun has made that practice illegal," Miguel stated, again appearing pale in the candle's flickering light. "Will you not draw unnecessary attention to yourself?"

"Distribution of Chinese silk from Macao into Nagasaki has always been a corrupt business, Miguel, and Portuguese merchants are always looking for higher profits."

"But how can you sell at prices above the Pancado system, Father?" Tonia asked. "I thought all the prices were fixed."

"Opportunities present themselves when wealthy families and warlords are willing to pay higher prices for access to the best."

"But why does Mateus not do it himself?" Miguel asked anxiously. "Mateus is a trader, *not* a Christian Father banned from Japan on pain of death. It is much riskier for you than for him."

"Mateus is familiar with wealthy families and daimyo, but his Japanese is weak and he does not properly understand Japanese etiquette and customs as well as I do."

"But he can speak a small amount of Japanese. I am sure Mateus would appreciate your help, but this practice is too dangerous. You are a Christian priest in hiding."

"It is dangerous, yes, but the village needs the money," Father Joaquim replied as he gently rested his right hand on Miguel's shoulder and looked directly into the nervous young man's eyes. "Without it, I believe Daimyo Shigemasa will do terrible things, particularly to our women and children. We cannot let this happen."

Catechists Miguel and Tonia sat silently in the dimly lit hut, obviously unsure of how to react to their leader's plan. Nervously, Miguel began to chew on his fingernails.

"I do not want you to worry. Everything will be all right,"

Father Joaquim stated as he placed his arms around Tonia and Miguel and gave them a reassuring hug.

"Like Saint Francis Xavier, the founder of our mission in Japan, I place all my faith and hope in the Lord and trust that He will protect us. You must do the same."

"We will try, Father," Miguel stated, sounding less than certain.

"Remember, we cannot ask the villagers to have a faith that we lack," Father Joaquim added.

"Yes, Father," Tonia replied earnestly. "I do have trust and faith."

Slowly, Miguel nodded.

"What time will you leave tomorrow, Father?" Tonia asked.

"As soon as the sun goes down. But first, I have a baptism planned for tomorrow morning. It is important to welcome our village newborn into the house of God. Children are a gift from God and are the future of the mission."

"We will help you get this organized," Miguel said, finally appearing a bit more comfortable.

"Thank you, Miguel. It is appreciated."

"You are welcome, Father."

"Also, Miguel, when I return, I would like to talk about your ambitions within the Society. I know you have been in Japan for only a short time and your experience has been challenging, but I would like to talk to you about becoming a Brother of the Society."

"Yes, Father," Miguel replied, again sounding hesitant.

Father Joaquim stood up, bowed his head to Tonia and Miguel, and walked out the door to return to his quarters. After a short period of pondering their future, and reassuring themselves that they were alone and no one was watching, Tonia and Miguel quickly blew out the candles, held each other, and gave each other a romantic kiss in the dark.

"Do not worry, Miguel; we will get through this."

Six

May 23, 1626
Arima Village, Hizen Province

With the clear blue morning sky as a backdrop, Father Joaquim stood on a small mound in front of the entire village, ready to perform a baptism. Adjacent to the dilapidated church structure, he stood close to a large wooden basin. In front of him stood a young Japanese couple, holding their newborn baby before an excited crowd.

"Holy baptism is the basis of all Christian life," Father Joaquim attested. "It is the gateway to life in the Spirit. It is also the door that gives access to other sacraments. Through baptism, we are freed from sin and reborn as sons of God.

"We become members of Christ and are incorporated into the Church and made sharers in her mission," Father Joaquim continued. "Baptism is the sacrament of regeneration through water in the Word."

"Come, let us sing a hymn together," Catechist Tonia said.

For the next few minutes, the villagers joyfully sang a hymn in unison.

"I would like to welcome everyone here today, especially the parents of this child," Father Joaquim stated when the singing stopped. He stretched out his arms, gesturing to the young couple, offering them a warm welcome. "This moment is joyous, for this child is a gift of God, the Source of life, who now wishes to bestow His own life on this little one."

Father Joaquim next addressed the parents. "What name do you give your child?"

"We name our child Peter," the father replied, casting a loving glance at his baby son.

"And what do you ask of God's Church?"

"We ask for baptism," the parents replied in unison. "We request *eternal life* for our child."

"You have asked that your child be baptized. In so doing, you are accepting the responsibility of raising him in the practice of the faith. Do you understand what you are asking?"

"Yes, we do," the young parents replied joyfully.

Smiling with enthusiasm, Father Joaquim looked at the child.

"Peter, the Christian community welcomes you with great joy. In its name, I claim you for Christ our Savior, by the sign of His cross. I now trace the cross on your forehead and invite your parents to do the same."

Father Joaquim made the sign of the cross on the child's forehead in silence, inviting the parents to do so as well.

"I will now read from our Holy Book." Father Joaquim opened his Bible, turned to the Gospel of Matthew, and began to read aloud. "Matthew 28:18–19 says, 'And Jesus came and spake unto them, saying, "All power is given unto me in heaven and in earth. Go ye therefore, and teach all nations, baptizing them in the name of the Father, and of the Son, and of the Holy Ghost."'"

"Amen," the crowd echoed as they bowed.

"Come, let us ponder on this passage and take a moment to pray."

★ ★ ★

24

Father Joaquim returned to the wooden basin next to the child's parents. "In the waters of the Jordan your Son was baptized by John and anointed with the Spirit. Your Son willed that water and blood should flow from His side as He hung upon the cross.

"After His resurrection he told his disciples, 'Go ye therefore, and teach all nations, baptizing them in the name of the Father, and of the Son, and of the Holy Ghost.' Father, look now with love upon your Church, and unseal for her the fountain of baptism. By the power of the Spirit, give to the water of this font the grace of your Son. You created man in your own likeness. Cleanse him from sin in a new birth to innocence by water and the Spirit."

Father Joaquim then touched the water in the basin with his right hand. "We ask you, Father, with your Son, to send the Holy Spirit upon the water of this font. May all who are buried with Christ in the death of baptism rise also with him to the newness of life. We ask this through Christ our Lord."

"Amen," the crowd responded.

Father Joaquim next gestured for the parents to come forward and approach the basin.

"Is it your will that Peter should be baptized in the faith of the Church, which we have all professed with you?"

"It is," the parents replied.

Father Joaquim scooped water with a wooden ladle, poured it on the child, and baptized him, saying, "Peter, I baptize you in the name of the Father, the Son, and the Holy Spirit."

Next, Father Joaquim silently anointed the crown of the child's head with sacred Chrism, took the child in his hands, and wrapped him in a small, white garment.

"Peter, you have become a new creation and have clothed yourself in Christ. See in this white garment the outward sign of your Christian dignity."

"Amen," the crowd roared again.

Father Joaquim handed the child back to the father and invited the child's mother to light the candle with a match.

"Receive the light of Christ," Father Joaquim proclaimed. "Parents, this light is entrusted to you to be kept burning brightly. This child of yours has been enlightened by Christ. He is to walk always as a child of the light. May he keep the flame of faith alive in his heart. When the Lord comes, may he go out to meet him with all the saints in the heavenly kingdom."

Everyone in the village cheered loudly and clapped their hands in excitement.

Assisting Father Joaquim, Catechist Miguel next walked the burning candle inside the disguised church and placed it on an altar.

"Let us conclude this wonderful celebration with a prayer," Father Joaquim said.

"Our Father, who art in heaven, hallowed be thy name; thy kingdom come, thy will be done on earth as it is in heaven. Give us this day our daily bread; and forgive us our trespasses as we forgive those who trespass against us; and lead us not into temptation, but deliver us from evil."

And all the villagers said, "Amen."

Seven

The villagers had become so accustomed to the incessant, monotonous *wah-wah-wah* sounds—more bird-like than the typical frog croak—that they hardly noticed the near presence of hundreds of hungry common brown toads on the village's periphery and extending to perhaps tens of thousands of the creatures calling out in the nearby rice fields. Certainly none of the villagers heard the *yamakagashi* snakes slithering through the fields in pursuit of the toads. Instead, in the cool evening air, nearly every village member was standing near the little church building—the one they'd become so skilled at quickly concealing when the need arose—with a singular focus: to pray for Father Joaquim before he set out on his trip to Nagasaki.

The father had traded his priest's robes for the more colorful high-quality silk attire of a Portuguese merchant. With large, baggy pants, a loose-fitting shirt, a long overcoat, and an oversized hat, he was hardly recognizable, even to these villagers who knew him well. He'd made this risky trip before, and each time he'd donned the same merchant's clothing, always with the same purpose: disguise.

As the last flicker of sunlight was eclipsed by the horizon, Father Joaquim bowed deeply to the villagers in appreciation of their support. He was humbled by these peasants he'd come to love, and who in turn cared deeply about his welfare and safety.

Next, Father Joaquim bowed deeply to the head of the village, Master Yamaguchi, a man for whom he held deep respect and admiration. More than just the village head and most senior male in the community, Master Yamaguchi was also a close long-time friend and mentor of Father Joaquim.

As a thick wedge of the moon began to provide a bit of illumination over his shoulder, Father Joaquim made a final bow to his beloved friends in the faith, picked up his European satchel, and departed up the mountain path.

Traveling a precipitous path in the dark of night carried its own set of risks, but the father deemed those risks to be less perilous than the threat of being caught by the daimyo's samurai if he traveled in the daylight. His plan was to avoid detection altogether. However, if detected, he hoped to pass himself off as a merchant. Although he also knew the local authorities and daimyo already suspected the Christian Fathers of disguising themselves in order to travel secretly throughout Japan.

All Christian missionaries were now banned from the country, and many years before, Japan's second shogun, Tokugawa Hidetada, had confined all European merchants to the port cities of Nagasaki and Hirado. Any foreigner discovered in the hills would certainly face the most intense levels of interrogation. One wrong answer—or even an interrogator's suspicion—could lead to banishment, imprisonment, or execution.

After praying throughout the first hour or so of his trek, Father Joaquim's mind turned toward thoughts of his early days in Japan, to times when Christians were free to walk through any part of the country, and free to share their faith with anyone who would listen.

When he'd arrived at the port in Nagasaki twenty-five years earlier at the age of seventeen, missionary life was completely different. Christianity was accepted. Missionaries were given the freedom to preach; they had no need to hide or sneak about in disguises.

Reaching out, Father Joaquim gripped a large rock, grunting a bit as he pulled himself up a steep part of the mountain, his thoughts, meanwhile, drawn again to the past. *Life then was bright and full of opportunity to spread God's Word. Now, only persecution, torture, and death await us.*

Tears began to form in the priest's eyes as he reflected on his many lost kinsmen, those who were persecuted and killed for their faith over the years. He pondered what he knew of the history of Christianity in Japan.

The mission in the country had begun half a century before his arrival, when Saint Francis Xavier took his first step in Kagoshima, near the southern tip of the country. In those early days, in addition to peasants, some feudal land-owners and warlords also embraced the Society's teachings. Even several influential daimyo converted to the faith.

With the exception of a few dark moments in the mission's early history, including an unfortunate martyrdom in 1597, religious freedom continued until 1614, when Japan's first shogun, Tokugawa Ieyasu, issued a series of edicts, prohibiting Christianity in Japan and banishing all foreign missionaries from the country.

By the year of its banishment, the Church's expansion was at its height in Japan and had converted more than 300,000 Japanese souls. At a time when Japan's total population was fewer than 20 million, the Church's mission had made extraordinary progress in converting Japanese to the faith— before politics and corruption took its course.

Father Joaquim recalled that during the early years of the banishment, the Society made a bold stand against the shogun's edicts as a means of protest. Concealment of one's Christian faith was expressly frowned upon within the mission.

However, in 1619, when arrests and martyrdoms of Christians took a dramatic upturn, it became clear that if Christianity were to survive in Japan, it would need to go underground and stay hidden from the shogun and his regime.

Thus, in a period of five short years, the mission had gone from public acceptance to complete banishment, suffering severe persecutions, and martyrdoms. The shogun and his *Bakufu* regime had ordered that any Christians caught remaining in the country were to be tortured and killed. European Fathers, who were viewed as the most subversive, defiant, and threatening to Japan's long-standing authoritarian culture, were special targets.

Surely, this was the largest Christian holocaust Rome had ever seen, and with little support coming from the papacy on account of a dwindling budget, the missionaries had only their faith, their wits, and one another to rely on.

But Father Joaquim would never complain. He knew missionary work in the Japans was dangerous, yet his loyalty and devotion to "the Company," as the Society of Jesus was known, was unwavering.

So, heading up the mountain alone, armed only with his faith, Father Joaquim pressed forward up the slopes, step-by-step, determined to save his village from death and destruction. A brother like no other, Father Joaquim was prepared to risk everything for the village—even if that price was his life.

Eight

May 24, 1626
Shogun's Castle, Edo, Musashi Province

While clouds darkened and wind swirled outside, inside at the far end of the Fujimi-tamon defense house on the grounds of Edo's Honmaru Palace, Shogun Iemitsu and his *eta* torturers were taking pleasure in their work, while several Buddhist monks and the five *Go-Roju* elders who comprised the Bakufu cabinet watched on.

Much like his father, Hidetada, young Shogun Iemitsu was a malicious man, probably even more obsessed with power and control than his father or even his grandfather. Officially, young Iemitsu had ascended to the title of shogun in 1623, at the age of nineteen becoming Japan's third shogun by hereditary title. From his early days, Shogun Iemitsu was given responsibility for exterminating Christianity in Japan, and he was ruthless in his quest to fulfill that duty.

"You will tell me where your flock is hiding," the shogun growled again at the Japanese father who was outstretched and bound by shackles on a metal table. The shogun and his cabinet members had already severely beaten the father with clubs. Because he'd continued to remain silent, they'd chosen a new torture technique. Shogun Iemitsu signaled to the Eta torturers to dispense their wooden clubs and grab their branding pincers.

31

The three eta torturers slowly removed the white-hot pincers from a nearby oven and moved toward the clearly unnerved Father.

"Do you wish to say anything before these eta brand your helpless body?" the shogun asked, grinning as he saw the fear in the man's eyes.

Despite his fear, the father remained silent, refusing to give the Shogun the satisfaction of any kind of a response.

Following a few seconds of silence, Shogun Iemitsu instructed the first eta to brand the father on his bare chest. The tortured man screamed and momentarily lost consciousness as the pincers sizzled against his chest for at least half a minute. Even the eta seemed a bit repulsed by the stench of the burning flesh.

"Do you not see the futility of your situation, Father?" the shogun asked, no empathy visible on his chiseled face. "Christianity can bring you nothing good in life. Look at where it has brought you." The shogun smirked. "It has brought you to the edge of death."

Grimacing in pain, the father looked at the Shogun impassively while trying to remain conscious.

"Christianity is a danger to the empire and a corruption brought by foreign barbarians!" the shogun bellowed. "Christians are spies for the pope and the king of Spain and all those who wish to invade my country." The shogun's eyes narrowed in contempt as he snarled, "You are a traitor for embracing this faith!"

He instructed the second eta torturer to brand the bruised, bloodied, and disfigured father, this time in his genital area. Within seconds, the father's genitalia began to melt. While he screamed out in pain, the Go-Roju cabinet members grimaced at the horrific sight and coughed at the stench that filled their noses.

"You are almost dead, miserable Christian." The shogun

reached out his hands, signaling the absence of any other Christians. "Where are your friends, Priest? Do they not wish to support you? Are they cowards? You are alone and about to die."

Breaking his silence at last, the Japanese father slowly opened his mouth and spoke in a soft voice. "Jesus watches over me. We are never alone."

"What did you say?" The shogun moved closer, his eyes riveted on the father's bruised and reddened eyes.

"Where I am weak, the Lord is strong," the father declared, with the little strength he still had. "I do not have to live by my own strength alone."

"Where is your Jesus now, you weak, pathetic Christian?" the shogun shrieked. "He will not save you. You are about to lose your life!" He looked around the room at his retinue, each of whom nodded approvingly.

"To find life, one must be willing to lose it," the tortured man gasped.

Sensing the end was at hand, the shogun grimaced. He felt frustrated at being cheated out of a more satisfying torture. He quickly walked across the room, fetched his own personal short sword, and with one swift stroke, the father's head fell to the ground and rolled to the feet of one of the Buddhist monks.

"Burn his body," the shogun ordered coldly, as he wiped the blood from his blade with a black cloth. "We must completely dispose of it. We do not want any Christians making a martyr of this traitor."

"Do not worry, Lord," one of his cabinet members answered. "He never existed."

Nine

May 28, 1626
Edge of Nagasaki Prefecture

Too late did Father Joaquim spot the six samurai standing on the path before him.

"Halt where you are!" one of them shouted as he ran swiftly toward the foreigner. The other five, seeming to be in an almost frenzied state, followed close behind.

"Do not try to escape," another samurai shouted as they quickly approached.

Analyzing his position, Father Joaquim quickly concluded it was too late to escape. So, assuming the role of a Portuguese merchant, as he'd planned to do in such an event, the foreign Jesuit calmly approached the samurai.

"*Konichiwa*," Father Joaquim said, showing no emotion or nervousness as he bowed and calmly walked toward the field's edge in an effort to greet his pursuers.

"We have you!" a zealous samurai bellowed as he arrived first, grabbing Father Joaquim and thrusting him forcefully to the ground. Standing above, the remaining samurai stared at him menacingly.

"I am on official trading business," Father Joaquim stated placidly, looking up to address his samurai captors.

"What official business?" a samurai demanded as he kicked

Father Joaquim in his side. "All foreign merchants are explicitly prohibited from leaving Nagasaki and Hirado!"

Another samurai quickly unleashed his *wakizashi* and pointed the short sword at Father Joaquim's head.

"I am on official business on behalf of Governor Hasegawa Gonroku," Father Joaquim replied sharply, doing his best to appear sincere.

"Of what do you speak?"

"What business do you have in assaulting a trader on official government business?" Father Joaquim retorted, again doing his best to appear offended that his official mission should be questioned.

"All foreign merchants are explicitly prohibited from leaving Nagasaki and Hirado," one of the samurai repeated.

"Yes, that is true, unless expressly authorized by the governor," Father Joaquim answered, still looking up from his place on the ground.

"We are not aware of any exceptions," one of the samurai countered, his eyes narrowed and appearing eager to harm the foreigner sprawled before him. "What evidence do you have?"

"Documentation in my satchel." The father lifted it toward his accusers.

"Grab the bag," one of the samurai instructed a younger member of the clan.

Instantly, the younger samurai snatched Father Joaquim's satchel and pushed him back down.

"I am on official government business. What right do you have to shove me like this?" Father Joaquim asked, hoping his feigned indignation would make his deception more convincing.

"Shut your mouth until you are spoken to, *gaijin*, or we will cut out your tongue!"

Two of the samurai brusquely rustled through the Jesuit's bag. Withdrawing a number of items, they produced a European compass, a map of Kyushu, some food, and a journal.

"Where is your documentation?" one of the samurai shouted gruffly as he continued to rummage through the satchel.

"It is there," Father Joaquim said, as he pointed inside the satchel at an envelope with an official seal.

Irritated, the samurai grabbed the envelope and tore it open, breaking the seal. The others were silent as the samurai read the letter.

"This letter is written to attest that the magistrate of Nagasaki provides official permission for Portuguese merchant Joaquim Martinez to travel on foot without restriction between Nagasaki and Hirado …"

"As I said—"

"Shut up, dog." The samurai resumed reading. "…to fulfil merchant duties as prescribed by the governor of Nagasaki, Hasegawa Gonroku."

"Is it signed and stamped?" asked one of the elder samurai.

"Yes, it is signed by the governor and bears the official seal of the magistrate."

"Why would the governor have you travel by foot and not sea?" a senior samurai demanded.

"It is private business," Father Joaquim answered evasively.

"You will answer the question!"

"I am a Portuguese representative of the governor. He has engaged me to gauge interest in new silks from some of his closest supporters in the region."

"For what purpose?"

"I am to visit with his supporters, determine their needs, and convey these to the governor. Then I am to monitor these requested items as they arrive on Portuguese ships into Nagasaki from Macao."

"What else?"

"In Nagasaki, I am to negotiate lower prices for these goods from my fellow Portuguese traders, as Governor Hasegawa Gonroku would like to secure them for his closest allies."

The samurai appeared to be deflated by the explanation.

"Grab your things and move on," the most senior samurai grumbled as Father Joaquim stood to his feet.

Another of the samurai thrust the Jesuit's satchel into his chest and pushed him in the direction of Nagasaki.

As Father Joaquim slowly walked away, he could see the samurai felt cheated of a potential catch. Surely, they would have been rewarded a small fortune of silver for apprehending a banned Christian in disguise. *Thank God they did not realize my documentation was a forgery. And thank God He gave me the inspiration to create that letter.*

As Father Joaquim picked up his pace toward the city of Nagasaki, he whispered, "Lord, I thank You for Your protection during this time of need. The village and mission are deeply thankful for Your shield. We praise You, Father. Oh, Lord, thank You!"

Ten

May 29, 1626
Arima Village, Hizen Province

In the cool morning sunshine, with a few wispy clouds hanging as if suspended above the nearby mountain, Master Yamaguchi was engaged in his favorite pastime, delicately clipping the leaves of the many bonsai trees in his garden. Carefully shaping the miniature trees relaxed him.

Bonsai was a tradition that dated back more than a millennium in Japan. And, as he had done in so many activities, Master Yamaguchi had become a master at the craft, excelling in all bonsai cultivation techniques, including pruning, root reduction, potting, defoliation, and grafting to produce small trees that mimicked the shape and style of full-size trees. Master Yamaguchi's private garden was spectacular in design and well-admired throughout the village.

A knock on his outside gate refocused the old man's attention. Catechist Miguel stood outside the yard.

"Master Yamaguchi, I am sorry to interrupt. Do you have a moment?"

"Ah, Catechist Miguel, of course. I am grateful for the visit." Master Yamaguchi walked over to the gate and opened it.

"Thank you," Miguel said as he followed his host inside.

Miguel gasped at the beauty of the garden. In addition to the abundant bonsai trees and other exotic vegetation, the garden was a magnificent display of colorful flowers, mostly pink, peach, and light blue in color.

On the right side of the garden was a small waterfall where a stream of water gently flowed from an adjacent mountain. On the left were a number of handmade miniature wooden houses, where several blue-throated *Ogawa-komadori* birds sat chirping.

"Master Yamaguchi," Catechist Miguel said, stopping to gaze about the garden, "your garden looks even more impressive than the last time I was here."

"You are too kind, Miguel, but I am sure that is not why you visit me today."

"No, it is not."

"What brings you here today, my friend?"

"I am full of worries, Master Yamaguchi."

"Let us start with the biggest one, Miguel. What is on your mind?"

"I am worried about many things, but I am most worried about Father Joaquim. Traveling to Nagasaki can be very dangerous. I am concerned he might not make it back."

"I worry also, Miguel. But I have faith the Lord will look after him, and he will return safely."

"But if they discover his identity, they will kill him."

"Try to keep your mind focused on positive outcomes, Miguel."

"I am trying, Master Yamaguchi, but the world has turned upside down on us in Japan."

"I admit, life has changed dramatically for Christians, but we must remain optimistic about our future. We must retain a degree of hope." Master Yamaguchi placed his hand on Miguel's shoulder.

"I feel the future is filled with death, Master Yamaguchi.

This is not what I expected in Japan." Miguel shook his head. "It is much worse than I imagined."

"Why did you come to Japan?" Master Yamaguchi asked. "What drew you here?"

"To spread the Word of God." Miguel took a deep breath, and as he exhaled he added, "That and the excitement of the mission."

"The excitement of the mission. What do you mean?"

"In Europe, the mission in Japan was always reputed to be the most exciting. It is one of the furthest outposts from Rome and held great prospects in terms of converts. We heard great stories about the missions here, despite the danger."

"I see." Master Yamaguchi nodded.

"Now I am finding it to be more than I can handle." Miguel looked down at the table, appearing ashamed. "From the moment I arrived, the mission seemed almost impossible." He looked at Master Yamaguchi again. "And the death toll has only risen."

Master Yamaguchi nodded again. "I agree that recent times have been difficult."

"I worry the mission will not survive here, Master Yamaguchi. And I fear I will not survive." Miguel dropped his gaze again.

"Times will help things improve, Miguel. God will see to it."

"I wish that were true, but I am afraid I do not believe it."

"What do you want, Miguel?"

"I want to go home. I am scared to death here. I can no longer sleep. I want to go home where I can live without having to fear persecution and torture … and death. I want to be free again."

Master Yamaguchi could see the conflict and fear in Miguel's eyes. "Then it is time for you to return home, Miguel."

"I wish it were that easy."

"What do you mean?"

"Father Joaquim … I cannot bear to tell him."

"Father Joaquim will understand."

"Father Joaquim is dedicated to the village and the mission, Master Yamaguchi. He is a very brave and committed leader. I cannot bear the thought of letting him down." Tears formed in Miguel's eyes as he continued. "There is also the question of getting out of here alive. The Society of Jesus was exiled a long time ago. We are not even supposed to be here. If I am caught trying to leave, they will kill me."

"Perhaps you should discuss this with Father Joaquim when he returns," Master Yamaguchi suggested.

"*If* he returns," Miguel whispered, giving voice to his worry. "And who will look after the village if he does not?"

"Miguel, we are not your responsibility. The village *will* survive. Our Lord Jesus looks after us."

Anxiously, Miguel buried his face in his hands.

"Is that the only thing keeping you in the village, Miguel?"

"What do you mean?"

"Catechist Tonia."

"What about her?"

"You have feelings for her."

"As a *sister…*"

"You may be able to hide your feelings for her from Father Joaquim, but not me, Miguel."

"I still do not know what you mean."

"Before you can be honest with others, Miguel, you must learn to be honest with yourself." Master Yamaguchi stood up and placed his hand on Miguel's shoulder. "I think you want to leave the mission, and Japan, but you cannot bear the thought of leaving Tonia behind in this dangerous place because you have deep feelings for her."

Startled by Master Yamaguchi's acumen, Miguel stumbled for a moment and paused.

"I really do not know what to think anymore," Miguel confessed as he held his head in his hands.

"Again, I think it best if you discuss these matters with Father Joaquim on his return."

"That is *if* he returns ..."

"Of what do you speak, Miguel?"

"Even *if* Father Joaquim *is* able to borrow enough silver from Mateus da Costa and able to make it back here alive, we *still* have to relocate to Yezo." Miguel shook his head again. "Yezo is too far, and the journey between here and there is much too dangerous. We will be discovered for sure."

"Miguel, you really should not—"

Miguel cut off Master Yamaguchi mid-sentence. "We will be discovered and captured. Do you know what they will do when they capture us? They will torture us. They will cut off our feet and burn us alive! I cannot stand the thought of torture."

"Miguel."

The young man sniffled and caught his breath before answering. "Yes, Master Yamaguchi."

"Would you like some tea?"

Miguel nodded. "Yes, I would like that." Miguel wiped his tears with his sleeve and calmed himself.

"Come, follow me," Master Yamaguchi said as he led Miguel through the back door into his small, but tidy home.

"Enough of worry. Let us talk about something else. Tell me more of your home in Portugal."

Soon, a sparkle emerged in Miguel's eyes as he began to reflect on home. "Ah, Portugal. How I long for home! Portugal is the most beautiful of all European countries. And Lisbon! Far more beautiful than Rome. How I miss home!"

Eleven

May 30, 1626
Nagasaki City, Nagasaki Prefecture

From the mountain's summit, Father Joaquim had a panoramic view of Nagasaki's residential quarters and the busy trading port. Weary from the climb, he slowly began his descent, contemplating the city's history.

Until recently, missionaries as well as traders often referred to this largest city in the south of Japan as the "Rome of the Far East" because of its beauty and international draw.

Lush, green mountains surrounded the huge, deep-blue bay, creating a serene setting, despite the port's bustle as cargo ships docked, unloaded wares, reloaded, and departed. The vibrancy of the city and port captivated Nagasaki residents, foreign traders, and all who happened to visit.

Originally, Nagasaki was a small fishing village, but during the latter half of the sixteenth century, the city had become the largest trading port in Japan, mostly on account of its strong trading ties with Macau in China and because of the Portuguese, who made it their trading hub for Japan.

The Portuguese were always the most powerful at sea, and they were the first to arrive in Asia. After rounding the continent of Africa, Portuguese traders stopped in Goa, then Malacca, then the Philippines, then on to China, and finally

Japan, establishing strong trading bases and footholds in both Macau in China and Nagasaki in Japan. Many Portuguese traders also made homes in Nagasaki.

Common imports into Japan included raw silk, silk fabrics, cotton, shark, deer skin, scented woods, dyes, sugars, lead, and tin. On the export side, Japan produced silver, copper, iron, sulfur, rice, and handicraft. The most popular trade, however, was trading Chinese silk for Japanese silver, and the profits from this trade were enormous.

Attracted by the vast trade and commercial profits, the Dutch also arrived, eager to gain a portion of the wealth. But they could never truly match the strong footholds already established by the Portuguese. Hence, by default, the Dutch were assigned the port of Hirado, a much smaller and less significant place. Not surprisingly, the Dutch envied the stronghold and trading prowess of the Portuguese, and tensions loomed in the region.

But Father Joaquim spent little time thinking of the impressive facts of the city, instead devoting his thoughts to prayer and thanksgiving.

Thank God I made it here alive, Father Joaquim reflected as he made his way down the mountain in the soft early-morning light. *I hope Mateus can help us.*

Two hours later, as Father Joaquim emerged from a trail at the base of the mountain, he was immediately confronted by two city officials dressed in samurai attire.

"Where are you coming from?" one of the officials shouted.

Holding a leash in his hand, Father Joaquim walked directly toward the officials.

"Have you seen my dog?" Father Joaquim asked loudly in perfect Japanese.

What?"

"Have you seen my dog? He ran up the trail ahead of me. Did you see him?"

"What?" The official squinted and shook his head. "No, we have not seen a dog."

Father Joaquim quickly dug into this bag and fetched some silver coins. "Here," he said as he handed two silver coins to each of the officials. "If you see my dog, a large black Portuguese dog, let me know. I reside in the foreign quarters, house number thirteen."

Father Joaquim then walked straight by them and quickly glanced back. "If you see my dog, please let me know. His name is 'Cão', and he has been with me a long time. I must get him back."

Content with the money, the city officials gripped their silver coins and continued along their route.

Father Joaquim grinned as he whispered, "Thank You, Father. It works every time." He strode confidently toward the foreign residential quarters.

Minutes later, he arrived at house number thirteen and instantly recognized the symbol on the door. It was the Chinese character for Buddhism—in Japanese pronounced *Budsu*. Studying the symbol in detail, Father Joaquim could observe that great care and diligence had been used to engrave the symbol in the wood. Surprised by what he saw, Father Joaquim decided to knock anyway.

Almost instantly, the door swung open and a smiling face greeted him. "Father Joaquim," the Portuguese man whispered excitedly. "What a surprise! It is wonderful to see you. Come in, please."

"Mateus, it is good to see you too."

Once inside, the two old friends embraced.

Of short stature and in middle age, Mateus had dark hair, dark skin, kind dark eyes, a thick dark beard, and an almost ever-present pipe, with pleasant-smelling tobacco smoke wafting about. Father Joaquim couldn't think of anyone who didn't like the jovial businessman.

"I am sure you saw the new engraving on my door," Mateus stated with some hesitancy.

"The Buddhist symbol."

"Clearly a decoy, but a necessity. The Portuguese must outwardly profess their following of Buddha to live in Nagasaki now. The symbol keeps the officers and authorities away."

"A sign of the times." Father Joaquim sighed.

Seeming to sense the regret, Mateus nodded and then asked, "What brings you to Nagasaki, Father? Nothing good, I am sure."

Smiling at the remark, Father Joaquim removed his shoes at the door and sat down at Mateus' small kitchen table.

"I am an optimist, Mateus; you know this. But my burdens have grown heavier, and I need to address some problems."

"What kind of problems?"

"Taxes."

"Oh." Mateus took a large puff from his pipe and fetched two wooden mugs. "Do not get me started about taxes." Mateus grabbed a bottle of wine and a pitcher of water. "Wine or water, Father?"

"I think I need some wine." Father Joaquim rubbed his whiskers.

Mateus poured some red wine into the mugs, and Father Joaquim took a big sip before continuing. "It is Daimyo Matsukura Shigemasa. He has driven up our taxes again and is putting even greater pressure on the villages to expose Christians."

"That does not sound good."

"It is not. The pressure is enormous, and communities are breaking."

"And your village?" Mateus asked, his brow furrowed with a look of concern.

"We are managing."

"Catechists Tonia and Miguel, are they still with you?"

"Yes."

"They are well?"

"Yes, both are still in the village, although I am worried about Miguel."

"What is the problem, Father?"

"I think the pressure is getting to him. He does not look well."

Mateus frowned. "What will you do?"

"I need a favor."

"Hah! I knew that was coming," Mateus joked. "What do you need?"

"Five hundred large silver coins."

"Five hundred large silver coins! Holy saints! You must be joking."

"I wish I were," Father Joaquim replied, raising his eyebrows and grimacing a bit at the audacity of his request.

"Well, that is much more than I have under my mattress," Mateus bellowed in good humor.

"I knew it would be."

"Not a problem, Father. I will borrow it."

"From whom?"

"Other Portuguese traders."

"Do you think they will lend that much?"

"I will find out tomorrow night."

"Tomorrow night?"

"Yes. Many Portuguese traders will be drinking in the gaijin bar in the port tomorrow night."

Father Joaquim knew the gaijin bar was where all the Portuguese traders liked to gather and drink. "Are you comfortable asking them this, Mateus?"

Mateus grinned and winked. "I will ask them when they are all drunk and in a good mood."

"I suppose traders will never change," Father Joaquim replied.

"No, they will not." Mateus laughed. "If there is one thing constant about traders, it is their love for money, alcohol, and women."

"It is certainly different from the missions."

"And how is the mission on the periphery, Father? Things are only getting worse for Christians hiding in Nagasaki. How is life on the outskirts?"

"I am sorry to say the situation is difficult and only likely to get worse on the account of politics."

"Because of the arrival of the new Nagasaki governor?"

"Yes. I have heard reports that the new governor, Mizuno Kawachi, is one of the shogun's most vicious men."

"His appointment does not sound positive."

Father Joaquim rested his forehead on the outstretched fingers of his right hand. "For the time first time, the shogun will have one of his own wicked men running Nagasaki, and he will not turn a blind eye."

"What will you do, Father?"

"After our taxes are paid, we will slip away and relocate to Yezo in the north."

"Yezo is a long way away. Do you think you can make it that far? Do you not fear capture?"

"Our Lord will guide us."

"Father, I am a believer and a good Christian, but I worry about you."

"Have no worries, Mateus. Think on Matthew 6:33–34: 'Seek ye first the kingdom of God, and His righteousness; and all these things shall be added unto you. Take therefore no thought for the morrow: for the morrow shall take thought for the things of itself.'"

"Thank you, Father. I like that verse."

"None of us need worry, Mateus. We need only seek God. Tomorrow is a new day, and He will answer our prayers."

Mateus nodded to Father Joaquim, taking a moment to think. "Father, we have been friends a long time, no?"

"Yes, Mateus, a very long time."

"Is it not time for you to return to Europe?"

"What do you mean?"

"You have done all you can here. The padres are no longer welcome. If you are caught, you will be executed."

"I will never abandon my converted brethren, Mateus—never."

Again, Mateus sat silent for a moment, obviously familiar with Father Joaquim's resolve. Once Father Joaquim was committed to an idea or principle, there was no changing his mind.

"I admire you, Father. Your strength and spirit are praiseworthy."

"Praise the Lord, Mateus. My strength comes from Him."

"Get some rest, Father. You have had a long journey. Please, take my bed."

"Are you sure? What will you do?"

"What I always do in the evening—visit the gaijin bar in the port. It may be a quiet night, but perhaps I will get lucky with some women." Smiling sheepishly, Mateus bowed and departed.

Twelve

May 31, 1626
Shogun's Castle, Edo, Musashi Province

Outside, a thick blanket of nearly stationary clouds locked in the day's warmth as evening settled upon Edo. Inside the castle, matters were intensifying as Shogun Iemitsu was about to conduct an official assembly in his grand meeting chamber. Like the rest of his castle, the shogun's meeting chambers were extraordinary, exuding excessive wealth and riches. The walls of the chamber's high ceilings were adorned with beautiful Japanese artwork and calligraphy, interrupted at precise intervals by strong mahogany wooden beams and light Japanese screens. No costs had been spared in designing, building, and decorating the shogun's magnificent castle.

High above in the rafters hung the shogun's flag and family crest. The flag itself was all white, and the shogun's symbolic family crest, or *mon*, was circular in form, containing three hollyhock leaves. The hollyhock leaf resembled wild ginger, and the triple hollyhock became a recognized icon throughout Japan, symbolizing the strength of the Tokugawa clan and the shogun's dominance over the country.

Shogun Iemitsu was proud of the triple hollyhock family symbol, which could be traced back to his grandfather, the great Shogun Ieyasu, the first shogun of the Tokugawa clan. Young Shogun Iemitsu was particularly proud that his grandfather had begun his rule of Japan after a courageous and famous battle—the great Battle of Sekigahara in the year of 1600—where Ieyasu had defeated all opposing forces, making him military master of the country.

Among attendees at the meeting this day were the shogun, the shogun's father, Hidetada, the shogun's Go-Roju advisory cabinet, multiple high-ranking samurai, and an administrative official, Mizuno Kawachi.

With few exceptions, the room contained the most powerful and influential figures in Japan. Not the least was the shogun himself, who was the richest and most powerful samurai in all Japan. As the country's military leader, he and his Go-Roju advisory cabinet tightly controlled Japan's finances. The daimyo were required to pay tax subsidies to the shogun in the form of pre-defined quantities of rice, called *kokus*, which principally acted as the country's currency in matters of trade and commerce.

Although other forms of currency or barter existed in Japan, including silver coins, the true measure of one's wealth and earning power as a feudal warlord was rice production. The most powerful daimyo had the most—and most productive—land; as a result, they could generate greater quantities of rice production. The key, of course, was to secure as much productive land from the shogun as possible, and warlords manoeuvered and even fought for this privilege. All the while the shogun and his powerful regime ruled it all.

As Shogun Iemitsu, kneeling on a beautiful golden satin cushion atop an elevated platform, gazed around the room, all became silent. To the shogun's left knelt his father, Hidetada. On the right, also adjacent, knelt administrative official Mizuno Kawachi, who had been extended a special invitation to the meeting. Directly in front of the shogun knelt his Go-Roju cabinet, along with a large number of high-ranking samurai, all of them lined in rows. Finally, many specially invited Buddhist warrior monks lined the room's periphery.

The shogun turned to his right. "Official Mizuno Kawachi-san, we have called this meeting because soon you will depart Edo for Nagasaki."

"Yes, Lord," Mizuno Kawachi replied as he bowed deeply to the shogun.

"Before you depart, we want to ensure you are clear about your role and our expectations in the south."

"Yes, Lord. I am here to serve." Mizuno Kawachi again bowed deeply to the shogun.

"Your role is to annihilate Christianity in Nagasaki and throughout Kyushu," the shogun rumbled. "You will do this by whatever means necessary."

"Yes, Lord."

"You are now officially appointed *bugyo* of Nagasaki. You will replace the existing governor, Hasegawa Gonroku."

"Thank you, Lord Shogun. Your appointment is a great honor." Again, Mizuno Kawachi bowed deeply to the shogun.

"You will also act as my official representative in Nagasaki, and I empower you to oversee all of Kyushu's warlords in exterminating Christianity."

"Yes, Lord."

"You will further keep a close eye on Kyushu's daimyo to monitor their eradication of Christianity. Do you understand your duties?"

"Yes, Lord. I understand."

"I want you to place spies in all the domains to ensure that none of my subjects give sanctuary to any Christians."

"Yes, Lord."

"I will also place my own spies in the region."

"Yes, Lord."

"If hidden Christians are discovered, I want to be informed."

"I will keep you abreast, Lord Shogun."

"If our daimyo are neglectful in their domains, I want to know," the shogun emphasized. "They will be punished and may lose their lands."

"Yes, Lord."

"Do you have any questions, Governor?"

"No, Lord. I look forward to exterminating Christianity," Mizuno Kawachi replied with a determined nod.

"When do you depart?" a member of the shogun's Go-Roju cabinet asked.

"In one week," Mizuno Kawachi replied.

"What will you do upon your arrival in Nagasaki, Kawachi-san?" the shogun's father, Hidetada, asked.

"On arrival, I will raise stakes and execute Christians as a warning to others."

"Good," Hidetada replied approvingly.

"When I arrive, I want to send a strong message to Nagasaki and all the domains. I want them to know that Christianity will not be tolerated. I want the whole island to know that Christianity will perish, and anyone who opposes us will either recant through torture or face death."

"I applaud your resolve, Kawachi-san," the shogun declared ardently. "Please make us proud of your appointment."

Light chatter broke out in the chamber as the attendees appeared pleased with their progress. The chatter was quickly silenced by the shogun's father, who raised his hands in the air.

"I would also like you to keep an eye on the foreign traders and merchants in Nagasaki," Hidetada stated in a serious tone.

"Yes, Lord Hidetada."

"You do realize *why* they must be closely watched, do you not?" Hidetada asked.

"To ensure they do not smuggle in any more priests or missionaries, Hidetada-san," the governor replied.

"Not only that," Hidetada continued. "We also need you

to gather intelligence about a potential raid or invasion of our lands by the foreign barbarians."

"Yes, Lord."

"This is very important. The Spanish have set up a base in the Philippines."

"Yes, Lord. I am aware of their base in Manila."

"Do not take this duty lightly, Kawachi-san. The Spanish are a conquering nation."

"I have been educated in their tactics, Lord. First they send Christians to infiltrate and gather intelligence. Then they send their army."

"Correct," Hidetada replied. "If the Spanish have conquered so much of the new world, why would they not also seek to conquer Japan?"

Silent, the governor nodded in understanding.

"I have studied the world maps of the Spanish, the Portuguese, and the Dutch," Shogun Iemitsu interjected. "Our country is very small and seems insignificant in the greater world. We could easily be invaded and taken over by foreigners."

"We must be very careful," Hidetada added. "Let us not forget that the English and Dutch have already warned us about the king of Spain."

"It is of grave concern to us," Shogun Iemitsu declared. "How do we know King Philip will not seek to conquer *us* next?"

"Yes, Lord," the governor replied. "I will deploy spies to learn all that we can."

"You must!" Hidetada said. "The Christians are the forerunners of the pope, but they report to the king of their native land. All of them are in league together to invade us. This is how they invaded others."

Whispers buzzed throughout the chamber.

"Do not trust anyone," the shogun interjected. "Imagine if

the Christians, the foreigner barbarians, and the *ronin* were to join forces!"

Again, murmurs broke out in the chamber.

"Let us not underestimate the ronin," a senior member of the Go-Roju cabinet spoke up. "They remain a serious threat to the empire."

"Precisely," Hidetada exclaimed passionately. "Imagine the ronin joining forces with a Spanish army. They could overthrow us!"

The murmurs in the meeting chamber grew louder.

"I despise these masterless samurai. With no lords to serve, they should commit suicide. Instead, they wander the lands, menacing the empire!" The shogun's face was red, and the veins in his forehead became visible.

"You have a very important role in the south, Governor," Hidetada added. "You must keep watch of everything."

"Yes, Lord Hidetada. I am a loyal servant of the shogunate. I will not let you down."

"First, kill the Christians," the shogun shouted. "Second, watch the Spanish and Portuguese traders carefully. They know things."

"Yes, Lord."

"Third, keep an eye on these unemployed ronin. They roam our lands without purpose and are dangerous. They must not conspire against us."

"Yes, Lord."

"Good. I will *not* lose my empire because of some filthy religion or foreign power. This is *my* country, and I will not give it up to anyone."

Thirteen

Despite the unfamiliar bed, Father Joaquim slept well at Mateus da Costa's. Unlike his own straw bed, Mateus's was comfortable and luxurious.

Before rising, Father Joaquim made the sign of the cross with his hand. "In the name of the Father, His Son, and the Holy Ghost," Father Joaquim whispered. "Please, Father, bless us with a loan that will save the village. We need this money to escape disaster and persecution at the hands of Daimyo Shigemasa."

Father Joaquim stood up, stretched his body, then knelt down beside the bed. Searching inside his jacket, he located a secret compartment and withdrew a small, worn-out Bible.

Opening to the book of Luke, he searched for a verse and began to read: "'Therefore said he unto them, The harvest truly is great, but the labourers are few: pray ye therefore the Lord of the harvest, that he would send forth laborers into his harvest. Go your ways: behold, I send you forth as lambs among wolves.'"

Father Joaquim turned his head as he heard a light knock at the door. Mateus da Costa entered. "Ah, Father, good morning. I see you are already awake. How did you sleep?"

"Good morning, Mateus. It is good to see you. I slept well, thank you. How was your night?" Father Joaquim arose and sat on the edge of the bed.

"It was very good," Mateus answered with a smile that hinted at satisfaction. "I always enjoy my nights in the port."

"Was it prosperous?"

"With the Japanese women? Always!" Mateus smirked devilishly. "Japanese women love Portuguese traders."

"Ah, Mateus, good for you, but you know my cup gets filled in other ways."

"Of course, Father. But we traders cannot help ourselves. We seek to enjoy the best Nagasaki has to offer."

"And how is Nagasaki, Mateus? What is new since my last visit?"

"More bureaucracy and barriers," Mateus replied, frowning. "The shogun appears bent on closing this country to outsiders."

"Tell me more."

"Did you know that Japan is now influencing ships departing from Macao?" Mateus leaned against the doorframe.

"What do you mean?"

"I am saying the shogun's cabinet has stationed a Japanese official in Macao."

"In Macao. For what reason?"

"They are inspecting all prospective passengers and preventing anyone who looks suspicious from proceeding to Japan."

Father Joaquim shook his head solemnly.

"They are creating pre-boarding lists along with personal descriptions of everyone on board."

"For what purpose?"

"A copy of the list is given to the ship's captain, who must deliver it to the authorities in Nagasaki before he is permitted to anchor. If there is any discrepancy between the list and the persons arriving, the captain could be killed."

"Another measure to prevent missionaries from arriving?"

"Regretably, yes."

"Unbelievable. The whole country is closing itself off," Father Joaquim exclaimed in frustration.

"It is ridiculous." Mateus shook his head and rubbed the back of his neck. "Look at the Spanish. They were expelled two years ago. How do we know the Portuguese are not next?"

"Because the Portuguese have a trading monopoly here. We have traded with Japan for over seventy years, longer than anyone else."

"Nothing lasts forever, Father. Trade has become much more challenging, for the Portuguese and even the local merchants. Did you see all those boarded-up houses on the way here?"

Father Joaquim nodded. "It looks like they are growing in number."

"Those are former homes of Japanese Christians. The local authorities have seized them because of their beliefs."

"But I thought Governor Gonruku turned a blind eye to Christianity."

"Only when he can," Mateus replied. "The governor cannot *always* turn a blind eye. When Christian worship is evident, he must act or face the shogun's wrath."

"I was not aware Governor Gonroku had become a persecutor."

"Not a deliberate one. But I do not think he has much choice these days. The shogun is firmly in control of religion now. He decides everyone's faith."

"It is very sad that religious freedom has ended."

"Unfortunately, I think it will only get worse here."

"Because of the expected arrival of Mizuno Kawachi?" Father Joaquim asked.

"Yes. Hidden Christians in Nagasaki are very worried about his arrival. And the traders as well."

"Why the traders?"

"We traders and merchants, particularly the Portuguese, used to run Nagasaki."

"And that is changing?"

"Unfortunately, yes. Through the new governor, the shogun will exert greater control over trade going forward."

"That is not good." Father Joaquim's shoulders slumped.

Mateus nodded. "It means the shogun will wish to limit our profits even more. He does not like the Portuguese making so much money at the expense of the Japanese."

"This has been the case for many years now," Father Joaquim answered. "That is why the shogun installed the Pancado system—to limit the profits."

"Yes, but it is getting worse. The Pancado price limits are coming down, and our profits are getting squeezed more and more."

"That is unfortunate."

"The governor and the authorities are increasingly meddling in trade issues."

"All the more reason to sell in the black market," Father Joaquim replied, with a bit of enthusiasm returning to his voice.

"Exactly," Mateus answered with a smile. "Some merchandise we will sell under the Pancado system, but we will sell our best items on the black market. The wealthy are always willing to pay more for the best silk from China."

"The Japanese love their Chinese silk."

"They certainly do, and right now everyone wants their silk in red and black."

"Indeed, the Japanese do like their fashion, and this is where I would like to help—with the silk trade."

"Oh?" Mateus raised an eyebrow.

"Surely my silver loan is not a gift. I want to repay you, and I have the language skills and knowledge of local customs to help you."

"What do you mean?"

"Let me do the negotiating for you in the black market."

Mateus paused for a moment as he thought about Father Joaquim's proposal. "It is a tempting offer, Father, but I am not so sure. There are more complications now. The Dutch are growing more jealous of our strongholds in Nagasaki and Macao."

"That is nothing new. Are they still sacking our ships at sea?"

"They are trying to, but they are also causing increasing trouble for us in Nagasaki."

"Are they still moaning about their lousy port in Hirado?"

"Of course. I suspect they will never be happy with that small fishing village. They want to control Nagasaki now."

"Some things never change."

"They do a little." Mateus shifted his footing. "The Dutch are frustrated and getting more aggressive in their tactics."

"That does not sound good."

"It is not, Father. They are jealous and very unpredictable in their troublemaking."

"I still would like to help, Mateus. I would like the ability to earn back the loan."

"Let me think about it, Father. It could be very dangerous for you as a padre. If you are discovered, they will execute you."

"Do not worry, Mateus. Our Father looks after us. We cannot live our lives in fear."

Mateus was quiet. "Let me think about it, Father. For the time being, let me secure the loan first."

"Very well, Mateus, as you wish. You will make enquiries tonight?"

"All the influential Portuguese traders with the deep pockets will be at the gaijin bar tonight. Let us see how the night goes."

"Thank you, Mateus." Father Joaquim bowed gratefully. "As always, your assistance to the mission is most appreciated."

"It is nothing, Father. It is the least I can do for the mission and my friend."

Fourteen

May 31, 1626
Arima Domain, Hizen Province

As Daimyo Shigemasa approached one of the larger farming villages on his domain, with a dozen of his most senior samurai also on horseback and another hundred or so on foot, the villagers scurried about, frantically preparing for the unexpected visit.

"Welcome, Lord Shigemasa!" a peasant farmer cried out as the detachment entered the village.

Behind the peasant many other farmers arrived along with their families in order to greet their daimyo.

"Welcome, Lord. Welcome, Lord," the crowd echoed as they bowed profusely to the man whose mere whim could decide their fate.

"I remember this village well," Shigemasa said as he eyed the village intently from his tall black horse. "You are the village that is always behind on rice production."

"We try our best, Lord Shigemasa," a peasant exclaimed in defense as he ran up to the daimyo, carrying a wooden pot filled with cold water. "Please, have some cool water after your long journey."

Ignoring the peasant and his offer, Shigemasa continued. "This village is the most unproductive in my entire domain. You have the greatest number of farmers but produce the least amount of rice."

"We work very hard for you, dear Lord, every day! Our fields may not be as fertile as others, but we work day and night for you," another man dared to say.

"Do not offer me excuses for your laziness!"

Another farmer approached Shigemasa and his large horse with a pot of water. "Please, Lord, take some cold water. You and your horse must be very thirsty."

"I am here for rice, not water," Shigemasa roared as he kicked the pot out of the farmer's hands, sending it to the ground, where it shattered.

The terrified peasant farmer took a few steps back.

"This soil looks perfectly fertile to me," the daimyo announced from atop his horse.

Another brave farmer stepped forward. "Lord, we would not lie to you nor make excuses, but the soil on these lands is not deep and there are many rocks."

"Silence, ignorant peasant!"

"Please, Lord, let us move to another parcel of land," a young peasant cried out. "We can improve our production on better soil."

"You will not move to other lands. *These* are your lands!" Astride his magnificent black horse, trotting around the village, the daimyo observed the filled rice bags. "Bring me your rice production—immediately."

"Yes, Lord," the peasants answered as they ran in all directions to collect every bag of rice in the village.

"How many sacks of rice do I see before me?" the warlord asked.

One of the peasants began to count the bags. "Nearly forty large sacks of rice, Lord," he answered, nervously.

"You are required to produce one hundred sacks of rice. This is less than half of your quota."

"Please, Lord, it is not possible," a distressed woman near the rear of the crowd cried out.

"Silence!" The daimyo glared at the peasants. "All across my domain I hear excuses for failing to meet quotas, but your village is the worst."

"Please, Lord, you own our entire lives," another farmer lamented. "It is not possible to work any harder."

"Nonsense. You are slackening in the fields, and there must be a reason. Are there Christians among you?"

"No, Lord, no," the village leader replied. "We are Buddhists. You know this."

"Then why are you slackening in the fields?"

No one dared reply.

"All the other daimyo are getting richer and producing more rice, but not me," the daimyo shouted in frustration. "If you are not slackening because of Christianity, then it means you are slackening because you are getting too old to work in the field."

"Please, Lord, no," a peasant begged.

"Who is the oldest amongst you?" the daimyo asked as he scanned the villagers.

No one spoke.

"Find me the oldest farmer in this village."

Quickly, Shigemasa's samurai began to rustle through the villagers as a few shouted in despair. After a few minutes of manhandling a number of older farmers in the village, the samurai pushed two elders to the front of the crowd.

"Bind their hands behind their back," Shigemasa commanded, then turned back to the terrified villagers. "If you are slow in the rice fields, it means you do not have the proper motivation."

The daimyo faced his samurai who detained the two elders. "Place a straw raincoat over their shoulders."

The samurai placed layers of straw over the bound older men as the other peasants wailed and cried in protest.

"Set them on fire," the daimyo ordered.

Terrified, the bound old men tried to run, but they were quickly apprehended by the daimyo's samurai. A samurai then approached the old farmers with a wooden match and lit their straw coats.

The bound men wailed and screamed in pain as their flesh burned. Helpless to escape the flames, they ran back and forth in agony.

"Look! They are dancing," a samurai declared as he laughed at the burning men.

"A *mino-dori* dance!" another samurai mocked as the other warriors laughed out loud.

Soon, the old men fell to the ground, and the stench of their burning bodies caused the villagers to cover their noses.

"I have no tolerance for unproductivity," Shigemasa stated coolly. "If you do not meet your next quota, we will find two more victims on my return. I trust this will be sufficient motivation for you to work harder."

Turning their backs, the daimyo and his samurai departed, leaving the charred bodies and the wailing villagers behind them.

Fifteen

In the back corner of a dark, smoky gaijin bar along Nagasaki's harbor front, Mateus da Costa sat drinking, smoking, and laughing with four other Portuguese traders. The establishment was run by a Portuguese merchant and consisted of a dozen small tightly packed tables. As most of the patrons were European, they typically wore colorful, oversized European clothes, with large boots, baggy pants, and majestic shirts sporting multiple buttons and excess cloth hanging from the shoulders. With just a hint of Japanese ambiance, the overriding theme and mood of the bar and its regulars was Portuguese.

As the evening wore on and Mateus judged that his friends had consumed enough liquor to be jovial but not so much as to lose their acuity, he decided it was time to ask. "Gentlemen, I need you to look deep into your hearts and then dig deep into your money purses. Father Joaquim Martinez and his village of Catholic converts need five hundred pieces of silver, quickly. If he does not get it, he might be killed." Mateus set down his mug sharply, as if for emphasis. "The villagers might be killed too—even the children and a newborn."

"Why should we help, Mateus?" one of the traders asked before swigging half his beer in one large gulp.

Mateus puffed on his pipe and exhaled. "Because it is the right thing to do," he answered.

"Mateus ..." The man leaned forward and grinned. "Mateus, I am a trader, a businessman. The right thing for *me* is to make as much money as possible in the coming trading season." He leaned back and took another large swig of his beer.

"He is right," a second trader agreed. "We are in May now, and the July trading season is on our doorstep. We will all need as much working capital as possible."

"Gentlemen, we need to think beyond trade and working capital. As Catholics, we have an obligation to help the Church." Mateus slowly turned his head to make eye contact with each of his fellow traders.

"Five hundred silver coins is a large amount of money," a third trader bellowed.

"Why does Rome not support the fathers?" another asked.

"Because Rome is half-way around the world and hopelessly behind on its promises. Father Joaquim needs our help now."

"Why is it so important for you to help this Father Joaquim?"

"Because we have known each other for more than twenty years, and he would do anything to help me. Please, gentlemen, divided five ways, it is just one hundred silver coins each."

"Just one hundred," the third trader thundered. "Do you know how many nights with Japanese whores one hundred silver coins will buy?"

"Of course he knows," the first trader quipped before turning back to face Mateus. "How do we know the father will pay us back? He could be dead in a week."

"Agreed," the second trader added. "The few remaining fathers in Japan are on death row. As soon as they are found in hiding, they will be executed."

"Then lend *me* the money, and *I* will pay you back. I will help the father."

"So we lend you the money, Mateus, not the father?" the first trader asked.

"Yes. You will take *my* creditworthiness in the loan, not the father's, and *I* will take responsibility for repayment."

"When do we get our money back?" the second trader asked, slurring his words.

"After the July trading season, but before 1627," Mateus answered.

The traders shot back their drinks and then puffed on their tobacco as they considered the matter.

"With interest?" the third trader asked.

"No interest," Mateus answered. "This is not a commercial transaction. This is for our Church."

The traders, still puffing on their pipes and cigars, began to nod.

"Very well, Mateus," the first trader said. "I will lend *you* the money on *your* creditworthiness, but not the father's. I do not think he will live long enough to pay us back."

"Agreed," the remaining traders echoed as they nodded and guzzled more spirits.

"So it is agreed upon." Mateus smiled and looked at each of the traders. "Tomorrow afternoon, I will visit each of your quarters for collection."

Mateus stood up, shot back a cup of *sake*, and stepped away from the table before removing his hat, bowing to the group, and exiting the smoky bar.

Outside, Mateus took a deep breath and felt relieved that his trader acquaintances had agreed to provide the loan. He poured some tobacco leaves into his pipe, gently lit it, and casually walked down the street, leaving the port area. *Father Joaquim will be pleased with the result. I am grateful these greedy traders agreed to provide the loan. Without it, I am sure Father Joaquim's fate would not end well.*

Mateus left the port area and ambled toward his home, just a bit tipsy. Suddenly, before he realized what had happened, he felt himself falling to the ground, his head throbbing. Warm liquid poured over his ear. He touched his fingers to his scalp and then, as he examined the red blood, he heard the distinct sound of a Dutch voice. He looked up and saw his two attackers, one slightly smaller than average and one much larger.

"Look what we have here," the big Dutchman said, glaring down.

"A bleeding Portuguese pig," the smaller one added.

Mateus moaned as he lay in the street, blood pumping forth from the gash the bottle had made when the big man slammed it against his head.

"Look, the pig is squirming in the dirt," the smaller Dutchman said before breaking into a hearty laugh. "We see too much of you, little pig. Every time we see trade, we see you."

"We have grown tired of your smell," the larger Dutchman said as he kicked Mateus forcefully in his chest.

"One by one, it is time to eliminate the competition," the smaller man added as he walked over to Mateus, delivering a forceful punch to his face and breaking his nose.

Holding his bloodied nose, Mateus gasped as he tried to catch his breath so he could speak. "You will not get away with this! Your actions are futile. Nagasaki is a Portuguese city and always will be."

"Not forever," the larger man said as he kicked Mateus powerfully in his side, breaking a few ribs.

Mateus cried out in pain. "Go back to Hirado or Holland!" Holding his ribs, Mateus lay immobilized in the street, bleeding from his nose and head.

"Stand him up," the small Dutchman directed his larger companion.

Effortlessly, the large, powerful Dutchman grabbed Mateus, stood him up, and held his arms behind his back.

"Your time is up, Portuguese pig," the smaller Dutchman said as he produced a sharp knife from his jacket. "It is time for you to visit the slaughterhouse."

Mateus struggled as he caught sight of the knife, but his injuries made him too weak to escape.

"Say a prayer, pig," the smaller man said coldly as he drove his knife into Mateus's throat. Taking no chances, the man continued to cut through Mateus's throat as blood gushed forth. Mateus made a gurgling sound, then fell to the ground, dead, his blood filling the street.

"Quick, fetch his bag," the smaller Dutchman directed his partner. "Open it and place the items inside. Hurry."

Swiftly, the large Dutchman opened Mateus's bag and placed some articles inside, including a Bible and a large crucifix.

Sixteen

Father Joaquim knelt against Mateus's bed in the early-morning light saying his prayers. Relaxed and at ease, he was reading from the book of Matthew in his personal Bible.

The same day went Jesus out of the house, and sat by the sea side. And great multitudes were gathered together unto him, so that he went into a ship, and sat; and the whole multitude stood on the shore. And he spake many things unto them in parables, saying, Behold, a sower went forth to sow; And when he sowed, some seeds fell by the way side, and the fowls came and devoured them up: Some fell upon stony places, where they had not much earth: and forthwith they sprang up, because they had no deepness of earth: And when the sun was up, they were scorched; and because they had no root, they withered away. And some fell among thorns; and the thorns sprang up, and choked them: But other fell into good ground, and brought forth fruit, some a hundredfold, some sixtyfold, some thirtyfold. Who hath ears to hear, let him hear.

Father Joaquim gently closed his Bible as he reflected on the passage and began to pray. "Oh, Lord, you have given me life so I may impart Your Word to others. I live for You, my Father. I lay down my life to serve You. Bless me this day, Father, to stand another day and do Your work. Oh, Lord, bless me with fertile soil to plant your seeds."

As the father uttered the last word of his prayer, Mateus da Costa's front door crashed down. Four armed officials stormed inside.

"Halt where you are," the first official shouted.

"What are you doing?" another demanded. "Are you Christian? Are you praying?"

"Who are you?" the first official asked. "Stand up!"

As Father Joaquim stood to face the officials, each placed his hand on the hilt of his sword.

"He is a foreign priest," one of the officials shouted as he observed Father Joaquim's Bible on the bed, quickly grabbing it.

"You are under arrest," another official shouted.

"Please be calm," Father Joaquim replied. "I am a colleague of Mateus da Costa, the man who lives here. He will straighten out all of this upon his return."

"Mateus da Costa is dead!" one of the officials declared.

"What?" Father Joaquim exclaimed, wide-eyed.

"He was murdered in the port area last night. And now you are under arrest."

"You will be executed, Padre," another official declared coldly.

"I do not want to hurt anyone, but I cannot go with you today," Father Joaquim answered.

"Do not do anything stupid, Padre. We will kill you if you resist." Quickly, in a show of force, the officials unsheathed their swords and advanced on Father Joaquim. But, drawing on his decades of study and practice with Master Yamaguchi, he evaded them. Father Joaquim deflected the first official's swipe of the blade and pushed him into the other three officials. In the tangled confusion, Father Joaquim seized a sword from one of them. Then, with two swift throat slashes, he quickly dispensed with two of them, their blood spattering the room.

"Put down your sword," one of the two remaining officials demanded.

"You first."

"Kill him," one of the officials bellowed as he charged at Father Joaquim, swinging his sword from left to right in a large swiping motion. The second official followed closely behind. With one deft swing, Father Joaquim knocked the sword from the first attacker's hand before kicking him in the chest, sending him flying into his colleague. Each lost his balance and stumbled sideways. As they reassembled for their attack, Father Joaquim quickly ended their lives with two precise slashes to their necks.

"Lord, forgive me, for I have sinned," Father Joaquim said meekly as he dropped the sword in his hand, grabbed his Bible and bag, and quickly fled Mateus da Costa's home.

Seventeen

At least the hot sun was not beating down on them. Instead a blanket of afternoon clouds shaded Arima's mountains and surrounding plains, including the village. Having worked in the rice fields since sunrise, all the villagers were exhausted. As usual, mud and dirt covered their faces, including those of the children, who were also forced to work in the fields. The peasants had no choice but to labor from morning to night in order to make their production quota. The daimyo had made clear the consequences of failure.

Taking a late break, all but one sat on the ground next to the rice fields, speechless and weary. Carrying a large old pot, Master Yamaguchi walked among the villagers, pouring water into wooden cups.

Master Yamaguchi finished pouring and stood up straight. "Listen," he said, "we have been working very hard lately. Let us take a short rest this afternoon."

Given the enormity of their rice quota, the villagers were hesitant, but they knew they all needed some rest.

"What shall we do?" young Shiro asked.

"Let us play a game," Master Yamaguchi responded.

The children cheered as they all leapt from the ground and rushed toward the beloved elder leader of the village.

"What game shall we play, Master Yamaguchi?" a young girl asked as she tugged at the old man's worn-out garment.

"I propose we have a competition: adults versus children. The winners get to take the rest of the day off." Master Yamaguchi smiled down at the children.

"What is the game? What is the game?" the children cried excitedly.

"The game is simple," Master Yamaguchi replied. "It is called rocks in the pot."

"What is that? What is that?"

"Quiet. Please. Let me explain." Master Yamaguchi held out his hands, beckoning the children to settle down and listen.

"Here is the pot, and there are the rocks." Master Yamaguchi pointed at a small pile of rocks near the edge of the rice field.

"From a distance of ten feet, you will throw rocks into the pot. The group with the most rocks in the pot takes the rest of the day off."

"Competition accepted," one of the parents shouted as he leapt to his feet and ran toward the rocks. "We are not going to let these little children beat us."

"You are right," a peasant mother added, laughing. "I think the adults deserve a day off, not these misbehaving children."

For a brief moment at least, the mood changed, and the villagers were actually living, not just working to avoid death.

"There are twelve children, so we need twelve adults," Master Yamaguchi shouted playfully as he set the rules. "Two rocks per player."

The children cheered as they ran to the front of the group, pushing to be the first to throw.

Master Yamaguchi intervened, settling the matter. Standing firmly at the front was young Shiro, who was fending off the other children.

"Well, it looks like Shiro-kun will be the first to throw," Master Yamaguchi declared.

Young Shiro was recognized as a very talented boy. Not only was he physically strong, but he was also regarded as exceptionally intelligent and spiritual. When Shiro wasn't working in the fields, he spent much of his time with Catechist Tonia, becoming proficient in Portuguese as well as memorizing verses from the Bible. At the young age of six, he had already developed a strong faith in God and become a leader and role model for the other village children. It was thus no surprise that Shiro would be the first child to throw a rock.

"Let us get started," Master Yamaguchi hollered.

Despite his anxiousness, young Shiro closed his eyes for a few seconds, taking a moment to pray. When he opened them, the other children cheered as they wished him well in his throw. With no hesitation, young Shiro threw his stone ten feet in the air, landing it dead center in Master Yamaguchi's pot.

The children again cheered, this time in delight. Master Yamaguchi and the parents in the village applauded.

"I will be the next to throw," Shiro's uncle stated as he paraded to the front, politely edging his nephew out of the way with a smile. "I think you will find the adults equally capable."

Confidently, Shiro's uncle threw his stone high in the air, and it also landed in Master Yamaguchi's pot. Laughing, most of the adults gave him a clap of congratulation while the children looked on in anticipation.

The games and throwing continued until almost all of the stones had been thrown. Not by accident, the adults kept the score equal until the final throws of the game. The score was seven to seven, with one child and one adult left to throw.

Finally, the last child walked up to the line. She was a young girl, age nine, with long dark hair and a cheery smile. The crowd chanted with enthusiasm, aware this would be the children's last throw.

"You can do it! You can do it," the children cheered.

"Go, Miwa-chan," Shiro shouted. "Visualize your rock in the pot, and it will be so."

Smiling, young Miwa grabbed her stone, poised herself, and threw it gracefully into the center of the pot. The children shrieked in delight, jumping and dancing around little Miwa.

"It is not over yet," one of the adults yelled. "We still have one more throw."

Slowly the children settled down as the final adult walked up to the line. Again, the villagers cheered in anticipation.

Wasting no time, the adult threw the stone … and missed.

For several minutes the children screamed in joy and danced before the adults.

"Catechists Tonia and Miguel have been hiding inside all day," Master Yamaguchi said. "I am sure they are very lonely. Who would like to join them for some playtime and stories?"

"Yay!" the children cheered again. "No more work in the field today!"

"Come with me then," Master Yamaguchi said as he led the children toward one of the small dwellings, where Tonia and Miguel kept cover.

Meanwhile, the adults knew what was in store for them. Like every other day, it would be non-stop work until the dark hours. The village simply could not afford to miss their new daily quota.

Eighteen

Owing to its trading ties and commercial significance, Nagasaki had long been an important port. Recently, however, because of the shogun's growing obsession with the prospect of a Spanish military invasion, Nagasaki had gained an even greater measure of the leader's attention. Dutch and English traders eager to take the lead in trade with Japan had repeatedly told the shogun and his cabinet that Spanish and Portuguese traders and missionaries were actually spies helping to prepare for a Spanish attack on Japan.

So the shogun wanted to have *his* man in this increasingly important post. Hasegawa Gonroku, the current bugyo, was not that man. He lacked the stomach for the kind of brutal, dictatorial rule—often including tortures and executions—the shogun demanded. Gonruku himself, in fact, knew he wasn't the right man for the job and had even suggested he should be replaced.

Thus, it wasn't long before the shogun determined Governor Hasegawa Gonroku was not fit for his post. The shogun's new appointment, Mizuno Kawachi, would arrive soon to take over. Until then, Gonruku had a job to do and, despite his distaste for the violent parts of the responsibility, he was determined to leave office without losing face.

That determination was tested when, in the middle of what had been a quiet day, two officials, nearly breathless, rushed into the governor's office. "Bugyo, we have serious news to report!"

"Speak," the governor replied.

"Four officials have been murdered in the residential quarters," the first official exclaimed.

"What?" the governor asked, realizing any hope he'd had of ending his term quietly had just been obliterated.

"They were murdered inside the home of a gaijin trader," the second official announced.

Stunned, the governor leapt from his relaxed kneeling position. "My officials were murdered? Have you arrested the gaijin?"

"No, the gaijin trader was murdered the night before. He was murdered in the streets near the port last night."

With his eyes closed and his forehead resting on his right hand, the governor asked, "What else do we know?"

"The gaijin trader was an avid Christian and was carrying a cross, a Bible, and other items of Christian worship," the first official said.

"When his identity was confirmed, our officials immediately went to his quarters to investigate," the second official added.

"Who was he?"

"A well-known and long-standing trader," the first official answered.

"What is his name?"

"Mateus da Costa, a Portuguese trader," the first official replied.

"I know this man. He has been trading in Nagasaki for decades."

"Is he a devout Christian, Governor?" the second official asked.

Deep in thought, the governor looked confused. "I do not think so," he replied slowly, shaking his head. "What did Mateus's home reveal?"

"When our officials arrived, all four were murdered," the second official said.

"What did you find in his home?"

"Blood and standard trading papers," the first official answered.

The second official then offered his assessment. "I think the murderers were professional killers, Governor."

"Why do you think so?"

"Because our four officials were all killed with single slashes to their throats. They had no other cuts or wounds, which suggests the murderers were experts in weaponry."

"How many criminals do you think were involved?"

"I do not know, Governor. But there must have been many. It would take several men at least to kill our officials like this. Our officials are very well trained."

The governor knelt down next to a small table and stared unseeingly at the wall. "This is horrible news. I do *not* need a Christian scandal during my last days as governor. It will be a humiliation for me before the shogun."

"What should we do, Governor?" the first official asked.

"Put every official in Nagasaki and the entire prefecture on high alert. I want anything out of the ordinary immediately investigated."

"What else, Governor?"

"Get the tracking dogs. I want to find these criminals immediately. I *cannot* suffer such embarrassment before the shogun."

★ ★ ★

The bright European clothing that had made Father Joaquim's disguise possible earlier now made his escape nearly impossible. So in the bright afternoon sun, the Jesuit sat on a rock in a thicket of shrubs, near the top of the mountain, hiding and contemplating—and mourning over the lives he'd ended. *Lord, Father, forgive me for my sins. While my transgressors were hostile, I have taken the lives of others and sinned. Please grant me forgiveness, Father. Is it right, Lord, to break Your law against killing in order to save the lives of others?*

He sighed then scanned the nearby terrain. Seeing no one, Father Joaquim continued to inch his way slowly up the mountain, away from the main trail. Soon it would be evening, and in the dark he'd be able to make better time on his way down the other side of the mountain, away from Nagasaki and toward the domain of Arima.

News of these deaths will spread quickly throughout Nagasaki and the domains. I cannot be seen. I must only travel at night from this point forward. No matter how long it takes … Father Joaquim removed his colorful jacket and began rubbing muddy soil on the garment as he tried to dull its brightness.

I cannot believe my dear friend is dead. Oh, Lord Father, please help me understand Your ways. Mateus da Costa was our only hope. Please, Father, please help me understand.

Father Joaquim paused and looked skyward as he began to pray aloud. "Oh, Father, please prepare a table for my dear friend Mateus. Welcome him into the kingdom of heaven as you have warmly welcomed all those before him. Mateus has always been a dear friend to me and a friend of the mission. Oh, Lord, please prepare a table for him."

Father Joaquim reached the mountain peak where he could see all of Nagasaki and the other neighboring mountainous peaks. Throughout the nearby mountains, Father Joaquim could also see other guard stations, where government guards watched over Nagasaki and all travelers entering and exiting the region. Since travel had become restricted in Japan, these look-out points and guard stations had become integral in keeping watch over anything suspicious throughout the empire.

While it was necessary for Father Joaquim to be patient and wait until dark before descending the mountain, it was also imperative he return to the village as soon as possible. Father Joaquim cared deeply about the villagers and their welfare, and he began to comprehend what lay ahead for his adopted people. Clearly, with Mateus da Costa dead, things had taken a turn for the worse.

What shall we do? With Mateus dead, all hope of a loan is gone. How are we going to pay Daimyo Shigemasa 500 silver coins? Should we escape Arima without paying our taxes? But Daimyo Shigemasa would hunt us down. Oh, Lord, show us the way.

Nineteen

Since young Shogun Iemitsu had come into power under appointment of his father, Hidetada, he had become obsessed with being adored and worshiped. So when he called for a celebration, it was only natural *he* would be the focal point, as well as the primary planner of the event.

The evening gala was taking place in the large outdoor courtyard of the shogun's castle. Hundreds of guests were assembled to exalt the shogun, including his entire family, members of Japan's imperial family, the shogun's Go-Roju cabinet, multiple daimyo and high-powered samurai from domains throughout the country, consorts, mistresses, hundreds of actors, performers, show-people, and other entertainers.

The evening's first show was about to finish. It was a display of archery, and dozens of samurai dressed in white uniforms were assembled in a long line next to the shogun.

Shogun Iemitsu had placed himself on an elevated platform at the head of the courtyard, next to his castle. The platform made him more visible, making it clear who was the center of attention. Next to the shogun, kneeling on the four corners of his platform, were four beautiful young Japanese girls. Those four were among the many other beautiful young girls standing nearby. All were his consorts.

Shogun Iemitsu nodded to the lead archer at the front of the line. A moment later, the lead archer let his arrow soar through the air. A split-second after that, the next archer let his arrow soar, and so on, down the line, until all three dozen archers had released their arrows. In a majestic scene, all the arrows flew through the air, one after the other, until each hit the same target, all in perfect sequence, several hundred feet away.

"Well done," the shogun shouted in exhilaration as he guzzled a shot of sake. "Perfect! My samurai make me proud."

The shogun had been drinking sake heavily since the evening began. When one of his female servants saw his cup was nearly empty, she quickly but carefully refilled it. The golden rule was simple: never let the master's cup run dry for more than a moment. Such an offense would be seen as disrespect for the shogun and would lead to serious repercussions.

"My samurai are the finest in the land," Shogun Iemitsu shouted as he smiled smugly and gulped another round of sake. "Bring out the animal show."

Moments later, the outside doors of the courtyard were opened and a long procession of animals began to enter, led by their animal keepers.

"These are all gifts for you, Lord Shogun," a senior retainer declared. "They have been brought from all over the world."

"I hope so," the shogun snarled. "The last animals you presented to me were embarrassing."

"I am sorry for your disappointment, Lord Shogun," the retainer replied. "These new animals are far more interesting. Some of them were even brought from the deserts of Africa."

"Let me see them," the shogun bellowed in a drunken tone.

"Please have a look, Lord. The first one is a giraffe. You have never been given one of these before."

Belching a deep alcoholic burp, the shogun laughed.

"Look at its stupid long neck. What a stupid-looking creature! No wonder foreigners are so stupid; their animals look stupid too!"

"We have many animals to present to you today, Lord. The next ones are colorful birds from India."

Behind the giraffes followed many servants and animal keepers carrying sticks to which beautiful birds were tied via strings attached to their legs.

"That one looks interesting," the shogun commented as he pointed at a colorful parrot.

"Yes, very beautiful, Lord. That one is from the south of India," the retainer replied excitedly.

"Bring that one into my quarters," the shogun demanded. "I like that one."

"Yes, Lord, I will do so immediately." The senior retainer quickly addressed the animal keeper and directed him and the parrot inside.

The shogun slugged another shot of sake before demanding, "What more do you have?"

"We have saved the best for last, Lord Shogun," the retainer answered.

"What do you have? Show it to me!"

"Bring in the tigers," the retainer called out.

Again the doors opened and three tigers were pulled into the courtyard. Each tiger was bound by rope and shackles and dragged in by multiple men. Feeling restrained, the tigers were restless and angry.

"These tigers are wild, Lord. They are not easy to control," the retainer explained.

"They look strong," the shogun stated, his interest evident. "Are they dangerous?"

"Very dangerous, Lord."

"Show me. What happens when they are provoked?"

"That is not a good idea, Lord. They are very wild."

"I want to see." The shogun glared at the retainer. "Tell those showmen to release a tiger and poke it with their sticks. I want to see the animal's reaction."

Obediently, the retainer stood up, walked over to the servants, and ordered them to remove the shackles from one of the tigers. They obeyed, albeit very carefully. Then the retainer approached the two showmen holding flags and gave them the shogun's orders to poke the tiger with their poles.

Despite their fear, the showmen reluctantly approached the tiger and began aggressively poking it with their long poles. The tiger let out a ferocious roar.

"Amazing," the shogun announced. "These creatures *are* ferocious!"

The tiger let out another huge roar as he tried to escape the grip of the many men containing him with the ropes.

"Let the tiger go," the shogun commanded. "If you two can kill the tiger with your poles, I will give your families a lifetime supply of rice," he yelled to the men with the flags.

Impressed by the offer, the showmen focused themselves. A lifetime of rice amounted to a small fortune, a good incentive. The other incentive was fear of the certain death that awaited them if they failed to obey. One of the showmen quickly slammed his pole on top of the tiger's head, jolting it to the ground. Almost simultaneously, the other showman pounded his pole into the tiger's throat. The beast fixed its furious eyes on that second man.

As the man raised the pole to strike again, the tiger lunged powerfully, breaking his swing and knocking him off balance. The tiger swiped at the man's chest with its huge paws, tearing him open and knocking him to the ground. Then, with one ferocious bite, the enraged creature severed the man's neck, sending his head rolling through the courtyard.

"Spectacular!" the shogun shouted in delight as his guests gasped in horror.

Stunned, the other showman took a step back and froze in fear, unsure what to do.

"Kill the tiger," the shogun roared as he stood and faced the lone man remaining with the pole. "Do not prove yourself a coward!"

Terrified, the showman took another step back. "Give me a sword," he shouted in despair.

"Nonsense," the shogun answered smugly. "You have a weapon. Use your pole."

The crowd looked on anxiously as the tiger and the last showman squared off. Taking a step back, the showman's fear showed in his eyes as the tiger emitted a deep-throated growl.

"Attack," the shogun demanded. "Attack!"

The showman gripped his pole hard and aimed it directly at the tiger's head. Lunging the pole forward, he slammed it into the tiger's nose, breaking it and drawing blood. Delirious in anger, the tiger pounced on the showman, knocking him through the air and landing on top of him. With his large paws, he tore away at the man's chest and face, before taking a bite out of the man's neck, removing half of it and filling his mouth with blood. The second showman was also dead.

"Wonderful," the shogun bellowed in pleasure. "These animals are killers. I adore them."

The other showmen slowly approached the tiger and threw many nooses around its neck. As the tiger was contained, other men removed the two bodies of their dead associates.

"What a great show!" The shogun rejoiced as he gulped another shot of sake and smiled. "I wasn't expecting this much excitement!"

"What would you like to see next, Lord Shogun?" a senior retainer enquired.

"I want to see a show of budo. I want to see the martial training of my samurai. But first, I must urinate."

Drunk, the shogun tried to stand up, but stumbled. In response, the four beautiful young girls quickly rose to aid him. Smirking, the shogun grabbed their chests, molesting them as he stood up.

"I need assistance to urinate." The shogun walked over to one of his servants, a frightened boy, twelve years old, and pulled him inside the castle.

"You will do just fine," he said and smirked in a devilish manner as they disappeared into the castle together.

Twenty

June 06, 1626
Arima Domain, Hizen Province

A few faint hints of dawn's light began to penetrate the night's black grip as Father Joaquim carefully worked his way down through the mountain's foothills, detecting the warmer temperature at the lower altitude. After a long and harrowing journey, the disturbed and disappointed Jesuit was finally approaching the village and its people, who had become his extended family.

As Father Joaquim reached flatland, the sun slowly started to rise, and he sought to console himself as his mind wandered. *Things will be okay. God, it is good to be back! This village is my home. Lord, thank you!*

As the father entered the village and walked by Master Yamaguchi's small, dilapidated home, he took a brief glance inside to see if his dear friend was awake. Approaching closer, he saw candlelight flickering inside.

"Is that you, Father?" Master Yamaguchi's voice penetrated the small window.

"Yes, Master Yamaguchi. I hope I did not wake you."

Master Yamaguchi stood up and walked to the window. "Nonsense, Father. You know I am an early riser."

"How did you know it was me? You did not even look out the window."

"I dreamed you would arrive today, and here you are. Would you like to come in, Father? You look tired. Please come in and rest."

"Thank you, Master Yamaguchi."

The old man walked to the door and opened it.

Stepping in, Father Joaquim bowed and took off his shoes.

"Would you like a cup of tea?" Master Yamaguchi asked.

"That would be nice; I am quite thirsty," Father Joaquim replied before kneeling on the floor, across from Master Yamaguchi.

"How was your visit to Nagasaki?"

"I have bad news, Master Yamaguchi."

"Oh?"

"Mateus da Costa is dead. He was murdered in the street, in the middle of the night."

"That is awful. Do you know who killed him?"

"Perhaps it was the Dutch, or a competitor. I do not know."

"Is that all the bad news?"

"Unfortunately not." Father Joaquim paused and took a deep breath. "When the authorities arrived to investigate, they discovered me in Mateus's home."

"And what happened?"

"They wished to arrest me and take me to the governor."

"And?"

"A fight broke out, and I killed them."

"But obviously you escaped."

"Yes, but it was very close. I suspect nearly every government official in Nagasaki is looking for the killer now."

"I had reservations about this trip, Father, but I did not want to prevent you from going."

"I know you did, Master Yamaguchi, but I had to see if Mateus could provide us with a loan."

"You did your best, Father. You cannot fault yourself for this."

"But I killed four men, Master Yamaguchi. I have sinned, and my conscience weighs on me."

"I understand, but I am sure they would have killed you first if they had had the chance. These are dangerous times."

Father Joaquim buried his head in his hands.

"You are alive because it is the will of the Lord. He looks after you."

Raising his head slowly, the priest replied, "Thank you, Master Yamaguchi. The Lord is indeed my salvation, and my protector, but I must admit I do not understand His ways."

"What do you mean?"

"I was sure Mateus would provide us the loan necessary to save the village."

"Perhaps the Lord has another plan for us," Master Yamaguchi replied before taking another sip of tea.

"My heart is filled with faith, and I know the Lord will look after us. I just do not know how."

"Nor do I, Father, but in the end I am sure we will be okay."

Father Joaquim nodded as he paused and sipped his tea.

"And how is the village, Master Yamaguchi?"

"Everyone is fine, Father. Although we continue to work incessantly."

"And how is that going?"

"The mood is low, and we are falling behind. It will be impossible to meet Daimyo Shigemasa's quota."

"We knew that would be the case. That is why we must pray."

"Then we will all pray," Master Yamaguchi replied. "And in the meantime?"

"We try to produce as much rice as possible. The closer we are to Daimyo Shigemasa's quota, the better."

"I agree, Father."

"And I am going to help."

"Help?"

"Yes, I am going to wear my farming disguise and work in the fields as well."

"That is not wise, Father." Father Joaquim could see the concern in Master Yamaguchi's expression.

"I will wear a good disguise."

"There are spies everywhere on Kyushu. You risk your life if you are exposed."

"My life is already at risk, and so is the life of everyone in this village if we fail to make our quota."

"Agreed. We are all at risk. But working in broad daylight is taking it too far."

"We must remember the Lord is with us. We *cannot* live in fear."

"It is too risky, Father."

"Please do not worry, Master Yamaguchi. God has a higher purpose for us. After we pay our taxes, we will move the village somewhere better. We will *not* be downcast under persecution forever."

★ ★ ★

Having returned home to change his clothes, then check on his young catechists, Father Joaquim made his way to the rice fields and stood on a rise, beckoning the villagers to come and hear his news.

As a few droplets began falling from the gray skies, Father Joaquim made the sign of the cross and signaled he was ready to begin.

"As you all know, for several years now a storm of trials and persecutions has assailed us. Unfortunately, it appears conditions will only get worse before they get better." He looked out at the many anxious faces in the crowd.

"What should we do?" Ayame, a young mother of two small children, asked nervously.

Father Joaquim looked directly at her, wishing he could make the approaching dangers disappear. "Maintain your faith, Ayame. Circumstances change, but our God does not. The God we serve today is the same God who parted the sea for Moses and the Israelites."

"What is the news from Nagasaki?" Kenta, an older farmer asked. "I thought we had a friend there who could help us."

"I will not lie to you," Father Joaquim answered. "Our friend, Mateus, was killed. There will be no help from Nagasaki."

Many in the crowd began to murmur uncomfortably.

"What happened to him?" Mitsu, an older woman asked.

"He was murdered, Mitsu." Father Joaquim grimaced a bit, involuntarily. "I do not know who killed him or why. I only know that door has been closed to us."

As the father looked at the surrounding faces, he saw many appeared terrified. Some were already in tears.

"We cannot produce Lord Shigemasa's new quota, no matter how hard we work," Shinobu, one of the older farmers declared. "What will we do?"

The murmurs intensified, and several women and children cried openly.

"We will do our best to meet the new quota," Father Joaquim answered calmly.

"But what about Lord Shigemasa? You know he has no mercy," Shinobu continued. "Our best will not be good enough. If we cannot meet his quota, he will destroy our families."

"We must try hard," Father Joaquim replied, moving his gaze from Shinobu and taking a moment to make eye contact with several of the village's elders before adding, "and pray to the Lord."

"But what if the Lord does not hear?" Tamiko, a mother of four young children, asked. "I cannot let the daimyo take my children."

"The Lord *always* hears your prayers," Father Joaquim answered confidently. "Even before you ask, the Lord has answered you."

"How do you know that?"

The father saw the desperation in Tamiko's eyes. "From the Scriptures," he answered. "The prophet Isaiah wrote this: 'And it shall come to pass, that before they call, I will answer.' This means that even before you pray, the Lord has heard you."

"What should we pray for?"

"Pray for the Lord to look after us—to protect us and ensure our survival."

"What else?"

"We must have faith that *He will answer*."

"That seems very wishful. What more can we do?" Noboru, a young father asked.

Father Joaquim turned his gaze from Noboru, closed his eyes, and lifted his head skyward before replying. "You can *see* God helping you and thank Him for it." Looking back at Noboru, he continued. "The greater your thankfulness, the stronger His response."

"What do you mean by *see*?" Noboru asked.

"I mean visualize our protection … our survival and freedom. *See* these things with your inner eye, and thank God for them. Remember, the stronger your gratitude, the stronger your faith. You and the Lord are in constant partnership, so trust Him. The Lord *always* responds to those who believe and have faith—*always*! This is His promise."

Hanako, a teenage girl, stepped forward. "Father, I prayed for the Lord's help, but He did *not* answer me."

"What do you mean, dear?"

"I prayed for help from Nagasaki, from your friend Mateus. But we did not receive it. Why, Father? Why did the Lord not answer?"

"The Lord *always* answers your prayers, Hanako-chan, but sometimes it may not be the way you like or expect."

"But why not in Nagasaki?"

"I do not know, but the Lord has infinite wisdom. Perhaps we are meant to follow a different path."

Sensing Hanako's confusion, Father Joaquim walked over to the young girl and put his hand on her shoulder. "The key, dear, is to *trust* the Lord and have faith that He *will* answer. Do not worry about *how* God will answer; just have faith that He *will*."

Slowly, Hanako nodded her head, as did several other villagers, looking a little more comforted.

Father Joaquim looked out over the crowd. "Let us all be aware and of clear mind. A dark storm is on its way, but if you have faith in God, He *will* answer you, and He *will* protect us."

Twenty-one

On an especially warm afternoon, even for mid-June, Governor Hasegawa Gonroku was quietly reading a document in his room at the Nagasaki magistrate's office. Outside the governor's door, two younger officials were serenely immersed in reviewing a number of trading documents that required official approval.

In just two weeks or so, Portuguese ships would begin arriving in Nagasaki from Macao—mostly with silk—for the busy trading season. So, as needed, the young men were affixing the magistrate's official stamp on various documents.

As the young officials concentrated on their paperwork, a large procession of samurai and other officials abruptly barged through the front door of the magistrate's office.

Startled by the unexpected arrival, the young officials immediately put down their paperwork and bowed to the high-ranking officials. "Bugyo Gonroku-san," one of the young officials called out, drawing the governor's attention.

"What?" Governor Gonroku responded slowly as he looked up from his work.

"We have an official visit. Please come quickly."

96

Surprised by the announcement, the governor leapt up and rushed into the front room, where he quickly scanned the delegation members.

Instantly, he recognized the leader. It was the new Nagasaki governor, Mizuno Kawachi, a cold and sinister-looking man with rough features and small, dark eyes. Despite his short stature, Mizuno Kawachi had a commanding presence, with strong, broad shoulders.

"Mizuno Kawachi-san." Governor Gonroku bowed. "Welcome."

With visibly less respect, Mizuno Kawachi and the members of his entourage bowed slightly in return.

"I was not expecting you for another week or two. Why the early arrival?"

"To make an impact," Mizuno Kawachi responded coolly. "Under the shogun's orders, I am here to relieve you of your duties—immediately. Go home."

"What?" Governor Gonruku was speechless for a moment before continuing. "This is very unexpected. I have work to complete, murders to investigate, documents to process." The governor's frustration and humiliation were evident in his voice and facial expression.

"That will not be necessary. You may leave now," Kawachi growled, his eyes narrowed in contempt at the man he clearly considered his inferior.

"Do you dishonor me?" Governor Gonroku returned his replacement's contemptuous glare. Several high-ranking officials of Mizuno Kawachi's party looked on, smirking.

"You dishonored yourself." Kawachi no longer even looked at Gonroku. He was busy scanning the office, planning how best to use it.

"Of what do you speak? Elaborate!"

Kawachi finally looked back at his soon-to-be predecessor. "Your main task was to exterminate Christianity in Nagasaki

Prefecture, but instead you closed your eyes to this disease infecting our land. Your dishonor is your own."

"That is nonsense. I have Christian prisoners, including priests, locked up now!"

"And why are they not dead?"

Kawachi locked his eyes onto Gonroku's, and the latter broke, shifting his gaze down to the table he stood behind. "Because it is not the right time."

"Nonsense! You delay executing them because you have a soft heart for them."

"I do not."

"For years, you have abstained from your duties!"

"What?" Gonroku began to shake with anger, frustration, and growing apprehension.

"You have pronounced a lack of evidence to convict; you have forewarned Christians to run; you have even let Christians go! You have failed the shogun!"

"I have not."

"It matters not. You wished to be relieved of your duties, and now you are." Kawachi waved his hand toward the door. "Go."

"But I have work to conclude, trading approvals to complete."

"Another area of concern to the shogun. Even this you cannot do satisfactorily."

"What do you mean?"

"The Dutch complain that you favor the Portuguese in trade. Even local Japanese complain that you favor them."

"This is trade. Someone is always complaining about their share."

"Are you taking bribes?"

"This is preposterous! What accusations do you make?" Gonroku's shaking became more pronounced.

"If the shame is too great, Gonroku, you may take your own life. Commit *seppuku*."

"I will not commit seppuku. I have taken no bribes!"

"It is clear you are not fit for your post. Why would we permit you to continue your work? Now go. Leave my presence."

Fuming in anger, Governor Gonroku quickly walked into the next room and grabbed his bag as Mizuno Kawachi and his officials looked on, their smug satisfaction apparent. Disgraced and humiliated, Governor Gonroku exited the front door with his head down. Nagasaki Prefecture had a new governor.

Twenty-two

June 18, 1626
Arima Domain, Hizen Province

Yori was sleeping peacefully, his back supported by a thick tree trunk, and shade from heavily leafed branches cooling the ground around him as the morning sun warmed the fields. So sound was the boy's sleep that by the time he noticed Daimyo Shigemasa and his detachment of mounted samurai, they were almost on top of him.

"Aaaaagghh!" Yori screamed out in fear.

"Shut up, boy!" Shigemasa snarled, glaring at him.

Straightaway, one of the daimyo's samurai rode his horse to within inches of Yori, scowling at him in silence but making his intentions clear.

Master Yamaguchi, working in the end of the field closest to the mountain, heard the scream and looked up, spotting the approaching samurai. Sprinting as fast as his old legs would carry him, he ran toward Father Joaquim, who was working at the other end of the field.

"Father, Tonia, Miguel, you must go hide. Shigemasa is coming!"

"Quick! Alert the village, and get as many of the women and children inside as possible," Father Joaquim said as he stood.

"You must hide as well, Father."

"I will hide behind my wall, as usual. I will need someone to seal it behind me."

"I will send someone. Now, quick, move!" Master Yamaguchi waved his hands, willing the father and the catechists to hurry to their hiding places before coordinating the remainder of the concealment efforts.

The peasants had only minutes to prepare, and all the arrangements had to be perfect or their ruse would be discovered and the consequences would be dire.

But with so little time, the coordination was poor and not fully effective. Some women tried unsuccessfully to place too many children into confined spaces, under floorboards, or in secret rooms behind hidden walls. The villagers also sought to hide as many of their Christian relics as possible, replacing them with Buddhist items of worship. To maintain their ruse, it was imperative to keep their Buddhist story consistent. Shigemasa and his men would be in the village within another minute or so, and preparations were not yet complete.

Master Yamaguchi walked to the edge of the village, where the warlord would arrive. Behind Master Yamaguchi several peasant farmers followed to pay homage to the self-serving man who could dictate their fate.

"Daimyo Shigemasa, it is a pleasure. We were not expecting you," Master Yamaguchi stated politely as he bowed deeply. Behind Master Yamaguchi, the villagers also bowed low.

"I know you were not expecting me. We were not due for two more weeks."

"Yes, Lord," Master Yamaguchi replied calmly. "How can we serve you, Lord?"

"I am here to collect the taxes you owe me."

"We are working very hard on your new quota, Lord. I am sure you will be proud of us."

"Then where is it?" Shigemasa bellowed from atop his horse.

"But it is not yet time, Lord. You gave us a month." Master Yamaguchi's eyes as well as his words pleaded his case.

"I need the production for trade and changed my mind, Yamaguchi-san. Show me what you have."

"But this is highly unusual, Lord. I must insist we be permitted the month given to us."

"Nonsense, show me what you have … *now!*"

"Fetch Daimyo Shigemasa's production," Master Yamaguchi said as he turned to face his fellow villagers. Promptly, a number of peasants ran off to various storage areas and the fields to retrieve every sack of rice they had.

As they waited, Shigemasa scanned the village and began counting the peasants.

"This presence looks light. Where are the rest of your villagers?"

"What do you mean, Lord?" Master Yamaguchi asked, hoping to delay until the others returned with the rice.

"Where are the rest of the women and children? I recall seeing more last time."

Men began to return, placing their bags of rice before the warlord and bowing, temporarily diverting the master's attention from his question about the missing villagers.

"Is that it?" Shigemasa snarled.

"We have more bags in the fields," Master Yamaguchi answered.

"Bring them."

"They are coming, Lord."

Moments later, a few more men arrived from the fields, breathing heavily as they dragged several more half-filled sacks behind them.

"Is that it?"

"Yes, Lord. I think this is a record production for us, given the time we had to work," Master Yamaguchi declared, quietly praying Shigemasa's concern over the rice production would cause him to forget his questions about the missing villagers.

"Silence, old man," Shigemasa said as he quickly examined the numbers of bags before him. "I see only a few dozen sacks here. This production is embarrassing for this village."

"It is a good production," a frustrated peasant shouted impetuously from the back of the crowd.

"Do you disrespect me?"

"No, Lord, of course not," Master Yamaguchi interjected. "We would never disrespect you. We serve you to the best of our abilities."

"This production is insulting! How dare you present this to me? You are all lazy dogs!"

"But, Lord—" Master Yamaguchi started to protest.

"Silence, or my samurai will silence you for me." Shigemasa looked around. "I know why your production is so low," he said turning as far as possible in the saddle to observe the village in the distance. "Some of your people are hiding from me when they should be out here working. Now where are the rest of the villagers?"

"We always honor your presence with as many as we can," Master Yamaguchi answered.

"Do not patronize me, old man."

Agitated, Shigemasa addressed his samurai: "Do whatever is necessary, but find the rest of the women and children!"

Dozens of samurai quickly dismounted from their horses and advanced on the villagers' homes, kicking down doors, punching through walls, and lifting up floorboards.

"Daimyo Shigemasa, I do not think this is necessary," Master Yamaguchi protested.

"Shut up, old man. I will deal with you in a moment."

Amid the crashing and destruction, Master Yamaguchi heard women and children screaming. Soon after, several samurai appeared, dragging the women by their hair, with their terrified children following and sobbing pitifully.

"You deceived me, old man," Shigemasa roared as he dismounted. "Keep looking," he ordered. "I am sure there are more!"

"Lord Shigemasa, we found gaijin!" Several samurai shoved Catechists Tonia and Miguel ahead of them.

Discovering a Japanese Christian was a triumph in itself, but to uncover two foreign Christians was an astonishing find for the daimyo. While the shogun would be angry over their discovery, he would nevertheless be pleased at their capture.

As villagers watched, crying, horrified, the catechists were beaten viciously with a flurry of kicks and punches.

"Let me see these Christian dogs," Shigemasa yelled as he cleared his way through the samurai.

"This is unbelievable," Shigemasa declared as he approached the two beaten catechists lying on the ground, Master Yamaguchi looking on helplessly.

Turning to his second in command, Shigemasa gave his order: "Tear down this village. I want every inch of this insidious village overturned. No one escapes!"

The villagers wailed as, systematically, the soldiers demolished every building and forcefully removed anyone hiding inside.

Suddenly, a samurai pushed his way through the crowd, making his way to the front as he pulled a man behind him, to where the daimyo stood, overseeing the destruction of the village. "Lord Shigemasa, look. I have discovered another gaijin. This one looks like a priest!"

"Bring the entire village to the landing," Shigemasa commanded.

Minutes later, with everyone assembled, the daimyo announced, "This village is no more. You have all deceived me."

Turning abruptly, Shigemasa walked over to Master

Yamaguchi, who stood calmly before him. "And you, old man. You have deceived me from the beginning. Your disrespect is the greatest of all!"

In one quick move, Shigemasa abruptly raised his sword and brought it down swiftly across Master Yamaguchi's neck, severing it and sending blood gushing as the old man's head rolled through the field.

★ ★ ★

Villagers were delirious in their wails and cries. Unable to control himself, Father Joaquim instantly rose to his feet. "What have you done? You have killed Master Yamaguchi!"

Immediately, several samurai pounded Father Joaquim to the ground and beat him mercilessly. Even so, the father still cried out, "You had no right to kill him. Master Yamaguchi was a peaceful man. You are a murderer."

Shigemasa's samurai resumed beating the father as villagers wailed and sobbed.

"Silence," Shigemasa yelled at the villagers, "or you will all perish." The daimyo turned his head, making eye contact with several villagers. "You are all under arrest for breaking the shogun's anti-Christian laws." He turned again to his second in command. "Burn the village."

Soon the entire village was ablaze. Dark smoke filled the sky as the villagers were rounded up, beaten, tied to long wooden poles, and dragged up the mountainside.

Twenty-three

June 18, 1626
Shogun's Castle, Edo, Musashi Province

When Masayoshi had to take part in his first torture as a member of the eta class, he vomited—and was immediately forced to clean up the vomit. He soon learned to control his stomach. It took several more months, however, before his soul became calloused enough to endure the torture sessions with no sense of remorse. Now, two years hence, he'd learned to block out all emotions as he carried out his work. So, on this dark, dreary afternoon in the capital city, Masayoshi was ready to do the shogun's bidding in the royal castle's torture chamber.

Also in the chamber were many members of the shogun's Bakufu cabinet as well as several Buddhist monks. Because of the increasing frequency of the torture sessions, even many of the cabinet members and monks were becoming calloused to the horrible injuries inflicted on prisoners—mostly Christians.

At the front of the room, a young Japanese man was shackled by his wrists and ankles to metal plates holding him tightly against a wall. After months of imprisonment, he was filthy and emaciated, but, given the circumstances, still surprisingly healthy. And, it seemed, his spirit was unbent. The shogun meant to break the prisoner's will by slowly, systematically, inflicting appalling pain.

Masayoshi stood to the side, awaiting orders as the shogun approached the torture subject. "What is your name?" the shogun demanded as he approached the shackled young man.

"My name is Akihiko," he answered softly.

"I understand you are strong," the shogun said as he looked intently at the young man who appeared to be no more than twenty. "They tell me you have survived for more than six months in my Edo jail. That is impressive."

Akihiko did not reply.

"They also tell me you are generous and even give your food to save others in the prison."

Akihiko remained silent, and Masayoshi watched him, knowing soon he'd be called upon to burn and/or dismember parts of the young man's body—it was his job.

As the shogun spoke to Akihiko, Masayoshi's contemplations betrayed him. He thought he'd moved past having any concerns for the prisoners—for his victims. But on this day, his mind wandered. He found his thoughts drawn to the deplorable conditions in the prison and to the many men he'd tortured.

The prison was narrow and dark, with only a small opening through which tiny amounts of food could be passed to the gaunt, hungry inmates. The ceiling of the prison was low, prohibiting anyone from standing fully upright. Outside, prison guards yelled and screamed at all hours of the day and night to deprive the prisoners of sleep. Inside, one hundred and fifty prisoners were crammed into a space of about seventy feet by thirty feet, where they were all lined up and kept in rows. Each prisoner had a space of no more than eighteen inches in width. If he wanted to sleep, he had to lean against his neighbor next to him. As a result of such accommodation, quarrels and fights were common in the jail.

The heat in the summer was blistering, and if a prisoner wanted to wear clothing, the others complained because

107

clothing took up more space and made their neighbors hot. Prisoners were given no water to wash themselves, nor were they allowed to cut their hair, their beards, or their nails. Food was sparse, and for some, nonexistent—they were allowed to starve to death. Corpses were sometimes left to decompose where they died, emitting hideous smells and disease-causing toxins.

Masayoshi had noticed that Akihiko was not only one of the strongest inmates in the prison, but also the most generous. On several occasions Masayoshi observed Akihiko give his food to others. He also saw the young man pray for men on their deathbed.

But not all the prisoners in the Edo jail were like Akihiko. Among them were murderers, rapists, thieves, and all other characters who offended the shogun or somehow posed a threat to his dominance, including Christians and ronin. So violence among the inmates was not uncommon. Among the jail's many inmates, young Akihiko was the least deserving of the torture he was about to endure—much of it at Masayoshi's hands.

★ ★ ★

The shogun stood close to Akihiko, staring at him with a demonic grin. "I have removed you from my prison in order to torture you. It seems my jail is not degenerating your body, so let us see how you respond to mutilation."

The shogun shifted his gaze from Akihiko to the Buddhist monks and eta torturers, including Masayoshi. "What do you think?" the shogun asked.

"I think he chose the wrong religion," one of the Buddhists answered coldly.

"I think you are right," the shogun replied. "At least, choosing a Buddhist path would not cost him his life."

"I do not fear death," Akihiko stated as he stared at the shogun, refusing to be intimidated.

"Your courage is admirable," the shogun commented. "It is too bad you do not serve *me*. I am always in need of courageous retainers."

"I serve only my Lord Jesus Christ."

"And that is the problem," the shogun replied coldly. "The peasants of this country exist to serve *me*, not some dead man named Jesus."

"Everyone should worship the *true* Lord," Akihiko answered.

The shogun's eyes narrowed, and his nostrils flared. "I am the almighty Lord in Japan and *I* am the only one who should be worshiped. Your worship of this Jesus imperils the very fabric of our entire society."

"Man was born free to make choices. I choose to follow my Lord Jesus Christ, Son of God."

"Let us see if we can make you choose differently," the shogun coldly stated as he walked over to a large table nearby, on which were displayed all the instruments of torture. Taking a moment to study them, he selected a large pair of sharp metal scissors and handed them to Yasu, the eta torturer standing next to Masayoshi.

Yasu grabbed the scissors and bowed to the shogun.

Together, the shogun and Yasu approached Akihiko.

"You are also a very pretty young man," the shogun stated as he stared at Akihiko. "Let us see if we can change that as well." The shogun began to eye various body parts of Akihiko. "Start by removing his ears," the shogun said as he returned to stand behind the table.

Blocking out his returning empathy, Masayoshi moved over and grabbed Akihiko's head, holding it firmly so Yasu could perform his grisly task. Despite their sharpness, the scissors could not cut through all the flesh and tendons quickly. The torturer had to chop repeatedly, as blood gushed and Akihiko screamed in hideous pain. Masayoshi's stomach turned, something he hadn't experienced in years.

Finally Yasu, smiling in triumph, held the severed ear up for all to see.

"Throw it on the floor in front of him," the shogun commanded.

The bloody ear made a slapping sound as it landed.

Nauseous and dizzy, Akihiko sagged in exhaustion, looking very pale, a dull gaze over his eyes.

"Whom do you serve now?" the shogun demanded. "Do you serve *me*, the ruler of all Japan?"

Unable to speak, Akihiko turned his head from side to side.

"No?" the shogun bellowed. "Cut off his other ear!"

For a moment, Masayoshi felt remorse, but he could not defy the shogun. As required, he again grabbed Akihiko's head and held it still while Yasu took the scissors to the bleeding young man's other ear and began chopping.

Akihiko screamed out in pain as, again, blood poured from his head.

Yasu threw the second ear on the floor in front of Akihiko.

Confused and disoriented, Akihiko continued to roll his head aimlessly from side to side.

"You do not seem so strong anymore," the shogun stated. "Are you ready to renounce this Jesus and pronounce *me* your true Lord?"

Akihiko's body collapsed. Only the chains on the wall held him up, as the metal shackles cut sharply into his skin. Unable to speak, Akihiko shook his head in denial as blood trickled down his face and nose and fell to the floor.

"Imbecile," the shogun yelled in frustration. "These Christians are far too unruly. How dare they deny me!"

The shogun walked briskly over to the table of torture devices. "What shall we choose next?"

110

Eager to serve, one of the Buddhist monks quickly approached the table and chose a sharp wooden saw. "I think we should saw off his feet," the monk offered.

"Do it. Bring the saw. Hold his feet," the shogun ordered the eta torturers. "Now saw them off."

Grabbing Akihiko's ankles firmly in their hands, the Buddhist monks readied his body for the removal of his feet. Akihiko awakened and started to resist, frantically trying to shake his legs free. And for a moment his struggling worked. The monks and eta torturers were unable to restrain him. In response, Yasu grabbed a metal pipe and pounded Akihiko's head and body until he was unconsciousness again.

The shogun gave Yasu an approving look. "Try it again," he said.

Reluctantly, but with a determination borne of fear for his own life and limbs, Masayoshi took a saw and began removing Akihiko's left foot, just below the ankle, while Yasu sawed just below the right ankle. All standing nearby were quickly spattered by the young Christian's blood, but after a few minutes of grueling and brutal work, Akihiko's feet were severed.

The torture proved too much. Akihiko hung limp and unconscious from his bloodied, shackled wrists.

"Place his ears and feet in that basket," the shogun instructed. "And bring in the physician. I do not want this man to die."

"But why?" a Buddhist monk asked.

"These Christians die too quickly, and I do not get enough out of them," the shogun answered. "I want to heal him so we can torture him again."

"As you wish, Lord Shogun," the monk replied as several of his comrades ran off to find a physician.

Smirking, the shogun stared proudly at the unconscious Christian hanging from the wall. "As Nami Amida Buddha himself will bear witness, this Christian man will profess *me*, the shogun of Japan, *his* Lord before his last day."

Twenty-four

As the early-evening air began to cool, Governor Mizuno Kawachi and a small entourage of senior officials walked up a long road toward the home of Deputy-Lieutenant Governor Heizo Suetsugu Masanao. Not surprisingly, the deputy-lieutenant lived in one of the nicest parts of Nagasaki prefecture.

Immaculately maintained, the road leading to the deputy-lieutenant's home was spacious, with grandiose landscaping. Elegant trees and shrubs lined the way, and large boulders and rocks were carefully placed to enhance the appeal of the pathway. Birds chirped in the trees, while squirrels chattered as they rushed up and down tree trunks.

Perched on a small slope on the mountainside, the deputy-lieutenant's home had a spectacular view of the city lying beneath it, affording a serene panorama of the sea and the surrounding lush, green mountains.

Gradually, Governor Kawachi and his entourage made their way toward the majestic gates of the deputy-lieutenant's home, where they were greeted by dozens of staff and samurai. As the contingent entered the grounds, everyone exchanged bows and cordialities.

Governor Kawachi and his officials were escorted through a beautifully maintained garden with a stream, waterfalls, and magnificent bonsai trees to the front entrance of Suetsugu's immense home.

Of traditional Japanese design, the deputy-lieutenant's home had an immense curved thatched roof, which was at least half the size of the overall structure. The roof was the most impressive feature of the exterior, which could be seen from great distances around Nagasaki. And, as with a temple, the slightly curved eaves of the roof extended beyond the walls, covering the verandas and creating a beautiful finish to the huge building.

As the governor and his delegation approached the front door, they were greeted again by more samurai, servants, and slaves. Suetsugu was highly involved in international trade and often seized illegitimate vessels, taking for his own any slaves on board.

Bowing cordially, the group members entered the deputy-governor's house, where all respectfully removed their street sandals. From behind a crowd of servants, Heizo Suetsugu appeared and approached the arriving party.

"Welcome to Nagasaki, Governor Kawachi," Suetsugu said deferentially. "I thought it more hospitable to host you at my home, rather than meeting at the magistrate's office."

"Thank you."

Within the Bakufu hierarchy, Governor Kawachi was a more senior figure than Deputy Suetsugu. However, as Kawachi would soon discover, the deputy-lieutenant was a far richer man by reason of his significant trading and commercial activities. Mostly through his hereditary family connections, Suetsugu had managed to build one of the most successful trading franchises of all time in Nagasaki.

Nevertheless, despite all the deputy's affluence and power, the structure of the Bakufu regime still ranked supreme and, at a moment's notice, the shogun could confiscate all of Suetsugu's wealth, if he chose.

The organization of the Bakufu regime was actually simple. At the top was the shogun, the chief warlord and military leader of the country. Supporting the shogun was his five-member Go-Roju cabinet, providing him with high council advice and support. Next, under the shogun and his cabinet, were his administrative officials and feudal daimyo.

Most feudal daimyo were very rich warlords who inherited their lands through family lineage, generating additional wealth by taxing the peasant class they ruled over. Driven by greed, most feudal daimyo resorted to bribery, corruption, and other exploitations in their quest for more money, land, and power.

Next to the feudal daimyo, but appointed directly by the shogun, were his administrative officials who helped administer and enforce the laws of the Bakufu regime. Equally corrupt, these official positions included governors and deputy-lieutenant governors. In addition to executing the shogun's laws and rules, these officials also existed to serve as spies. In this way, the shogun established a direct presence in the five major shogunal cities: Osaka, Kyoto, Edo, Sakai, and Nagasaki.

Thus, for each town, the shogun appointed a governor to keep watch, rule, and administer. And to assist the governor, the shogun also appointed a *daikan*, a deputy-lieutenant governor.

As newly appointed Governor Kawachi studied Deputy Suetsugu's magnificent home, he quickly grasped the extent of Suetsugu's incredible wealth. Hanging from his walls were dozens of pictures of exceptional Chinese art. Also found in his home were multiple outlandish Buddhist statues, exotic art, and exceptional calligraphy. But although such striking items were on display, the home was designed primarily to minimize distractions and allow the beauty of the building itself to shine.

The governor had heard the deputy-lieutenant's riches did not end with his home. To store his more significant assets, Suetsugu had multiple warehouses throughout Nagasaki. It was rumored his wealth consisted of dozens of boxes of gold and silver, vast piles of precious lumber, boxes of coral and exotic foreign tea-sets, hundreds of hanging pictures by Chinese artists, thousands of boxes of Chinese articles, dozens of folding screens, and hundreds of swords and other high-quality weapons.

"Please make yourself comfortable. May we offer you some tea?" the deputy asked as he lowered himself into a kneeling position before a large sitting table in the midst of a vast room.

The governor nodded affirmatively as he also lowered himself on the opposite side of the table.

"And how do you find your time in Nagasaki thus far, Governor?"

"I am not bothered with pleasantries. I am here to execute the shogun's orders."

"You mean the Christians?" the deputy asked.

"Of course."

"The shogun was disappointed with Governor Gonroku," the deputy stated. "I know. I told him all about Gonroku's failings."

"*You* told him?"

"Yes, but I was not the only one who communicated this. The shogun has many spies in Nagasaki."

"It appears nothing goes unnoticed in Nagasaki."

"The shogun knows everything," the deputy replied as he signaled his servants to pour tea for all his guests, starting with the governor.

"So tell me of your plans, Governor. How will you conduct your administration differently?"

115

"Tomorrow, I will raise some stakes and execute several Christians."

"Oh?"

"Yes, I want my presence to be felt immediately. I want any remaining hidden Christians to know that a holocaust is coming."

"I am impressed." The deputy nodded his head and smiled. "I am sure the shogun will be pleased."

"The shogun has honored me with this appointment and I will not disappoint him. I want him to know that under *my* name, the Christians will be completely exterminated from Nagasaki and surrounding areas."

"And what will be your tactics, Governor? How will you accomplish this?"

"Death and torture."

"That is it?"

"Far from it, deputy."

"Then what else? Not all Christians fear death. Some even relish it."

"I will use every means available, Deputy-Lieutenant. At first, I will use death and torture to show I am not averse to bloodshed."

"And then?"

"I want apostates. Killing is easy."

"What do you mean?"

"It is easy to create large piles of dead bodies to put on display as forewarnings, but I want *apostates!*"

"You prefer them to apostatize rather than suffer death?"

"Yes, I would much rather force these Christians to renounce their useless faith."

"I am intrigued. How will you do this?"

"Unless they recant, I will take everything they own. I will make beggars of them. I shall conduct raids and routine searches of all homes in Nagasaki."

"For what purpose?"

"Each home will be overturned to discover the occupants' true identity."

"That will take a great deal of men," the deputy replied.

"I will offer incentives for families to betray one another. If one family betrays another, they will inherit the other family's home and all their belongings."

"That is very wise," the deputy replied, smiling. "You will give them a strong incentive to act as informants."

"Of course. Money is always a powerful reward."

"And if a family is adept at hiding their faith, how will you discover them?"

"I will put pressure on communities and place the onus on them."

"And how will you do this?"

"Every community will be forced to investigate its neighbors. If a Christian is later discovered hiding in a community, I will randomly kill the neighbors as punishment." The governor sipped his tea before continuing, unemotionally, as if he were reading a dry narrative. "I will also take their homes and deprive them of work, food, and sustenance. I will take everything they have in order to force them to inform on their neighbors."

"Very thorough, Governor. And if all these measures are insufficient?"

"Death, Deputy. If they do not recant, they will face torture and death."

"It may be the only way."

"And can I count on your assistance, Deputy?"

"Of course, Governor. I have no reservations about persecuting Christians."

"Are you sure, Deputy?"

"Indeed, Governor. Why would you question my resolve?" the deputy asked, appearing uncomfortable as the governor sat quietly.

"Because you used to be Christian, Deputy. I need to know where your loyalties lie."

"I apostatized a long time ago," the deputy replied defensively. "My loyalties lie with the shogun and the Bakufu now."

"The shogun sincerely hopes that is the case, Deputy."

Looking offended, Suetsugu placed his tea on the table. "Governor Kawachi, look around you. Do you really think I would give up all this wealth because of a repulsive religion?"

Briefly, the governor looked around with envy at the deputy's enormous, lavish home.

Suetsugu gazed intently at the governor. "I made my decision long ago, Governor. I chose money over God."

"Are you sure, Deputy?"

"I will never forsake my riches for a dead man named Jesus. Never!"

"I am pleased with your response, Deputy."

"Rest assured, Governor, that my apostasy is irrevocable and resolute, and I will prove it to you."

"Oh?" Governor Kawachi replied, a bit surprised. "How?"

"With your own eyes you will witness me executing Christians with my own hands."

Twenty-five

June 19, 1626
Fields of Arima, Hizen Province

Sliding along through the mud, a bit like a small anchor, Haruko learned quickly not to cry out loudly. A samurai backhand to the side of her tearful face had made a convincing impression. But her tired little legs simply could not keep up, and her whimpering was mostly involuntary as the other nineteen villagers attached to the pole dragged her along through the pouring rain, yanked from the front by another burly, short-tempered samurai.

Tied by their wrists to one of three bamboo poles, all the villagers were being moved as rapidly as possible in the soggy conditions. At the front of each pole were the tallest men, followed by the women, and the children at the rear. At the very back, the youngest children, like Haruko, hung from the poles and were dragged like debris if they couldn't keep up.

Haruko's mother, Shizuyo, tied by her wrists to the same pole but nearer the front, could only pray, as she occasionally sought to twist her neck enough to catch a glimpse of her weeping, struggling six-year-old.

With no food and the falling rain as their only water source, the villagers had been tugged, pulled, pushed, and whipped along non-stop since their village was burned, nearly twenty-four hours before. In addition to their physical exhaustion, depression at the death of Master Yamaguchi had overtaken nearly every villager. The kind old man had been more than the village leader; he'd also been an intimate friend and confidant to young and old. Once a samurai and high-ranking retainer, Master Yamaguchi was always ready to share his time and humor with others, imparting wisdom to any willing to hear it.

★ ★ ★

When one of the samurai abandoned his section of a pole to urinate off the side of the path, some of the prisoners saw an opportunity to whisper.

"Father, where are they taking us?" Miguel asked anxiously from behind Father Joaquim.

"I do not know, Miguel. Probably to the court in Nagasaki."

"What will they do to us?"

"I do not know," Father Joaquim replied, barely able to hear over the splattering rain and the sounds of myriad feet pulling against the sucking mud.

"They will torture and kill us, will they not?"

"Try to rid your mind of these thoughts, Miguel. They will not help you."

"But what is the point? We are captured. There is nothing we can do now."

"Precisely, Miguel. It is out of our hands. We are in *God's* hands now."

Miguel slipped and fell into the mud, but quickly righted himself and resumed walking lest a samurai beat him for slowing the procession.

"What shall we do, Father?" Jiro, a tall farmer, asked.

"We will do the only thing we can do; we will pray."

Simultaneously, Father Joaquim heard a sharp snap and felt a burning pain across his back.

"I told you to shut up," a samurai snarled at Father Joaquim, leather whip in hand.

The samurai then put a rope around Jiro's neck and began to strangle him. "When you speak," the samurai said, "he will not breathe."

Turning blue, Jiro slumped down, clamoring for air.

"Let this be a warning. When *you* open your mouth, *he* will suffer." Seconds before it was too late, the samurai released his grip on the farmer's throat, allowing him to breathe.

As the group moved on, many of the children, including Haruko, continued to slip and fall in the mud, causing delays and frequent stops.

"Damn this weather and these stupid children," another frustrated samurai cursed as he approached Haruko, who had just fallen again. "Get up, stupid girl," the samurai commanded as he hit her hard on the side of the head with his fist. She crumpled to the ground, face down in the mud, where she struggled to stay conscious and breathe. Frustrated, the samurai approached Haruko, grabbed her by her hair, and yanked her to her feet.

Crying and holding her head, Haruko was injured and terrified. Her mother looked on, crying, but helpless.

"If you fall one more time," the samurai growled, "I *will* beat you to death!"

Angered by yet another child being beaten, Father Joaquim could no longer contain himself. "What kind of samurai are you to strike a child?" Father Joaquim shouted from the front. "Why do you not hit *me*? Let us see if you are brave enough to hit a man!"

Outraged, the samurai charged at Father Joaquim, knocking him to the ground, and forcing the entire pole of victims to fall over into the mud. With tremendous force, the samurai then kicked Father Joaquim repeatedly in his sides. Still fuming, he withdrew his sword and delivered a series of devastating blows with the butt end of his weapon to Father Joaquim's head and back.

"That is enough," Shigemasa said as he calmly walked over to observe Father Joaquim, who was bleeding and coughing. "We can beat these dogs just so many times."

"But this dog barked at me, Lord," the furious samurai protested. "He should be killed for dishonoring me."

"This padre will be executed at the hands of the authorities. I do not want to deliver dead Christians. His death sentence awaits him in Nagasaki."

The samurai took a step back, rumbling in frustration.

Slowly, Father Joaquim picked himself up off the muddy ground, and the remainder of those on his pole also rose.

"Everyone, listen," Shigemasa ordered. "This journey is taking far too long."

Equally exasperated, all the warlord's samurai grumbled in agreement.

"This cursed weather will force our journey to take three days instead of the usual two, but I see no reason why it should take any longer."

"Hai! Hai!" the samurai echoed in agreement.

"From this moment forward, all my samurai and retainers will keep their thrashings to a minimum in order to hasten our travel."

Responding to the grumblings from the ranks, Shigemasa added, "Have no concern, men. I can assure you all these Christian dogs will meet their end very soon."

★ ★ ★

Meanwhile, in Nagasaki, Governor Kawachi, Deputy-Lieutenant Suetsugu, and a large number of officials and samurai were on the edge of the city, in the rain, watching samurai erect stakes for a mass execution.

"How many stakes do you wish to raise, Governor?" the deputy-lieutenant asked.

"At least fifty."

"You want to execute that many?" the deputy-lieutenant asked, wide-eyed.

"We should erect more than we need."

"For what purpose?"

"To remind everyone in Nagasaki that other stakes are vacant—ready to execute at a moment's notice."

"It is a wise plan, Governor."

"Christians should constantly fear for their lives. These extra stakes should remind them to live in fear."

"How many shall we execute tomorrow?"

"I am not sure yet."

"How about thirteen?" Suetsugu suggested.

"Why thirteen?"

"Because thirteen is an unlucky number for Christians."

"Why unlucky?"

"Because their Lord, Jesus Christ, was betrayed by His thirteenth disciple, Judas," Suetsugu answered.

"Your knowledge of Christianity is useful, Deputy-Lieutenant."

"It makes me a better anti-Christian. I know their weaknesses."

"And thus you are like Judas," the governor replied, nodding his head approvingly.

"No," the deputy answered with a hint of a chuckle. "I am *far* richer than Judas."

Both then laughed openly at the joke.

"Very well, thirteen executions," the governor declared. "But make sure we have more stakes available."

"We will raise at least fifty."

"Good. Tomorrow will be a momentous day." The governor looked at the progress. "Under *my* watch, let all of Nagasaki see that Christianity will die."

Twenty-six

At the front of the group being marched through the streets was Bishop Francisco Pacheco, Provincial in the Society of Jesus, and the highest-ranking Catholic in Japan at the time. The seventy-year-old Portuguese father had been captured and arrested in Kuchinotsu, Arima, a year earlier. He'd been in Omura prison awaiting his execution ever since.

Governor Kawachi had selected for his victims the most prominent and influential Christians at his disposal, along with others who had aided them. Awaiting their deaths, most of these victims had been confined and incarcerated in nearby local jails.

Despite their destitute condition, before the march, all of the victims were beaten severely with a variety of weapons, including slabs of wood, scraps of metal, knife handles, ropes, and other heinous devices. Owing to their horrific condition and lack of sanitation in the jails, the victims were already pale and gaunt. Multiple ulcers covered their bodies, and the skin that hung from their frames was pale white, with green pus exuding from various sores. Nevertheless, despite their already deplorable condition, Governor Kawachi insisted they be beaten prior to their execution.

Next, the governor instructed his officials to shave the victims' heads and paint their scalps bright red in order to make them distinguishable and to indicate their impending death. Finally, he commanded that rags be shoved into their mouths to ensure they could not make any inspirational statements during their death march. The governor considered it imperative to keep them silent, to instill fear in any hidden Christian who witnessed the gruesome display. But while the victims were paraded throughout the streets, the execution would take place in private. He would not let these people be martyrs as they died.

The governor recalled the last public execution, which took place three years before, in 1623. Most of the Christians had faced their executions with amazing resolve, and sometimes even rapturous joy. Contrary to intentions, the public martyrdoms tended to inspire others to embrace or recommit to the faith rather than extinguish it. So at that point the authorities decided that executions should take place only in front of the proper authorities.

From the moment he learned of his appointment as the new governor, Kawachi had greatly anticipated this day. Thus began the march. Down the streets of Nagasaki walked the death procession, with Bishop Pacheco at the front. Next was Balthasar de Torres, a sixty-eight-year-old preacher from Spain. The third priest was Iwan Baptist, fifty seven-years old, from Italy.

Also among the company were five Portuguese victims, including Albremen Fosse and his fourteen-year-old son. In addition, there were two ship's captains, Balthasar de Sousa and Iwan de Coste, who had been caught aiding Christians. The final victims among the thirteen were several Japanese individuals who had been found sheltering priests.

Each victim was tied to the next to keep them all in line. Several officials dragged them all down the streets like dogs, kicking them and scolding them whenever they felt inclined. As the governor had instructed, the victims were humiliated incessantly along the way.

The streets were swarming with the curious, with those opposed to the Christians, and with many who silently supported them. But their supporters had to remain quiet and undetected. A similar fate might await any who showed sympathy. Nevertheless, hidden Christians greatly admired the martyrs. Like soldiers of the sword who were venerated in Japan, so too were soldiers of the Cross. In the eyes of the Japanese Christians, the ways of the samurai were not too dissimilar from the ways of the Cross in terms of honor, discipline, and service.

Slowly, the thirteen victims proceeded through the crowded streets of Nagasaki. Ever so subtly, some onlookers discreetly bowed to the martyrs; others offered silent prayers.

Father Pacheco tried to approach a small child he saw crying, off to the side. But a guard quickly lashed him, leaving a deep, bloody gash in his leg.

For nearly two hours, the death march and humiliation proceeded through the streets until the procession reached the private execution ground. Finally, after their long, arduous march, the thirteen victims were directed into a private area where their execution stakes had been erected.

★ ★ ★

Contrary to Governor Kawachi's expectations, however, as the procession entered the place of execution, the soon-to-be martyrs looked surprisingly calm and fearless. Walking into the fenced execution area, where the public was prohibited, Father Pacheco calmly led the prisoners toward the stakes where they would meet their end. Standing firm and upright, his head erect, and looking unfalteringly forward, Father

Pacheco seemed to pay no attention to any of the officials. He walked straight past the governor and deputy-lieutenant, never even glancing in their direction.

Governor Kawachi was astonished that no one in the procession had to be dragged unwillingly to the stakes on which they would soon die. Amazed by their courage, the governor and many of his officials looked perplexed and perturbed. At the direction of the deputy-lieutenant, the victims were then tied and bound to their stakes.

Making sure none of the victims could position themselves away from the fire, all of the ropes binding them were checked and then checked again. No mistakes would be made. Each victim would die this day. About three feet from each stake was a stack of wood that would slowly incinerate the victims. Since the Christian holocaust in Japan had begun, the distance from the fire had been carefully calculated to ensure a slow and painful death for each unfortunate victim.

The governor watched as, after the victims were firmly bound to their stakes, the deputy-lieutenant fetched additional pieces of wood and placed them in front of each of the victims, then walked up to Father Pacheco and spat in his face. Despite the grave insult, Father Pacheco maintained his composure, continuing to stare forward bravely.

The deputy-lieutenant then approached the governor, who held the wooden matches. Bowing, Suetsugu took the matches, approached the victims, and lit the kindling in front of Father Pacheco. Through Suetsugu's overt actions, the governor understood the deputy-lieutenant's resolve to display his unquestionable loyalty to the shogun's edict.

"You are all criminals of the empire. May you all die with shame," Suetsugu shouted as he lit the remaining wood piles.

"You have violated the shogun's laws. Consider this your end," Governor Kawachi roared as he approached the victims.

As the fire burned, Governor Kawachi paced around the

victims, hoping to observe signs of weakness and fear, but he was not rewarded; the victims maintained their calm resolve, and the governor stepped back, deflated.

As the fire roared and the heat became unbearable, the governor, the deputy-lieutenant, and all the officials had to back up still more. The end was near for the martyrs, but Father Pacheco managed to chew away the rag lodged in his mouth, and in one quick blow spat it out and began to speak. "Brothers in faith," he shouted, "despair not! The Holy Spirit is with us and sends us supernatural strength."

"What is happening?" Governor Kawachi yelled furiously.

"I am not sure, Governor, but I think they are smiling," Suetsugu answered, looking confused.

"How did the leader's rag come out? Get someone to put it back in!"

"It is too late, Governor. The fire is burning above their waists," Suetsugu replied.

Despite the horrific pain, Father Pacheco was determined to bolster the spirits of his comrades. "Brothers in faith," Father Pacheco shouted over the roar of the flames. "These men cannot do more harm to us than permitted by God. Hold no ill-judgment or anger against them, for they know not what they do."

Standing tall, the martyrs nodded their heads.

"Shut him up," the governor yelled.

"I am sorry, Governor, but it is too late. The fire is too strong now to approach," the deputy-lieutenant answered.

"Brothers, the end is near, but have no fear," Father Pacheco continued. "The Lord stands with us—at our side. Oh, Lord," he quoted from the twenty-third Psalm, "Thou preparest a table before me in the presence of mine persecutors: thou anointest my head with oil; my cup runneth over. Surely goodness and mercy shall follow me all the days of my life: and I will dwell in the house of the Lord for ever."

The raging fire quickly consumed all the bodies of the victims, and some of the officials vomited in revulsion at the smell.

Furious at his victims' courage and resolve, Governor Kawachi approached a group of officials, declaring, "I want *all* their ashes shoveled into sacks—nothing remaining."

"Yes, Governor."

"Then I want those ashes scattered in the deep sea."

"Yes, Governor."

"Before you return, I want every man to bathe twice, at length, before touching shore."

"Bathe twice, Governor?"

"Yes. Not one ash should remain. I will not have anything from their bodies endure. Japan is to forget these Christians ever existed!"

Twenty-seven

June 21, 1626
Edge of Nagasaki City, Nagasaki Prefecture

The rain subsided as Daimyo Shigemasa, on horseback, led his samurai and their captives to the first official guard station at the edge of Nagasaki. Given his prominence as a powerful warlord, Shigemasa was well-recognized almost everywhere around the south of Kyushu.

Scurrying forward, two senior guard officials approached the daimyo and bowed out of respect, extending him a warm greeting. Behind the two senior officials a larger number of samurai and officials looked on with fascination at the arriving party, particularly at Father Joaquim and his foreign catechists, who were tied to the bamboo poles. The capture of a foreign priest and his catechists was a rare occurrence in 1626.

"Daimyo Shigemasa, it is an honor," the most senior guard stated. "How may we assist?"

"I have uncovered an entire village of Christians. They have sheltered this foreign priest and his aides."

"It is an impressive capture, Lord," the guard answered with admiration.

"I take them to the Nagasaki court of justice for sentencing by the governor."

"Please proceed, Lord Shigemasa," the senior guard said,

131

motioning them forward. "Several officials will happily escort you."

Bowing cordially, the guards and officials moved out of their way, and Daimyo Shigemasa's procession began to make its way down the mountain toward the city. Soon, the villagers would arrive at the court of justice, where they would face judgment. Fear began to show on their faces.

"What will happen at the court of justice, Father?" Catechist Miguel asked, whispering anxiously.

"Judgment and sentencing, Miguel, but worry not."

"So the end is near?"

"No, these men have no power over us. We are in *God's* hands now."

★ ★ ★

Magistrate's Office, Nagasaki City

Down at the bottom of the mountain, Governor Kawachi and Deputy-Lieutenant Suetsugu had arranged a meeting at the Nagasaki magistrate's office.

"I never said the shogun does not want you to make money," Governor Kawachi stated sternly. "I only said he does not wish for your activities to disadvantage the regime."

"What does that mean?" the deputy-lieutenant asked, sounding frustrated.

"It means your decisions need to be more closely aligned with the Bakufu."

"Please, Governor, give me an example."

"The Portuguese."

"What about them?"

"You favor them in trade and give them special privileges."

"My family has long-standing ties to government officials in Macao."

"So?" The governor glared, unblinking.

"The Portuguese have long been established as the intermediaries between Japan and Macao."

"And what about the Dutch?"

"I do not trust the Dutch."

"Why?"

"Because they ransack our ships at sea. They are troublemakers."

"Maybe they cause trouble because they cannot get a legitimate foothold in Macao or Nagasaki. The shogun may not want to trade only through the Portuguese. He may wish to have it more balanced."

"I do not see how that makes sense. It was the shogun who expelled the Spanish three years ago."

"That is different," the governor replied, growing irritated. "The shogun has good reason to suspect Spain may try to invade Japan."

"Ah, but who planted that idea in the shogun's mind?"

"What do you say?"

"It was the Dutch." Suetsugu exhaled noticeably, also displaying apparent frustration. "It was the Dutch and the English who planted that thought in his mind."

"It matters not. He is shogun, and he decides policy."

"So what would the shogun have me do?"

"Provide the Dutch with more opportunity in Nagasaki."

Suetsugu shook his head and sighed again. "It does not make sense."

"From whose perspective?"

"What do you mean?"

"The shogun is interested to learn the real reason why the Portuguese are doing all the trade in Nagasaki."

"I already told you. The Portuguese have the foothold in Macao, our largest trading partner."

"Is that the only reason?"

"I do not understand."

"The shogun has concerns you are taking bribes from the Portuguese to give them a monopoly on trade in Nagasaki."

"Bribes?"

"Are you taking bribes and not sharing the proceeds?"

"Absolutely not! I am dishonored by the insinuation."

"The shogun has a right to ask questions. His regime controls trade in Japan, not the merchants."

"I do not dispute the shogun's control."

"Perhaps there is another reason why you give a monopoly to the Portuguese."

"Of what do you speak?"

"You have too many outstanding loans to them. The only way the Portuguese can pay you back is if you continue to allow them a monopoly."

"That is absurd!" The deputy-lieutenant's agitation was becoming more pronounced.

"It is not absurd. You are making too much money from these loans, Deputy. Your loans to the Portuguese are extended at interest rates much higher than the shogun considers proper for you."

"Give me an example."

"Some of your interest rates are nearly thirty percent."

"It is my own money; I can lend it out at rates I want."

"You are making far too much money, Deputy. The shogun is concerned that you may be profiting too much from your position."

"I do not see why I should lower my interest rates."

"It is not only your rates," the governor replied. "The shogun thinks you may be in too deep now with your loans, and your personal interests may not be fully aligned with the regime."

"That is preposterous," the deputy-lieutenant shouted in frustration. "My business is good for Japan. I bring our country the best silk from China!"

The governor turned at the sound of runners approaching.

"Governor, we have an urgent message from a guard on the edge of the city," the official blurted out. "Daimyo Matsukura Shigemasa has captured an entire Christian village in Arima domain. He is bringing them to the court of justice now."

"He also captured a Portuguese Christian father and his foreign aides," a second messenger announced.

"Escort them into the court immediately," the governor commanded.

"Yes, Governor."

"The deputy-lieutenant and I will be there shortly."

"Another foreign priest?" asked Suetsugu, stupefied.

"It appears so," responded the governor. "Come, let us go. It is time to destroy some more Christians."

★ ★ ★

Court of Justice, City of Nagasaki

To maintain order in the overcrowded court, all the villagers were crammed into a corner of the room and forced to kneel. Most looked overwhelmed, exhausted, and anxious as they awaited the arrival of the new governor, Mizuno Kawachi, and the deputy-lieutenant.

Battered over the last three days, the villagers were filthy and bloodied. With dark circles under their eyes, all waited in silence.

Moments later, Governor Kawachi entered the building with a very stern look on his face. He gazed harshly at Father Joaquim, his catechists, and the villagers. Approaching the front of the room, he was followed by Deputy-Lieutenant Suetsugu, who swaggered behind him.

"You will all bow in my presence," the governor commanded as he addressed the village. "How dare you fail to acknowledge my presence?"

Quickly, the villagers bowed deeply to the new governor.

"You are all very lucky," the governor proclaimed. "Had you arrived yesterday, you would have all perished in our great fire. Yesterday, I celebrated my arrival by executing thirteen Christians." The governor smiled. "Deputy, can you please remind me of some of their names?"

On hearing the victims' names, Father Joaquim felt a deep sense of sorrow. Reflecting for a moment, he recalled how genuine and caring these priests had been and how much they had given to the Japanese people. But now they were dead, like hundreds of other Christians before them.

"This court of justice will not convene long today," the governor declared. "You are all criminals by law of the shogun." Governor Kawachi then addressed his officials and samurai. "Take these dogs to the prison. Tomorrow, we will pronounce judgment on them."

Twenty-eight

June 22, 1626
Nagasaki Prison, City of Nagasaki

Father Joaquim studied the surroundings and his fellow prisoners as best he could in the dark. It was past midnight, of that he felt certain, and many of the exhausted inmates were struggling to fall asleep, given the horrid conditions and putrid smell. The overcrowded, cold, dark, filthy concrete prison building had no beds or even blankets. The prisoners had to make do, some of them lying next to, or in some cases on top of, their own excrement.

The father was still mourning the loss of his friend, Master Yamaguchi. Adding to his grief was the newly discovered loss of his friends in the Society. *Oh, Lord, I do not understand Your ways,* he prayed, staring into the darkness. *Please grant me vision. Please grant me comprehension. Please do not forsake Your people in this time of need. Now, more than ever, we need You.*

"I do not understand," Catechist Miguel said, sitting up and turning toward Catechist Tonia. "Why did Master Yamaguchi not defend himself against the daimyo?"

"I do not know," Catechist Tonia replied, also sitting up. "Master Yamaguchi had defended himself against such an attack a thousand times."

"Yes, and he even taught us that technique again several weeks ago," Miguel continued.

"Do you think it was because of us?" Tonia asked. "Perhaps he did not want to incite further violence, as the daimyo and his samurai would have retaliated against the village."

"I do not know the reason," Father Joaquim stated. "But I am sure it was for our benefit. Master Yamaguchi always placed others first."

"I guess it does not matter anymore." Miguel shrugged. "Master Yamaguchi is dead, and we are next."

"Miguel, please have faith," Father Joaquim said to the worried young man.

"Faith in what?"

"That we *will* survive."

"Do you really believe that, Father?"

"Yes, Miguel."

"How?"

"I do not know how; I just *know* that we will."

"How can you realistically feel this way, Father? Look around us; this is the end."

"It is important to keep faith, Miguel."

"I do have faith, but I am just being realistic."

"If you feel this is the end, then you do not have faith, Miguel. If you have faith, you need to believe."

"Believe in what?"

"Our survival, Miguel. Do you believe the Lord will protect us?"

Miguel sighed deeply. "I want to believe, Father. But look at our reality. We are in prison, facing a death sentence, with no way of escape."

"Our reality is what we *believe*, Miguel. I have asked the Lord for help, and I believe we *will* survive."

"I believe, Father," Catechist Tonia interjected. "I believe we will be free again one day."

Catechist Miguel shook his head in frustration. "I am sorry, Father. I have the greatest respect for your faith, but I have seen nothing but bad luck since I arrived in this God-forsaken country."

"Then pray, Miguel. Pray for our survival, and pray for Japan."

Sighing again, Miguel closed his eyes to retreat from the conversation. "I am tired. I will try, Father—I will try."

Father Joaquim and Catechist Tonia also closed their eyes and sought to get some sleep. They knew their fate would be revealed soon.

★ ★ ★

Governor Kawachi, Daimyo Shigemasa and his son Katsuie, Deputy-Lieutenant Suetsugu, and a number of other officials were gathered in the Nagasaki magistrate's office.

"So what do we do with them all?" the governor pondered aloud from behind the magistrate's desk.

"We execute them immediately," the deputy replied.

"I do not really care," Shigemasa stated. "Execute them, torture them—it does not matter to me. Just as long as I get credit for their arrest."

"You already have credit for this," the governor answered.

"But I want *the shogun* to know I captured and arrested them."

"Yes, yes, you will get your credit," the governor replied, grunting slightly.

"This is very important, Governor. I want the shogun to know that I am doing everything possible to capture these despicable Christians on my lands." Shigemasa looked intently at the governor. "And I want him to know I am producing results."

Visibly perturbed, the governor huffed: "Yes, Lord Shigemasa, I will make him aware."

"So are we all agreed?" Suetsugu interjected. "We will execute the entire village tomorrow."

"Slow down, Deputy. We should think carefully about this," the governor answered.

"What is there to think about? The answer is simple; we exterminate them."

"I know you want them dead, but I want what is in our best interests, Deputy."

"What do you mean?"

"I mean, how can *we* gain the most favor with the shogun?"

"The shogun wants us to execute hidden Christians." Suetsugu shook his head, suggesting his impatience. "There is nothing more to discuss."

"The shogun also likes to torture Christians himself," the governor replied.

"So what are you saying?"

"Why not send them all to the shogun and let *him* torture and execute them?"

"That is a very good idea," Shigemasa agreed, smiling. "But there are too many. The women and children tire easily, and it would take far too long to get them to Edo."

"Then maybe we should split them up," the governor suggested. "Split the men from the women and children."

"Yes," Shigemasa agreed quickly. "The men can easily be brought to Edo."

"Then it is decided." The governor leaned back, satisfied.

"And what about the foreign priest and his aides?" Shigemasa asked. "One of them is a young woman."

"Is she strong?" the governor asked.

"Yes, she is the strongest among all the women of the village."

"Then bring all the men and all three foreigners to the shogun. The shogun has never tortured a foreign woman before."

All the men in the room smiled. Apparently the governor was not the only one amused at the thought of the shogun torturing a young Portuguese woman.

"The real prize will be the torture and death of the foreign priest." The governor seemed almost giddy. "The shogun views the priests as the primary agents poisoning Japan."

"Who will take the men to Edo?" the deputy-lieutenant asked.

"I will!" Daimyo Shigemasa blurted.

"Edo is almost a two-week journey, Daimyo."

"It matters not. I personally want to hand these dogs over to the shogun."

"Very well, you have earned it. You take them to Edo," the governor answered authoritatively.

"And what about the women and children?" the deputy-lieutenant asked.

"What about them?"

"Shall we execute them?"

"I prefer apostates over martyrs."

"Surely, if we are sending half the Christians to Edo, we can execute the women and children."

"I was not pleased by our execution yesterday, Deputy."

"Why? The Christians are dead. Even their ashes do not remain. It was a great victory."

"Not quite, Deputy. They were fearless; this bothers me. They would rather choose death than recant their faith."

"It is still a victory," the deputy replied stubbornly.

"A complete victory would be for them do something against their will. I want apostates, not martyrs."

"And how will you achieve this?"

"Torture, Deputy. It will be achieved through unbearable torture."

"Splendid, Governor. And I would like to be in charge of this."

"Are you sure you have the stomach to torture women and children?"

"If I can torture my own mother and sister, who were previously Christian, then I can easily torture some unknown women and children."

"Did you really torture your own family, Deputy?"

"Yes, their Christian beliefs were compromising my business."

"Then it looks like we have the right man for the job." The governor smiled and nodded his approval. "Wake the Christian dogs and remove them from the kennel."

Twenty-nine

June 22, 1626
Nagasaki Court of Justice, City of Nagasaki

Most of the villagers standing in Nagasaki's court of justice had barely slept. Having spent the entire night crammed together and surrounded by, and sometimes resting on, excrement and waste, the villagers looked and smelled horrible. Many were sick and exhausted.

Governor Kawachi quickly marched into the courtroom from the magistrate's office. Behind him were a large number of senior officials, including Daimyo Shigemasa, Deputy-Lieutenant Suetsugu, and many guards.

"Line up these dogs so they may face their judgment," the governor ordered as he made his way to the front of the courtroom and took his seat as prosecutor and judge.

Quickly and brutally, several officials forced the villagers into rows near the front of the courtroom. They shoved the children forward, followed by the women, keeping the men at the rear.

"This hearing will be very short," the governor exclaimed firmly. "By law of the shogun and the Bakufu regime, you are all criminals and will suffer greatly for your crimes. There is only one way to reduce your suffering: you will renounce your useless faith."

Apart from the sound of a few whimpering children, the room was silent.

"Who among you will recant?" The governor scanned the room, looking for those most likely to break.

More silence.

"The governor asked you a question, you stupid dogs," the deputy-lieutenant bellowed. "Who will recant?"

Clearly terrified by the deputy's frightening voice, many of the smaller children began to cry. But the adults remained silent.

In the back of the room, Father Joaquim saw the governor's eyes lock onto his own, the man's rage apparent. "Bring the foreign priest to the front," the governor commanded.

Two samurai guards grabbed Father Joaquim and yanked him to the front.

"State your name," the governor ordered.

"Father Joaquim Martinez."

"You admit to being a priest?"

"Yes, I am a father in the order of the Jesuits."

"Why are you in Japan? Your time here has expired."

"My mission is to spread the Word of God and to shepherd the converted." The father heard mumblings from the guards.

"Will you recant?"

"No, sir, I will not."

Governor Kawachi stared menacingly at the Jesuit. "And what of your flock? Will they recant this false religion?"

"These men and women are free to make their own choices. Ask them if they wish to recant."

"Which of you will recant and live? Step forward immediately!"

The villagers remained silent and still.

"Read your sentences. We will not recant," Father Joaquim answered resolutely.

"Do you not wish to save their lives, Priest?" the governor sneered. "You should *make* them recant."

"Only God can truly save."

"Your faith will not help you here," the deputy-lieutenant interjected before walking rapidly toward Father Joaquim and staring at him coldly.

"Our Lord Jesus cautioned his disciples they would meet with opposition when they spread His word. I am not afraid."

"You should be afraid, Priest, for your death will be the most painful and gruesome of all," the deputy-lieutenant sneered.

"You should never have voyaged to Japan, Priest," the governor said. "The shogun is the Lord here and there is no place for your Jesus. Your teachings have corrupted the minds of our people."

"The people of Japan have a right to choose whom they serve."

"Wrong, Priest. The people of Japan exist to serve the shogun and the daimyo who own the lands they work on."

Daimyo Shigemasa grinned.

"Well, then ..." The governor shook his head as he gazed over the assembled villagers. "Here is my sentence: The village will be divided into two groups. The men and foreigners will be marched to Edo, where the shogun will have the pleasure of choosing the manner of their torture and death."

Several women and children began crying.

"The women and children will remain incarcerated in Nagasaki, where they will recant through torture or face death."

The samurai and officials began to divide the villagers, pushing the men and foreigners to one side of the court and the women and children to the other.

The crying and wailing grew louder as families were torn apart. Several villagers were assaulted as husbands and wives tried to embrace for the last time.

"This court is dismissed," the governor shouted. "May you all lament the day you adopted this useless faith!"

Thirty

June 23, 1626
Nagasaki streets

Crying only inflamed the samurai, who forced the women and children down the street toward the deputy-lieutenant's empty warehouse near the harbor. Every moan or whimper led to a blow on the back of the head by one of the samurai. As they moved through the streets, the samurai purposely yanked on the ropes binding the prisoners, causing them to trip and fall to the ground. They'd been ordered to treat the women and children like animals, to mock them.

Leading the march was Deputy-Lieutenant Suetsugu, who strutted down the street with great bravado. Most of those he passed on the streets quickly ran off in another direction. No Nagasaki resident wished to mingle with this horrific persecution.

"This is what happens to Christians," the deputy-lieutenant shouted as he paraded past a group of locals who had gathered near the center of the city. "All Christians will be treated like dogs—tortured and killed!"

Several local women looked on, speechless at the degrading spectacle before them. Noticing their reaction, Suetsugu smiled at them. "Christians are criminals and enemies of the regime. They will be humiliated before they are purified through torture. These dogs have far too much dignity. Remove the women's clothing!" the deputy commanded.

"Here?" one of the officials asked, visibly surprised.

"Yes. What better place to humiliate them?"

Scores of Nagasaki residents looked on in horror and disgust. Parading a woman naked in public was a grave insult and great dishonor. Suetsugu saw their revulsion and fed on it.

The samurai did as ordered. The women dared not resist. They could only cry.

"Christians are dogs. Why should dogs wear clothes?" Suetsugu asked, grinning.

"Leave my aunt alone," young Shiro shouted before running over to kick the samurai who had torn off her clothing.

"Discipline that brat," the deputy yelled.

With the butt end of their swords, several samurai hammered away on Shiro's little back and head until he was nearly unconscious.

"Do not touch him," his aunt screamed as she tried to run over and protect him.

Another samurai quickly knocked her to the ground, where she lay naked, sprawled out on the street.

"Look at this pathetic show," Suetsugu said, laughing. "These helpless dogs wish to protect one another."

Standing over the naked woman, whose name he did not know nor was inclined to learn, Suetsugu continued. "Criminals will not be spared my wrath. Even small children. No one will be spared."

The woman tried to get up.

"Stay down there," the deputy-lieutenant commanded as he stood above the woman with a large whip in his hand. "I want you to crawl like a dog!"

The woman stared back at the deputy, wide-eyed and unmoving.

"You dogs are far too disobedient. You need to listen to your masters," Suetsugu shouted again. "Now crawl!"

Still the woman remained motionless.

"Crawl, I said! Crawl like a dog!" Suetsugu ordered as he began whipping the woman. As his whip drew blood, she cried out and began crawling, reluctantly, down the road, naked and humiliated before the crowd.

Motivated by the laughter of the many samurai, Suetsugu ordered all the women to crawl down the road naked, like animals. After several minutes of amusement, Suetsugu signaled for the samurai to pick them up from the ground.

"We cannot let these dogs crawl all day," the deputy-lieutenant declared, grinning. "We would never arrive at the warehouse."

Walking again, the group soon arrived at Suetsugu's empty warehouse near the water in the harbor. Inside, the warehouse had tall ceilings and was almost void of light—and of sound.

"It is time to lock up these dogs. Shove them in."

Following the deputy's instructions, the officials untied the ropes that had bound the women and children together, then shoved them into the dark warehouse, tossing their clothes in after them.

"You can recant or suffer a revolting death," Suetsugu announced before slamming the door closed and locking them in the dark.

Thirty-one

June 24, 1626
Omura Prison, Hizen Province

Under different circumstances, anyone would have marveled at the brilliant orange-and-red sunset seeming to rest upon the mountain up which Daimyo Shigemasa, his son Katsuie, and the warlord's samurai forced their band of ragged, hungry, exhausted Christian prisoners. But Shigemasa was too intent on obtaining the shogun's favor to observe the splendor. His men were too focused on doing the daimyo's will, and the prisoners were simply too fatigued and miserable to notice anything. Omura Prison, their destination, was located approximately twenty miles north of Nagasaki, and Shigemasa had marched them nearly non-stop from the court in Nagasaki to their present location.

As the daimyo, his samurai, and the prisoners continued up the hill, they were greeted by several prison guards walking down toward them. Up at the top, nearly concealed by a number of trees, stood Omura Prison, guarded by twelve more guards.

"Daimyo Shigemasa, welcome to Omura Prison," Ozuru Matsumoto, the prison master, said as he bowed deeply. "I see you have more prisoners."

"Yes, and they are all Christians."

149

Discreetly, Shigemasa led Matsumoto away from the group in order to speak privately. "They were all found on my lands in Arima," the daimyo confided.

"I am sorry, Lord, but it is a good capture for you, is it not?"

"Yes, always better captured than in hiding."

"How many do you have?" Matsumoto asked as he looked over the prisoners.

"Twenty-one, including three foreign dogs. Each will be a delightful gift for the shogun."

"So how can we help, Lord Shigemasa?"

"I need to visit my castle tomorrow before I lead our long march to Edo. I have more gifts for the shogun that I need to collect. I also need to gather supplies for the journey, so I would like to leave these prisoners here for two nights while I make preparations. Do you have the space to imprison them?"

Half turning his head and scowling a bit, Matsumoto answered: "Hmm ... I do not know. The prison is already well over capacity. I do not know where I could put twenty-one new prisoners. Perhaps we could execute some."

"No, I do not want to kill any." Shigemasa shook his head vigorously. "They are valuable gifts for the shogun. I want him to see all the fruit of my labors."

"I cannot execute any of our existing prisoners," Matsumoto replied. "I have instructions to make them suffer more."

"Well then, let us force them all in together for a few days. They will all suffer more, and I can get what I need."

"It will probably mean piling them on top of one another."

"Why do I care?"

"They will not be able to sleep. Some go insane and kill for more space."

"But my prisoners are gifts for the shogun."

"Perhaps we could also use a new underground prison cell I have built. It is nearly complete."

Shigemasa was pleased by Matsumoto's enthusiasm almost as much as by the offer itself. "A new prison cell?"

The man nodded, obviously proud of his accomplishment. "I built it for the most vile criminals. It is a deep concrete hole in the ground. It can fit one or two, possibly three if they stand and lean against each other."

"Why is it for the most vile?"

"Because there is almost no air in the hole, and it is unbearably hot, and sometimes we fill it with human waste, so it is grotesquely foul."

"Good. We will put my most despicable criminals in it— the Christian priest and his aides. I cannot risk them being killed."

"Very well, Lord. But they will get very sick."

"Sick dogs are less likely to run away." Shigemasa grinned at his good fortune.

"And the rest of the Christians?"

"Shove them into the main prison. I do not care if we have to pile them on top of one another. It is not me in there."

"Very well, Lord. It will be like hell for them."

Thirty-two

Masao sat in a corner of the dark, cold, smelly prison cell, staring blankly and trying to shut out the many groans and occasional wails and heated arguments around him. Sleep called to him, but his mind refused to relax enough to surrender. How could he possibly sleep, he wondered, as he sat with his back tight against the wall and his legs drawn up equally tight, his arms wrapped around his legs, and his head resting on his knees. He and his fellow village men were crammed in so tightly that if he even tried to stretch out, his legs would come to rest on top of several of his neighbors.

How had this happened to him—and to his fellow villagers? They'd never had an easy life. For as long as Masao could remember, and surely long before that, his village had been at the mercy of greedy daimyo. But, until a few days before, at least they'd been free to sleep in their own little homes, surrounded by their immediate family members. Now they were in a miserable prison awaiting torture and death. Perhaps they'd been wrong to convert to this new religion brought to them by foreigners. But he'd seen lives changed. His own life had changed. Before he was nothing more than a slave for the daimyo, making rice day after day, but now, for the first time in his life, he had something of his own—his faith.

Masao's thoughts shifted as a stench assailed his nostrils and triggered a hint of recognition. He'd smelled decaying flesh before. It was a different scent, unique and distinguishable from the many other horrid smells that surrounded him. When he and his neighbors had been hastily shoved into the prison, he'd had little opportunity to note his surroundings. But he recalled now, seeing as they entered, perfectly stationary bodies lying on the floors. Those motionless forms, he now realized, hadn't been sleeping. They were corpses, rotting piles of dead human flesh.

Masao also recalled seeing some prisoners who lacked a foot or a hand. At least one, he seemed to remember, was missing an entire arm. The limbs appeared to have rotted off, no doubt diseased and neglected. Soon, he was sure, the bodies those diseased limbs were attached to would die as well. Soon, he consoled himself, *all* of them would die, and leave this horrid place forever.

★ ★ ★

As prison master Matsumoto, Shigemasa, and most of the guards and samurai no doubt slept, a few hundred feet away, in a hole nine feet deep and no more than three and a half feet in diameter, Father Joaquim and the two young catechists stood. They were soaked in the urine Matsumoto and several of his guards had earlier drained on them.

Exhausted but lacking the room required to sit—and not wanting to recline in the vile waste that surrounded them even if they had had the room—the three stood and discussed their situation.

"When will this end, Father?" Tonia moaned as she stood pressed tightly against the side of the hole.

"When we are dead," Miguel replied, sounding utterly despondent.

"I know I have said this before, but have faith, my friends. We *will* survive this," Father Joaquim answered, hoping to rally his young apprentices.

153

Miguel mumbled: "I am sorry Father, but things have gone from bad to worse for us. I do not believe anymore. God has abandoned us."

"That is precisely the time to renew your faith, Miguel. Perhaps you need to pray."

"I have already prayed, *every night* since our capture. Yet still we are persecuted. And it is only getting worse!"

"Give the Lord a chance to respond, Miguel."

"I already have, Father. He has had plenty of time."

"The Lord will respond in *His* time, Miguel, not yours. Never lose faith. God will answer." He embraced the young catechists. "Let us all pray together. Let us recite The Lord's Prayer from the book of Matthew."

Our Father which art in heaven, Hallowed be thy name.

Thy kingdom come, Thy will be done on earth, as it is in heaven.

Give us this day our daily bread.

And forgive us our debts, as we forgive our debtors.

And lead us not into temptation, but deliver us from evil: For thine is the kingdom, and the power, and the glory, for ever. Amen.

"Amen," Tonia echoed firmly.

"I do not need to be taught how to pray," Miguel grumbled. "I am a catechist. I know the Bible."

"You are right, Miguel," Father Joaquim said. "Words are only words. It is how you *feel* about them that matters."

"What do you mean?"

"God's Spirit lives inside you. When you have genuine faith, and feel it, He will know."

"And why does this matter to me?"

"Because one day it could save you."

Thirty-three

June 25, 1626
Omura Prison, Hizen Province

Just after sunrise, while the two young catechists, still on their feet, appeared to actually be dozing a bit, Father Joaquim heard voices above, not far away. Standing motionless and focusing his attention, the priest listened carefully.

"Keep these dogs securely in their cages while I am away," Shigemasa ordered. "I will be back before sunset tomorrow."

"Yes, Daimyo," Father Joaquim heard Matsumoto answer. "I will not open the door even to feed them."

"And keep the lid on the pit. I do not want the padre or his aides to see daylight."

"The lid will remain locked until you return, Lord. The only contact with the priest and his aides will be my men urinating on them," Matsumoto boasted smugly.

"I am pleased that we stopped at Omura Prison," the daimyo said.

"Thank you, Lord. It is an honor to assist you," Matsumoto said as Father Joaquim heard the hoof beats of Shigemasa's horses moving away.

"Come," the priest then heard the prison master say, "let us give the dogs an early-morning shower."

Father Joaquim began praying as he anticipated Miguel's reaction to the abuse they were about to suffer.

The laughter from Matsumoto and his guards aroused the dozing catechists just in time to look up into the streams of urine raining down on them from their tormentors.

"Stop, you heartless bastards!" Miguel yelled.

But his words only encouraged the chortling guards.

"Have no worries, Miguel. Our torments will end."

"When, Father? When will it end?!"

"Soon, Miguel. The Lord will wash us clean."

"How can men treat other humans like this?" Tonia sobbed in distress as she shook the waste from her hair.

"Foster no ill-feelings for them, Tonia," Father Joaquim said as he wiped the tears from her eyes.

"I want to kill them," Miguel yelled out in a sudden outburst. Frantically, he tried to shake his body in a futile effort to clean himself.

Tonia reached out her hand and placed it on Miguel's shoulders to console him.

"Mind your emotions, Miguel," Father Joaquim said. "Anger is self-destructive. Focus on love. Love your enemy as the Lord loves us."

"But these men should pay for their inhumanities!"

"It is not your job to carry out vengeance, Miguel. Focus on our freedom, and we will have it."

★ ★ ★

As the sun began to set and strong winds picked up, signaling the approach of rain, Hideo, one of the guards, spotted an older man with the bearing and gait of a samurai approaching the prison from a nearby field. As he neared the prison from the bottom of the hill, Hideo and several other guards intercepted him. They saw that he was carrying a small box.

The man had gray hair and looked to be in his sixties. Despite his age, however, he appeared strong, and his dark skin suggested he spent most of his time outdoors. As he neared them, he smiled, suggesting he came with good intentions.

Noticing the crest of Daimyo Shigemasa on the man's shoulder, the guards bowed to him. "Welcome," the senior guard said, acknowledging the samurai's allegiance. "What brings you to Omura Prison?"

"I am here to present a gift to the prison master and all the guards on behalf of Lord Shigemasa."

"We are greatly honored," the senior guard answered. "What do you have for us?"

"It is Lord Shigemasa's finest imported tea. It is his hope that you will all partake in this fine tea tonight. He said it should keep you awake to look after his dogs."

"We are delighted to look after the lord's dogs. And we are greatly honored by this gift. Please profess our deepest gratitude to Lord Shigemasa."

"Of course. And thank *you* for looking after his mutts."

★ ★ ★

In their cramped hole in the ground, steady rain seeped through the cracks in the slab that covered Father Joaquim and the catechists. It wasn't enough to wash away the waste that had been poured over them; instead, it was just enough to give them chills.

"Apart from the rain, it is very quiet tonight," Tonia noted. "Nothing like last night."

"Shhhh," Father Joaquim interrupted. "Did you hear that?"

"It is probably a guard," Tonia said.

"No, it is not a guard. A guard would be cursing at us," Father Joaquim answered. "This noise is something else."

"Look!" Tonia focused on a bright blue flame visible through the cracks in the slab.

"What is that?" Miguel asked, appearing fearful.

"I do not know," Father Joaquim answered, bewildered by the light.

Remarkably, the mystical blue flame burned through the wood, despite the heavy rain.

Soon, the lid popped off and a man appeared hovering above the pit. Heavy rain continued to pour down, and the filth was washed from the three surprised prisoners.

Silently, the man gazed down into the pit, observing Father Joaquim and the catechists.

"Who are you?" Tonia broke the silence.

"My pupils call me Master Watanabe. Hurry, take this rope." Master Watanabe threw one end of a rope into the pit.

"Do it," Father Joaquim told Tonia. "You go first."

Master Watanabe yanked Tonia out of the pit in a matter of seconds, before tossing the end of the rope back in.

"Who is next?" Master Watanabe asked.

"You are, Miguel. Quick, grab the rope."

As instructed, Miguel grabbed the rope and was also quickly yanked out of the pit, followed by Father Joaquim. Each, in turn, wobbled momentarily, trying to regain their balance.

"Where are the guards?" Miguel asked, still looking fearful while casting a quick gaze at Tonia.

"Resting," the old man answered cryptically and with a hint of a smile.

"Why are you helping us?" Father Joaquim asked their benefactor.

"I am here to help you escape, but we do not have much time."

"I cannot leave the others." Father Joaquim looked toward the main prison building, which housed the remainder of the village's men.

"We are out of time, Father. We must go. You will have an opportunity to save them later, but not now."

"Why should we trust you?"

"You need only trust your own intuition," Master Watanabe answered. "For now, you need to make one choice: Do you wish to escape or not?"

"Yes, we do!" Miguel answered as he stared down at the pit.

"Yes, we want to escape," Tonia echoed. "We want to leave here as soon as possible."

"Fine," Father Joaquim agreed, though reluctantly. "But this is only temporary. I will *not* abandon the others."

"Very well," Master Watanabe agreed. "But for now, let us go quickly!"

Thirty-four

June 26, 1626
Omura Prison, Hizen Province

Matsumoto finally awoke to the sound of birds outside his window. He shook his groggy head—several times. Panic began to well up inside as he tried to remember—something, anything. His name. Where he was. What he was supposed to do. Shaking his head a few more times, he began to recall. *I am Ozuru Matsumoto. I am the master of Omura Prison.* He took a few steps to his bedroom door and walked outside. The guard stationed outside his door was on the floor, unconscious. Matsumoto kicked the guard, and the man began to wake up. Suddenly Matsumoto remembered the prisoners Daimyo Shigemasa had left under his watch.

Rushing to the main prison building, he inspected the sealed lock, entered and found all his prisoners still inside. He breathed a sigh of relief.

Then he remembered the pit and quickly dashed over to it. To his horror, the pit was empty! Panic set in as he cursed and ran to the guard house. Opening the door, he burst inside and began yelling, "Wake up! Wake up, you imbeciles! The Christian foreigners have escaped!"

Slowly, the other guards roused themselves. Like the prison master, they too seemed groggy and confused.

"Get up." Matsumoto paced frantically around the guard house. "The Christian priest and his aides are gone!"

"What happened?" the most senior guard asked as he stepped forward, shaking his head just as Matsumoto had done when he awoke.

"Drugged, poisoned … I do not know, but it all started with that tea!"

"But that was a gift from Daimyo Shigemasa," the senior guard answered.

"It does not matter now. All that matters is that we find the missing prisoners before the daimyo returns!"

"What shall we do?" the senior guard asked.

"I want our six strongest and fastest to gather arms and depart for the forest immediately."

"Yes, Master. I will take care of it. Why the forest? They could have escaped in any direction."

Matsumoto glared contemptuously at the guard. "Use your mind. These Christians are fugitives. They *must* run to the forest to avoid detection."

"Yes, Master, you are right. I am sorry."

"Bring them back alive," Matsumoto ordered. "The daimyo will be furious if we return them dead."

"Yes, Master, but what if it is not possible to return them alive?"

"Then kill them. It is better to return them dead than not at all. Go, and find them quickly! They are tired and ill, so it should not take you too long. Remember, the daimyo will return before sunset, so make sure you bring the dogs back before then."

★ ★ ★

Shigemasa was surprised to see Matsumoto walking down the path to meet him.

"Welcome back, Lord Shigemasa," the prison master said, bowing to the daimyo and his samurai.

"Yes, and how are my prisoners?"

Matsumoto paused for a moment. Finally he answered: "We have a problem."

Shigemasa dismounted. "What problem?" he asked, glaring at Matsumoto intensely.

"All the Japanese prisoners are still safely incarcerated in the jail, but the foreign priest and his aides are missing."

Shigemasa's glare expressed his fury.

"I am sorry, Lord. They escaped, but I am confident we will recover them soon."

Without a word, Shigemasa pounded Matsumoto's face and drove him to the ground, where he delivered a ferocious kick to his chest.

"Get up," the daimyo ordered. "Take me to the pit. I want to see what happened!"

Terrified, Matsumoto rose to his feet and scurried up the hill, with Shigemasa and his samurai following.

"Look," Shigemasa exclaimed when they arrived at the pit. "The lock is intact!"

"Yes, Lord, I know."

"Then how did they get out?"

"They burned the wood, Lord. Look, they burned one of the planks, just enough to slip out."

"Do you mock me? You are telling me they cultivated a fire as rain poured down on them?"

"Yes, Lord, so it seems."

"And, if they did start a fire in the middle of the night, how is it that none of your twelve guards noticed it?"

Afraid to answer, Matsumoto looked down, silently.

"It was your tea, Lord," the senior guard, standing nearby, said shamefacedly.

"My tea?"

"Yes, Lord, we were drugged by your tea. Yesterday, your retainer delivered us a gift of English tea."

"*I* presented you with a gift of *English* tea?"

"No, Lord, your *retainer* presented us with a gift of English tea. He knew about the Christian dogs and offered us an entire box to keep us awake."

"Is this a hoax? Do you dare play with me on such important matters?"

"No, Lord, I swear it is the truth," the senior guard replied. "Your retainer even bore your family crest on his shoulder."

"So this mysterious retainer offered you English tea—to keep you awake—yet you all fell asleep. And while you were sleeping, three Christians at the bottom of a pit managed to create a supernatural fire with their bare hands, masterfully burn one plank of wood in the rain, and crawl out with no one noticing."

Still afraid to look Shigemasa in the eye, Matsumoto remained silent.

"Stand over here." Shigemasa pointed to a spot next to the pit.

Trembling, Matsumoto did as ordered.

Shigemasa unsheathed his long sword and slowly turned his head, scanning the row of guards before turning back to face Matsumoto.

"Never in my life have I witnessed such incompetence as this. Your explanation is beyond lies! You are either too stupid or too disobedient to go on living!"

Swiftly, the daimyo drove his long sword into Matsumoto's stomach.

Bleeding profusely, Matsumoto began to wobble. As Shigemasa stared into the prison master's eyes, he slowly released his sword, before raising it and expeditiously bringing it down and through the back of Matsumoto's neckline, sending his head and part of his neck to the ground with a thud. It rolled toward the pit. Shigemasa kicked the head in, where it splashed in the waste at the bottom. Then, with another powerful kick, he shoved Matsumoto's body down after it.

"Come over here," the daimyo said as he pointed at the senior prison guard. "You are next."

With terror in his eyes, the senior guard refused to approach. In response, two powerful samurai grabbed his arms and dragged him toward Shigemasa, who still stood at the edge of the pit.

"No! No! It is not my fault!" the guard screamed.

Straightaway, Shigemasa drove his sword into the senior guard's stomach. The man's body went limp, and the two samurai released his arms.

"Never mock your lord," Shigemasa shouted as he swiftly decapitated the guard. After wiping the spattered blood off his face and hands, Shigemasa kicked the senior guard's head and body into the pit, before spitting after him in contempt. "These men have jeopardized my lands and do not deserve to live," Shigemasa shouted. "Now we must catch these wild dogs."

"What about the remainder of the guards?" one of the samurai asked. "Shall we also throw them into the pit?"

For a moment, the daimyo thought carefully.

"No, throw them into the prison with all the inmates. We might have questions for them later. If they do not provide satisfactory answers, we will let them rot as lepers."

"And who will run the prison?" a retainer asked.

"We will. It is time to run this prison properly."

★ ★ ★

In the guard house, Shigemasa spoke to his samurai. "The Nagasaki magistrate sent a letter to the shogun informing him we have a gift of twenty-one Christians for him to slay, including a foreign Christian priest. What will the shogun say when we arrive with only eighteen and no priest?"

"I do not know, Lord. Perhaps he will be upset," a retainer replied.

"Upset? He will be furious. He will probably take all my lands. I will be a peasant!"

"What is our plan, Lord? We must decide quickly."

"We will mobilize every samurai at my disposal."

"All three thousand?"

"Yes. We will scour every piece of land and forest until we capture them. We will use our horses to outrun them."

"We will find them, Lord," the retainer assured.

"Yes. They are on foot, tired, and outnumbered. Three is no match for three thousand."

$\star\star\star$

"I cannot go on," Tonia said, taking a deep breath and shaking her head. "I need to rest."

"We are not far from rest," Master Watanabe replied. "Do you see that small hill?"

"Yes," Tonia said, nodding.

"Underneath, there is a cave where we can rest. So, please, we must continue. Soon, you will be able to rest."

Pushing themselves, the group continued for another mile or so, until they arrived at the edge of the hill where they found a small hidden cave.

As they entered, Tonia fell to the floor, exhausted, followed by Miguel, who lay down next to her.

Seating himself against the cave wall, Father Joaquim began to speak. "Now I must ask, Master Watanabe: who are you, and why did you come to rescue us?"

Master Watanabe sat on the ground, across from Father

Joaquim. "I am an old friend of your good friend, Master Yamaguchi. And, like Master Yamaguchi, over the years I have learned to listen carefully to the still, small voice when it speaks to me. The voice told me something terrible had happened to my old friend and his village. When I arrived and found all the houses burned to the ground and the village empty, I began to pray. I prayed the entire day, and then the still, small voice told me to make my way to Omura Prison—and to bring Master Yamaguchi's sword. I have learned that miraculous things happen when I obey that still, small voice."

Fascinated by Master Yamaguchi's sword before him, Father Joaquim looked over at his young apprentices, eager to see the impression Master Watanabe had on them. Both had fallen asleep.

"Perhaps, Father, we too should get some sleep now," the old man said.

"What will we do when we awaken? What is our plan?"

"To continue our retreat and re-group in a place of safety."

"Where?"

"The Goto Islands. They are not far, and some of them are sanctuaries for Christians."

"What will we do there?"

"We can take refuge from our pursuers and plan the rescue of your villagers."

"Good," Father Joaquim replied. "Do you think a large force is hunting us?"

"By morning, Shigemasa will have no less than three thousand samurai on our heels. He will summon his entire force."

Thirty-five

June 27, 1626
Shogun's Castle, Edo, Musashi Province

Having inherited his reign, the current shogun, Iemitsu, was not the equal of his grandfather, Ieyasu. While Ieyasu had been brutal and dictatorial like his grandson, unlike his grandson the elder Tokugawa could back up his bluster with true strength and courage. Young Iemitsu had only the bluster. He depended on his family name and his intimidation to enforce his rule.

This morning another ruthless torture was under way, the shogun surrounded by his usual retinue of senior Bakufu government officials and warrior Buddhist monks. This day's torture victim was not only a Japanese Christian, but also a ronin, an ex-samurai.

The shogun viewed ronin as dangerous troublemakers. He'd effectively made beggars of these former samurai who had opposed his family's regime. Then, because these ex-samurai had no place in the societal structure the shogun had created, he felt threatened by them. If united, they could cause an uprising and destabilize his absolute rule.

The man in the shogun's torture chamber became a ronin after the death of his warlord, Konishi Yukinaga, many years before. Iemitsu knew his history well: back around the turn of the century, Daimyo Konishi Yukinaga, also known by his Christian name, Dom Agostinho, was one of the most powerful warlords in Kyushu, and he had become a devout Christian. A quarter century before, Yukinaga had fought against Tokugawa Ieyasu during a time of political uncertainty and a vacancy in Japan's military leadership.

Yukinaga led four thousand samurai to the Battle of Sekigahara, one of the most decisive battles in the country's history. But Tokugawa Ieyasu won that battle and became shogun, and Ieyasu's grandson, Iemitsu, held his grandfather in the highest regard, regarding him as almost God-like status.

Iemitsu was certain the ronin tied before him had fought against his grandfather in the Battle of Sekigahara, so this day's torture would be particularly brutal. This ronin was tall and had only a little gray hair on the sides of his distinguished face. He had broad shoulders, and his arms were quite defined for a man nearing fifty. Having been captured recently, he still looked healthy. While thin, he was not emaciated from a long prison term.

Like most samurai in the Edo era, the man's hair, featuring a shaved pate, signified his warrior status. The remaining hair, which was long and oiled, was tied into a small queue, folded onto the top of the head in a characteristic topknot. Originally, this hairstyle was used to hold a samurai's helmet steady atop his head in battle. But, over time, it became a status symbol in Japanese society.

Kneeling confidently in the seiza position, Shogun Iemitsu oversaw the torture session. With burning-hot metal swords, several eta monks were in the process of scorching the shogun's family crest of three hollyhock leaves into the skin on the ronin's chest and arms. Despite the excruciating pain, the ronin only groaned. As a hardened ex-samurai, he was accustomed to extreme pain and mental discipline.

Frustrated and rising to his feet, the shogun interrupted

the session, approaching the ronin and spitting in his face. "Remind me who you served?"

"I proudly served Daimyo Konishi Yukinaga," the man said, blood dripping from his mouth as he spoke.

"Konishi fought against my grandfather, the deity of Japan, so you are an enemy of the Tokugawas!"

The ronin looked on in silence.

"Did you raise arms against Ieyasu?"

"I followed my leader into battle."

"Then face the consequences of your treachery!" Iemitsu again spat in the ronin's face.

"Burn this traitor's forehead. Let him bear the mark of the Tokugawa family on his face so he is constantly reminded who won that battle."

As instructed, the eta torturers placed a white-hot sword on the man's forehead, burning the shogun's family crest deeply into his skin. Putrid smoke rose from his scalp as blood trickled down his face.

"Daimyo Konishi lost the battle of Sekigahara," the shogun reminded all listening. Then, looking intently at the ronin, the shogun demanded, "Why are you still alive? Why did you not kill yourself? You suffered shame in your defeat."

"I am a Christian. I will not kill myself."

"Another reason this religion is banned in Japan," the shogun proclaimed as he turned to address his Go-Roju cabinet. "This religion has corrupted our traditions! When *I* die, I will demand that all my retainers take their own lives to honor *me*."

The shogun then turned to the ronin. "The execution of your daimyo has brought you great shame. You should kill yourself."

"I will not. I serve the Lord Jesus Christ now."

"Wrong. I am your Lord. I am the supreme leader of Japan! You will worship and serve me!"

"I serve only Jesus Christ."

Furious, Shogun Iemitsu quickly approached a table full of weapons and torture devices, chose a sharp knife from the table, and returned to the ronin. "If you disrespect me one more time, I will personally cut out your eyes."

The ronin stared back at the shogun, his defiance apparent.

Roaring, the shogun drove his knife deep into the ronin's thigh.

Grinding his teeth, the ronin grunted and moaned.

Pleased with the ronin's discomfort, the shogun left the knife lodged in the ronin's thigh and smiled. "I do not know why I have torturers to help me. It is much more enjoyable to torture you myself. I cannot have your kind, serving no lord, wandering around my country." Approaching the ronin again, the shogun gripped the knife in his thigh, twisting and turning it. Blood spurted, covering the shogun's hand. A retainer quickly handed the shogun a towel to dry himself.

"Imagine the consequences of the Christians and ronin uniting with the king of Spain and his forces."

"It is a threat to the empire, Lord. We will not allow this to happen," the retainer said.

"No, we will not. Like the filthy Christians, these ronin must be eliminated from our lands!" The shogun withdrew the blade lodged in the ronin's leg, and quickly stabbed it into the man's throat, again sending a spray of blood. "Anyone who does not serve *me* will die."

Thirty-six

June 28, 1626
Fields of Hizen Province

Near the north end of a carefully calculated search perimeter, peasants in a small, poor village—much like the one Father Joaquim and the catechists had ministered to before it was desecrated and burned—labored wearily but steadily in the hot afternoon sun. But their quiet, tedious labor was abruptly interrupted by the thunder of rapid hoof beats and the rattle of armor as a regiment of one hundred samurai hastily approached the busiest area in the rice fields.

Lord Shigemasa's plan to recapture the escapees was simple. Based on the density of Nagasaki and the number of officials in and around the city, he had determined that Father Joaquim would not head south. So he directed his perimeter toward the north of his domain. He and his retainers had carefully calculated how far Father Joaquim and his aides could have traveled, given the time available to them, and thus established a perimeter based on their expected distance from Omura Prison. He would send his regiments to the edges of the established perimeter and have them sweep inward from there until their prey was captured.

Chokichi, a large and heavy-set man, with a battle-scarred face that attested to his long military background, sat atop his massive black stallion, examining the village. He wore the same kind of full armor and colors as his master, Daimyo Shigemasa. And, motivated by the warlord's promise of generous rewards as well as by his orders, Chokichi was determined to be the one to find the escaped Christian dogs. He considered no action too callous in the course of achieving his goal. Motioning toward the village, Chokichi and his men moved forward, the villagers obediently following behind.

As the samurai arrived in the ramshackle little village, most of the children ran to hide behind their mothers. Meanwhile the male farmers scurried into the center of the village to pay homage.

"Where are they?" Chokichi shouted, still astride his stallion.

"Who?" a frightened farmer asked, his head bowed and his eyes downcast.

"Do not play stupid, worthless peasant. Where are they? If they are here, tell us immediately or we will torch your village and everyone in it!"

Chokichi gave a hand signal, and immediately twenty samurai dismounted and charged into the disheveled homes, ransacking them in their searches. Inside, terrified women and children could be heard screaming in distress. The male farmers wailed in protest, and several ran to their homes to try to help their families, but they were quickly beaten to the ground.

"Set that one on fire," Chokichi commanded as he pointed to a large old home built of straw and wood in the center of the village.

Several samurai quickly obeyed. As smoke arose, a woman and two children ran out, crying.

"Round up all the children in the village," Chokichi yelled. "Bring them to me immediately."

Throughout the village, samurai shoved mothers to the

ground and yanked away their crying children. Chokichi scarcely noticed the panic among the villagers, as his thoughts were too focused on reaping the reward for finding the escaped Christians.

"You will tell me where they are or we will shove your children into the burning house."

"Please! What do you speak about? Who are you looking for?" a farmer desperate to save his family cried out.

"Three escaped foreign Christians. Where are they?"

"We do not know. I promise you, we have not seen any foreigners."

"Look at that fire. Look at it closely," Chokichi ordered the villagers. "If we discover you have lied to us, we will incinerate every child in this village. As commander of this unit, this is my word!" Chokichi turned slowly in his saddle, surveying the villagers. "Now, I will ask one more time. Have you seen three run-away Christians?"

"No," several of the peasants replied.

"Harboring Christians is harboring *criminals*," Chokichi bellowed. "Violation of this law will result in immediate death. Do you understand?"

"We have not seen any foreigners. We promise you," a farmer yelled, his voice cracking with fear and pleading.

"Do you pledge your children's lives on this?"

"Yes. It has been years since we have seen *any* foreigner," the same farmer replied.

Chokichi again scanned the faces of the clearly terrified and submissive villagers. "Do not get too comfortable. We *will* return to verify your claims." Turning his enormous horse around, Chokichi positioned himself to face his samurai still on horseback.

"How are our supplies?"

"Low," his second-in-command answered. "The men are hungry."

"Help yourselves to whatever we need," Chokichi said. "These peasants exist to support us."

Straightaway, dozens of hungry samurai raided the village supplies, taking nearly all of the food and filling their metal water containers. Demoralized, the villagers could only watch as the army emptied their stock of food and water.

"Do not look disheartened," Chokichi joked as he observed their forlorn faces. "You still have your fields. Get out there and harvest some more." As Chokichi and his fellow samurai turned to depart, the commander yelled out, "I order you to keep your eyes open for them."

"But what can we do?" a downcast farmer asked.

"You can send men into the forest to look for them."

"But we have a new, strict quota to meet."

"That is not my problem. Until they are captured, no one is safe—and we will keep coming back!"

Thirty-seven

June 29, 1626
Plains of Hizen Province

As the morning sun began to make its presence felt, Father Joaquim, his catechists, and Master Watanabe emerged from a forest onto a large, open plain. They could not wait out the daylight. They had to cross the field before the pursuing army caught up with them.

Half a mile or so through the field Tonia's pace slowed significantly. "I am exhausted," she declared, breathing heavily. "I need to rest. When can we stop?"

"Not now, Tonia," Master Watanabe replied, shaking his head in warning. "We cannot rest in an open field. It is too dangerous."

"But I am too tired to continue. I just need …" She took another deep breath. "… a short rest." Tonia stopped, placed her hands on her thighs, and hunched over.

"Here, drink." Master Watanabe offered her a skin filled with water.

Father Joaquim and Miguel, who had been walking ahead of Tonia and Master Watanabe, halted and returned to check on her.

"Are you okay, Tonia?" Father Joaquim asked.

Observing her state, Miguel suddenly appeared very anxious.

Still hunched forward, Tonia breathed a large gasp as she dropped to her knees on the soil.

"I cannot go any furtther," Tonia answered as she placed her palms over her face.

"It is all right, Tonia. We will rest for a while," Father Joaquim said as he helped her find a place to sit. "We will take care of you."

Miguel approached Tonia and put his hands on her shoulders. As he gave her a gentle massage, he suddenly raised his head. "Oh, my God," he said, pointing to the edge of the forest. "Oh, Lord Jesus! Look at the size of their force! There are hundreds. We are doomed!"

"We are far from doomed, Miguel," Master Watanabe replied calmly. "How can we be doomed if we are united with God?"

"Now what, Master Watanabe?" Father Joaquim asked.

"The Chikugo-gawa is a large river close to here. We can escape them on the water."

"Can we get there before they catch us?"

Master Watanabe nodded. "If we hurry, we can make it."

Extending their hands to Tonia, Father Joaquim and Master Watanabe pulled her to her feet.

"Can you make it, Tonia?" Father Joaquim asked. "Can you run?"

"I will do my best."

Master Watanabe led the group in a jog across the large field.

Roaring with determination, the legion commenced their pursuit. A small group of samurai on horses led the charge and quickly left the ground forces behind as they raced full-speed ahead. Behind them, hundreds of samurai quickly followed at full sprint.

"The horsemen are gaining on us," Miguel cried, nearly tripping as he looked back.

Equally anxious, Tonia ran as quickly as she could, but tripped and crashed to the ground. Quickly, Father Joaquim and Master Watanabe yanked her to her feet.

The fugitives somehow increased their pace, but still the gap between them and the horsemen narrowed.

"We will not make the river at this pace. Give me Master Yamaguchi's sword," Father Joaquim said to Master Watanabe.

"What will you do, Father?"

"I must slow them down."

"I will help you," Master Watanabe offered.

"No, you must continue with Miguel and Tonia. Quick, pass me the sword."

Holding the sword, Father Joaquim turned to face the enemy. "Lord, grant me skill to defend my people."

Within seconds, the first horseman arrived. Father Joaquim stood squarely in the field, facing him. With his sword securely hidden behind his back, Father Joaquim stood motionless, encouraging the samurai to approach him.

Then, swiftly, almost faster than the eye could see, Father Joaquim turned his body, and threw his sword through the air at the attacking samurai. With lightning speed, the sword flew above the horse's head and passed straight through the samurai's shoulder, throwing him from his horse. As the samurai flew from the horse, the horse lost its balance, and both crashed to the ground, creating a large cloud of dust.

Father Joaquim quickly ran over to the unconscious samurai and grabbed his bow and arrows. Taking cover behind the horse, the skilled Jesuit then readied the bow and fired a series of arrows at the remaining horsemen.

One after another, the attacking horsemen fell from their horses as they suffered great wounds in their chests, arms, and shoulders, until none were left but the samurai footmen, still some distance away. Even Father Joaquim was surprised by his success.

Looking back over his shoulder, he could see he had gained his friends some time before the main ground forces would arrive, so he ran towards the river.

Minutes later, Father Joaquim caught up with Master Watanabe and the catechists, but the gap between them and the ground force was narrowing. Pushed to her limits, Tonia was struggling to keep up.

"The river is but minutes away," Master Watanabe shouted as he encouraged her to continue. "Our escape is at hand."

Tonia pushed on as Father Joaquim and Miguel ran alongside her, grabbing her hand and pulling her forward. Within moments, they arrived at the edge of the wide and powerful Chikugo-gawa River.

"This is where we will escape them," Master Watanabe said as he approached the river's edge and put his hand in the water.

"Where is it?" Miguel asked anxiously.

"Where is what?"

"Our boat. Where in God's name is our boat?"

"We do not have a boat," Master Watanabe answered.

"Then how on earth are we going to cross?"

"With our feet, Miguel."

"What? I do not see a bridge."

"There is no bridge. We are going to walk across."

"Are you mad?" Miguel blurted frantically. "Do you think I am Jesus?"

"Please, I have no time to explain. You must trust me. I will help you take the first step."

"Very well, we trust you," Father Joaquim said, giving his young aides a look of confidence.

"Quick, Tonia, grab my hand," Master Watanabe said, reaching out. "Miguel, grab her other hand. And finally, Father, please grab Miguel's hand. Form a line."

Hesitating, Tonia and Miguel stood motionless. But,

looking behind them, they could see hundreds of samurai approaching across the great field.

"Quick, do as he says," Father Joaquim said.

Tonia and Miguel formed the line. As they did so, Master Watanabe closed his eyes, lifted his head toward the sky, and meditated for a moment. Then, assured and composed, he opened his eyes and walked toward the water, leading Tonia, Miguel, and Father Joaquim forward.

"Maintain your inner eye on God," Master Watanabe said as he took his first step on the water.

Slowly, one after the other, each stepped on the surface of the river as though it were a plank and began to walk.

"Is this a dream?" Tonia asked as they progressed across the river's raging current.

"It is as real as you are," Master Watanabe assured them.

"The current is very strong here in the middle," Miguel shouted anxiously as he began to struggle.

"Fasten your inner eye on the power of the God, who transcends any power of the deep. When you do this, the water will become as firm as a rock."

Miguel held tightly to Tonia's hand, holding his eyes firmly closed. At the end of the line, immersed in prayer, Father Joaquim held his eyes serenely closed and walked calmly across the water. Just as they took their final steps off the water and onto the riverbank, the samurai arrived at the other side.

★ ★ ★

"Did I just see that?" the first Samurai who arrived at the river bank asked, rubbing his eyes.

"What do you mean?" the next samurai replied.

"I think they walked across the water," the first samurai ventured.

"Do not be ridiculous. They swam across."

"But how? Look at the current."

As dozens more arrived, many, eager to impress Shigemasa and gain a rich reward, ran into the water and tried to swim to other side. But the current was far too strong, and all were swept to their death in the raging river.

Thirty-eight

June 29, 1626
Plains of Hizen Province

Despite being grateful to have made it across the river and eluded their pursuers, each of the escapees understood their reprieve was temporary. Shigemasa's men knew where they were and where they were likely headed. It was only a matter of time before they found a way across the river and resumed their hunt. Meanwhile, the hunted intended to put as much distance as possible between themselves and the samurai, who'd become even more enraged after seeing many of their comrades swept to their death in the turbulent waters.

As they ran with renewed vigor, Father Joaquim and the two catechists silently pondered the strangest experience of their lives. Had they really walked on water, over a wide and rapidly flowing river? Could one really perform impossible feats simply by believing in God's power?

"I cannot wait any longer," Tonia finally said, breaking the silence as she caught up to Master Watanabe and they continued at a jog. "I must know. How on earth did you perform that miracle?"

"Of what do you speak, Tonia?"

"How did you walk us across the river?"

"By myself, I can do nothing."

Father Joaquim and Miguel quickly ran over to join the conversation.

"What do you mean?" Tonia asked.

"Everything I do is in communion with the Source."

"You mean, God," Father Joaquim suggested.

"Yes, God, the Creator, the Source, or whatever you wish to call Him. I can use all these names interchangeably if you wish."

"Why interchangeably?" Father Joaquim asked.

"Because we should not get too concerned with the *name* we call Him. We need only be concerned that we *do* call Him."

"But why call Him the 'Source'?"

"Is God not the *source* of all Creation?"

"Yes."

"Then we can also call Him 'the Source', or even other names as well."

Scratching the top of his head, Father Joaquim appeared deep in thought.

"What do you mean by '*in communion* with the Source'?" Miguel asked.

"I mean it is through Him that I accomplish these deeds. I cannot do these things on my own."

"Then why cannot I do them?" Miguel asked.

"You can."

The young man shook his head. "No, I cannot."

"You are correct, Miguel. If you tell yourself you cannot, then you cannot. First, you must tell yourself that you can."

"It seems impossible."

"Does your Bible not say, 'Greater works than these shall you also do'?"

"That is John 14:12," Father Joaquim commented.

"Help me with the passage, Father," Master Watanabe asked.

The padre nodded. "In the book of John, Jesus said, 'Verily,

verily, I say unto you, He that believeth in me, the works that I do shall he do also; and greater works than these shall he do; because I go unto my Father.'"

"Precisely," Master Watanabe replied. "Jesus understood this very well, and He was constantly in communion with the Father."

"But I cannot do this," Father Joaquim protested. "I am a normal man."

"Are you suggesting that Jesus was lying or trying to deceive when He said that?"

"Of course not. But I am just an ordinary man."

"So Jesus spoke this passage only to supernatural men?"

The padre hesitated, then shook his head. "No, I did not say that."

"Then it is time to put away your doubts and start to truly believe in your inherent powers."

"It sounds like fantasy," Miguel interjected.

"Did you not just walk on the river, Miguel?"

"Yes, but that was only because of *you*."

"Remember, by myself, I can do nothing. Everything I do is through the Source, but the belief starts in you."

"How does it work, Master Watanabe?" Tonia asked.

"First, believe in the Source and that He resides in you."

"I believe this," Father Joaquim avowed.

"I know you do, Father. And you are very close to manifesting your capabilities. Your faith is very strong, and you are very close to doing these great works on your own. Soon you will not need me to help you cross the river."

"What must I do?" Father Joaquim asked.

"To cross the river, you will need to cross the bridge."

"What bridge?"

"It is not a physical bridge."

"Then what kind of bridge are you talking about?"

"It is a spiritual bridge. It is crossing the bridge from

believing to knowing. You have great faith, Father, and you are a great believer, but now it is time for you to *know* you can do these things yourself."

"I will try," Father Joaquim replied.

"Do not try, Father. *Do.* There is a difference between the two. When you try, the outcome is uncertain. When you know, you simply do, and the outcome is assured because of your belief in the Source."

"What do you mean?"

"Your belief in the Source completes the circle. When your belief in the Source is so strong that you *know* He will complete the act, the outcome is assured and the circle is complete."

"How can I know for sure?"

"Thank Him for it. Thank Him for it even before it is complete."

Father Joaquim's eyes were fixed on Master Watanabe. "Is it not haughty or arrogant to give thanks for that which has not yet been granted?"

"No. By thanking, you affirm your knowing it is done. Thanking is the greatest form of faith."

"So when I pray, I should also thank."

"Yes."

"What about asking?" Miguel inquired. "Is it not important to ask?"

"If you wish, ask once, but only once."

"Why only once?"

"Asking is like trying. If you ask too many times, it means you are uncertain about the outcome. When you are uncertain about the outcome, you cannot know, and the circle cannot complete itself. Remember, the circle can be complete only by knowing. And the best way to know is to thank. Thanking is the strongest form of knowing."

"But what if I thank and do not mean it?" Miguel asked.

"Then it will not work."

"Why?"

"Because you have to mean it. You have to feel it in every part of your being—physically, mentally, and spiritually."

"Why?"

"Because these are the three parts of your being. When you feel thankfulness at all three levels of your being, you have certainty and the circle is complete. When the circle is complete, the act is done."

"But why must you feel it?" Tonia asked as she edged closer to Master Watanabe.

"All of life is energy. This life force energy flows through all of us and causes us to be alive. We are alive because of it."

"Why does this matter?" Miguel asked.

"It matters because this life force flows around us in an energy field. Some may call this our aura. This aura is very responsive to thoughts and feelings. It becomes disrupted when we accept negative thoughts or feelings."

"Why is this important to me?" Miguel asked.

"It is important because if your thoughts and feelings are negative or uncertain, you cannot be truly thankful. And if you are not truly thankful, you do not yet know. Remember, it is the knowing that completes the circle. And thanking in advance, at all three levels of your being, is the best way to know."

"That is a lot to remember," Miguel stated.

"It is enough for now. These are the principles of the universe. Let them guide you."

"It is wise counsel," Tonia suggested. "But now what?"

"Now we must outrun a legion of the daimyo's samurai."

Tonia took a deep breath. "Can we not rest a short while?"

"No. The legion has just found a way to cross the river."

Thirty-nine

June 29, 1626
Shogun's Castle, Edo, Musashi Province

"I should kill you! I gave very clear orders that I was not to be disturbed. Give me a good reason not to kill you," Shogun Iemitsu roared as he arose from his bed and wrapped his naked body in a plush silk robe. Two pre-teen boys looked on nervously from beneath the blankets.

"Forgive me, Lord. I would never disturb you unless it was to bring you news of the greatest importance," the anxious retainer answered.

"Well, what is the news? What is so important that you violate my strict order?" the visibly intoxicated ruler asked.

"One of your spies on Kyushu sent a carrier pigeon. The note said some of your new prisoners have escaped."

"Which prisoners?"

"Your new Christian prisoners on Kyushu escaped from Omura prison."

Furious, the shogun grabbed his elegant sake flask and smashed it against the wall, sending glass flying. "Get out of here," he shouted at the half-clothed boys lying frightened on his bed. "Under whose command did these prisoners escape?"

"Daimyo Matsukura Shigemasa, Lord, but he was at

his castle when it occurred. They escaped under the prison master's watch."

"Fools," the shogun shouted. "They are all fools. There will be consequences for their incompetence!"

"The prison master is already dead. Daimyo Shigemasa executed him."

"Good." The shogun began dressing himself as he continued. "And perhaps Daimyo Shigemasa should also be sanctioned."

"Daimyo Shigemasa has organized a massive manhunt, my Lord. He has deployed a force of three thousand samurai to recapture them."

"Which prisoners escaped?"

"The foreign priest and his aides, Lord."

In a second burst of anger, the shogun kicked over an expensive Chinese table, sending all the exotic sculptures resting on it flying to their destruction. "That foreign priest was the prisoner I wanted most. Him and his foreign helpers."

"I am sorry, Lord."

"I despise those foreign dogs more than anyone. They carry a disease that challenges *my* dominion. They are the ones I most want to mutilate!"

"What shall we do, Lord?"

"Fetch my sword. I must vent my anger."

★ ★ ★

An hour later, still fuming and swinging his long sword wildly, Shogun Iemitsu led dozens of his samurai and retainers down the streets of Edo, as residents and passers-by ran away frantically to avoid him.

"Who can I strike down?" Taking a turn down a street, the angry dictator caught a glimpse of a man sleeping beneath an old filthy blanket, and immediately dashed toward him.

"Stand up, worthless vagrant!" The shogun kicked the man repeatedly in his chest and side.

"What? Who is it?" the intoxicated man asked as he woke up incoherently.

"Get up, I said. Useless man!"

The homeless man tried to rise to pay the shogun respect, but because of his decrepit condition he moved slowly, which greatly vexed the shogun, who had found a good target for his fury. Instantly, he stabbed the homeless man in the stomach. As blood spurted from the man's wound, the shogun quickly withdrew his sword.

Shocked by the blow and losing consciousness, the homeless man fell forward, landing on the shogun, grabbing his garment.

"Do not touch me, filthy creature," the shogun roared in disgust. "Get away from me!" Kicking the man in his chest, he knocked him to his knees. "Die, useless man," the furious tyrant shouted as he raised his sword again. With a swift swing, the shogun severed the man's head, sending it rolling a short distance away.

"Homeless are society's waste," the despot declared as he handed an aide his sword to wipe off the blood. "Let us go find some more."

"What should we do with his body?" a retainer asked.

"Nothing. Let the residents clean it up."

"But, Lord, the residents will complain again. They become embittered when you kill to test your blade."

"These homeless make my city look bad. If the residents want to complain, let them come to *me*. Now, what else can we find to test my blade?" the shogun asked as he walked briskly away down the street.

"Look, there is another, rummaging through that garbage," the shogun shouted as he ran like a child eager to play with a new toy. Quickly, his samurai sprinted after him.

"Halt where you are," the petulant ruler hollered as he approached a decrepit old man. "What are you doing?"

Startled, the old man quit his rummaging and turned to face the shogun. "I am looking for food. Can you please help me?"

"I will *not* help you. You are an embarrassment to my city!"

"Please have mercy, Lord Shogun," the old man pleaded as he dropped to his knees, bowed, and opened the palms of his hands.

"I will help you." The shogun smiled. "By putting you out of your misery." He raised his sword.

"No, please, please—"

The old man's pleading fell on deaf ears. In two ferocious blows, the shogun first opened up the man's chest, then tore through his neck, killing him immediately.

"Excellent," the shogun declared, nodding and grinning. "This blade is very sharp."

Calloused by their leader's frequent displays of brutality, his samurai looked on placidly, showing no emotion at the slaughter.

"Perhaps this is enough for one day, Lord," one of his retainers suggested. "We would not want to dull your blade."

"One more," the shogun said, turning around and scanning the streets. "I am still enraged by this priest's escape. Daimyo Shigemasa had better catch him!"

Forty

Having learned that one of his regiments had spotted and nearly caught the fugitives, Daimyo Shigemasa and the 1500 samurai accompanying him hurried to the region of the Chikugo-gawa River. As the regiment's commander, Fuyuki Yamada, noticed the daimyo's approach, he stepped forward and bowed deeply. "Lord Shigemasa, welcome. We are ready for your instructions, Lord."

"In what direction are they moving?" Shigemasa asked as he dismounted.

"They are still heading west, Lord."

"Good. What happened yesterday? How did they escape you?"

"I am sorry, Lord. They escaped us on the river."

"Give me an explanation. How could three exhausted Christians escape a force of three hundred samurai?"

"My men spotted four, my Lord. They are receiving help."

"What difference does it make? Three or four. Your regiment has three hundred warriors!"

"They eluded us on the river, Lord."

"How is that possible? What can they do that you cannot?"

"We do not know how they crossed the river, Lord."

"Did they take a boat or swim?"

"We did not see a boat, Lord, and it is not possible to swim. Several of our samurai tried, but they were swept downstream."

"Then how did they cross?"

Yamada sighed and shook his head, his shoulders hunched in acquiescence. "We do not know, Lord. Our horsemen chased them across the field, but they were ambushed by an expert bowman."

"Their helper is a ronin?"

"He must be a warrior because our horsemen suffered great wounds. Some are still disoriented as they believe it was the Christian priest who wielded the bow."

"A foreign priest wielding a bow? That is ridiculous."

"It is what some reported, Lord."

"Then they are imbeciles. Now tell me how they crossed the river."

"Our fastest samurai who arrived first thought he saw them walk across, Lord."

"Have your men been drinking, Commander?"

"No, Lord. They do not drink on duty."

"Then why is their judgment impaired?"

"I do not know, Lord. It all happened very fast."

The daimyo huffed. "Now that I have arrived, we *will* get them. With nearly two thousand samurai on their heels, there will be nowhere for them to hide."

"What is our plan, Lord?"

"We will use our great numbers, spread out, and circle in on them. We will scour every piece of land westward, leaving no stone unturned."

"Yes, Lord."

"We will not rest until these run-away dogs are back on their leash. Then we will drag them to the shogun."

★ ★ ★

191

"They are closing on us, are they not?" Miguel asked as he glanced anxiously over his shoulder, scarcely noticing the magnificent, deep-hued sunset over the distant Pacific Ocean.

"Have no fear, Miguel," Father Joaquim answered as the quartet plodded on. "If God be for us, who can be against us?"

"But there are so many, Father. The samurai have such great numbers."

"Worry not, Miguel, but be thankful that God will take care of us."

"Yes, Father."

"Master Watanabe, I would like to thank you again for your help," Father Joaquim said as he turned to their rescuer. "Without you, we would not have made it this far."

"Eventually, you will not need me."

"I wish that were true."

"Do not wish it to be true, Father. *Know* it to be."

"Yes, you are right," Father Joaquim answered, smiling at his new friend. "I remember what you said. Knowing completes the circle."

"Very good," Master Watanabe replied, nodding his head affirmatively. "And please do not underestimate yourself. You have great potential, and you are also very skilled with the bow. If it were not for *you*, we would not have made it this far."

"I thought it wise to disable them. Fortunately, I do not think I killed any of them."

"Yet they seek to destroy you."

"It is of no matter," Father Joaquim answered. "Their actions will determine their own fate. If they live by the sword, they will die by the sword."

"And while they live by the sword, you live by the Cross?"

"Yes. I have given my life to serve our Lord Jesus Christ and to carry the Word of God."

"Perhaps the way of the Cross is not so different from the way of the sword. Both ways involve a life of service."

"Are you suggesting the lives of Christians and samurai are the same?"

"Not the same, but similar."

"How are they similar?"

"Absolute devotion. A samurai serves his warlord unconditionally and will die for him. The same could be said of Christians. A Christian also serves his Lord Jesus Christ unconditionally and would die for his faith."

"Agreed, there are similarities," Father Joaquim acknowledged hesitantly. "But there also many differences."

"Oh?"

"Samurai serve greedy warlords who thirst for more lands and power. Christians serve a loving God, who is all-powerful and has no need for land."

"It is true."

"Samurai also kill on orders from their daimyo. God does not allow Christians to kill."

"But Christians do kill."

"It saddens me to see Christian sin, but sometimes killing is necessary."

"Killing is rarely the highest choice," Master Watanabe commented.

"I would kill only in self-defense or to protect the innocent. In no other way would I seek to kill another."

"I make no judgment, Father."

"I am simply emphasising that Christians are different from samurai despite some similarities."

"I prefer to focus on similarities, not differences," Master Watanabe answered placidly. "Focusing on similarities in people brings us together. Focusing on differences separates us."

"It is a wise philosophy—"

"Look!" Miguel's sudden shout interrupted the

conversation. Pointing to the woods before them, the young catechist declared, "The forest is on fire! We will have to turn back!"

Walking next to Miguel, Tonia had already turned to observe the forested hill from which they'd emerged a few minutes before. "We cannot go back. Look there," she cried.

Daimyo Shigemasa and his massive army of samurai were emerging from the thick forest behind them. They were hemmed in.

"What shall we do?" Miguel yelled, panic-stricken.

"We will escape them in the forest fire," Master Watanabe replied.

"We cannot run into that fire," Miguel yelled. "It will burn us alive!"

"Calm yourself, Miguel," Master Watanabe answered. "The daimyo has many men at his disposal. He must have some samurai ahead of us."

"And for *that* reason I should be calm? We have a fire and samurai in front of us and Shigemasa and his hordes behind us. We have nowhere to go! Why would I be calm?"

"Trust me, Miguel. As before, you will all follow me," Master Watanabe said calmly as he stepped toward the forest, which was now fully engulfed in roaring flames.

"The fire is too thick. We cannot survive it!"

"Do not let your fears determine your decisions, Miguel. We *will* survive."

★ ★ ★

"That fire wall is their end," Shigemasa asserted smugly as he stared down at the group trapped by the flames. "Send the samurai down to collect them."

As ordered, the senior retainer gave the signal for the legions to charge.

"Bring them back alive," the daimyo shouted.

Immediately, hundreds of samurai rushed down the hill to capture their prey.

★ ★ ★

"But it is impossible," Miguel exclaimed as he backed away from the burning trees. "Nothing could survive that fire!"

"We *will* make it, Miguel. We will use the power of the Source to raise our energy above that of the fire. Raise your consciousness to a higher level."

"What do you mean?"

"Raise your consciousness to a place where you and the Source are one."

"I do not understand," Miguel answered. "I cannot do it."

"Please trust me. We *will* pass through unharmed. Again, let us hold hands and I will guide you."

Shigemasa's samurai were charging full-speed down the hill toward the group.

"Miguel, we are running out of time. Why do you see me as different?"

"Because you *are* different! I do not possess your powers."

"You *do* possess them, Miguel. It is only a matter of consciousness. For now, I can only offer you my hand. But it must be *you* who grabs it and takes the first step."

"Please, Miguel, we have little time," Father Joaquim interjected. "Our Lord Jesus walks with you. Have trust and place your faith in Him. He *will* be at your side."

"But Father, fire terrifies me. I was burned as a child. I cannot do it!"

Father Joaquim made the sign of the Cross on his forehead and chest. "Have faith in the Lord, Miguel. He *will* save us."

The legion of charging samurai had reached the bottom of the hill and were quickly closing in.

"Quick, let us hold hands again," Master Watanabe called out.

"Do as he says," Father Joaquim urged as he took the lead by grabbing Master Watanabe's hand. Tonia quickly followed suit, Miguel reluctantly joining at the rear.

Master Watanabe led the group into the flaming forest. Despite the heat, all remained untouched by the flames. But, overwhelmed by his anxiety, Miguel dropped Tonia's hand and ran back, escaping the forest but running straight toward Shigemasa's forces.

"What happened?" Father Joaquim asked as he tried to see through the heavy smoke.

"He dropped my hand," Tonia cried. "Miguel dropped my hand and ran back."

"We have to go back for him," Father Joaquim yelled.

"We will be apprehended, Father," Master Watanabe replied. "Is that what you want?"

"We cannot leave him!"

"What about your plan to rescue the others?"

"God will show us another way. We *must* go back."

"Are you sure?"

"What God has set His hand to do must triumph—even with setbacks."

"Very well. Do not drop your hands. I will lead us out."

As they emerged from the burning forest, they discovered Miguel lying in a pool of blood, captured by the samurai, who were kicking him in the head and chest.

"There are the others," a samurai hollered, as devilish cheers rose from their ranks.

Forty-one

After allowing his samurai to beat and bloody the captives for several minutes, Shigemasa commanded, "Get these dogs up! It is time to put them back on their leash and re-join the others."

As Father Joaquim was yanked to his feet, Shigemasa walked over to face him. "Did you really think you could escape me?"

"There is nothing to escape from," rebuked Father Joaquim. "Our faith is our freedom. You have no power over us."

"Your words are empty," the daimyo replied as he struck Father Joaquim with his fist, sending him to the ground.

Father Joaquim could taste blood.

"You run because you are afraid. But no force in the world could prevent us from capturing you."

"You underestimate the power of God."

"And you underestimate me!" the daimyo roared as he kicked Father Joaquim again. "You *will* regret your escape, Priest. I promise you."

"I am not worried. Our fate rests with God."

"Your God does not exist. Where is your Jesus now? He is nowhere to be found—just like His empty promises."

"Our Lord's promises are more real than your sword. Metal can bend and break, but not the Word of our Father."

Again, Shigemasa kicked Father Joaquim. "Watch your tongue, Christian dog. I am the daimyo of these lands. No force here is stronger than mine!"

"There has always been a force stronger than you, Daimyo. You are just not aware of it," Father Joaquim answered firmly but calmly as he composed himself and stood up.

"You live in the past, Priest. There are no more Christian daimyo any longer."

"That is not the force I speak of."

"Then who? These troublemaking ronin?" Shigemasa turned and sneered at Master Watanabe. "You filthy ronin. Have you been helping these Christians?"

"Yes."

"Then you will be executed with them. The shogun despises ronin who are in league with Christians."

Unperturbed, Master Watanabe returned Daimyo Shigemasa's gaze.

"Too much talking," Katsuie, the daimyo's son, suddenly interjected impatiently and pushed his way to the front. "We need to punish these runaway dogs. Their escape has caused us great embarrassment!"

"They will be punished, Katsuie-san, rest assured," the daimyo replied.

"How?"

"We will kill their women and children. For each escapee, we will kill a woman and a child from their village. They need to understand that any escape will kill their dearest ones."

"Please, no, Daimyo!" Father Joaquim cried out in distress. "They have done nothing wrong. Take my life instead."

"Silence, filthy Priest, or I will cut out your tongue!"

"A clever idea, Father," Katsuie added enthusiastically. "Let *them* feel the consequences."

"The runaway dogs nearly cost me my lands. It is only fitting their beloved should die."

"I want to be the one to deliver the message to Nagasaki," Katsuie announced. "Let me be the one to choose the women and children to perish."

"Granted, son," the daimyo answered, smiling. "Speed your way to Nagasaki, and deliver the message. Choose your victims well."

Forty-two

July 01, 1626
Port of Nagasaki, Deputy Heizo Suetsugu Masanao's Warehouse

"I do not think I can take much more," Chinatsu confessed to her longtime friend Etsuko as they, along with the remainder of the women, were forced outside their warehouse prison.

Etsuko took Chinatsu's hand in hers. "Stay strong. Maintain your faith. We can get through this."

"But I am so hungry, and I cannot sleep." Tears flowed down Chinatsu's cheeks. "And my skull hurts so much."

Etsuko looked sympathetically at Chinatsu's burned, blistered, hairless skull. Over the previous two days Deputy Suetsugu had chosen several women for especially brutal torture in his effort to get them to recant. Chinatsu and two others had been chosen to have their hair set on fire.

"Stay strong," Etsuko answered. "As Saint Francis Xavier once said, 'They cannot do more to us than God permits.'"

"But why does God permit so much torture? Even one of my eyeballs was scorched. I can barely see."

"Remember what Father Joaquim said. Our faith will get us through this storm. Our Lord is with—"

Chinatsu cried out in agony as a pole thumped both women on top of their heads. "I told you whores to shut up! No speaking," a guard shouted as he rapped them one more time.

200

As several women and most of the children cried, Deputy Suetsugu spoke up from the front of the courtyard, next to the water's edge: "Welcome to another day of hell. I hope your night was filled with nightmares and horror."

Etsuko looked around at her fellow villagers, well aware of the atrocities they'd witnessed and experienced in recent days. And the psychological terrors they suffered as they drifted in and out of sleep throughout the nights were every bit as horrible as the physical tortures they endured during the days.

"Yesterday, I set hair on fire," the deputy declared. "Who has had enough? Who would like to recant this useless faith?"

While some whimpered, none of the women or children spoke.

"We can continue. We can keep going until I have mutilated every one of you. I can remove your hands, your feet, your legs, your arms. I can cut off anything I want!"

Again there were more whimpers, but still no one spoke.

"Or I can burn you or puncture you. Whom shall we start with today?" Suetsugu walked back and forth, examining the women and sending fearful chills through each.

"What about her?" a senior guard asked as he pointed at Hatsumi, the prettiest woman among the villagers. "I think we have ignored her thus far because of her good looks."

"You like her?" the deputy asked with a chilling smile.

"Perhaps we can enjoy more private time with her?"

"She is very pretty, is she not?"

"Yes, the prettiest peasant girl I have seen."

"Perhaps she is *too* pretty," the deputy stated, smirking. "Perhaps we should make her less pretty."

"But, Lord Deputy, all the guards enjoy spending time with her. She is the prettiest Christian prisoner we have ever had and her whimpers make her even more stimulating."

"Nothing lasts forever. Bring her to me."

Several guards dragged Hatsumi before the deputy, as tears flowed from her eyes.

The deputy withdrew a wooden cross from a bag and threw it on the ground before her. "This forbidden item was recently found in the streets of Nagasaki." Suetsugu stared coldly into Hatsumi's tearful eyes. "Step on it."

"No, I will not."

"Step on it or we will disfigure you," the deputy shrieked.

Crying, Hatsumi said nothing.

"Grab her and hold her tight," Suetsugu said to his guards, who quickly obeyed. "Give me a knife." The deputy-lieutenant grabbed Hatsumi's throat with his left hand, and with his right, put the blade above her nose and sliced down forcefully. Blood spattered and poured, and several women and children cried openly.

After a brief scream of shock and pain, Hatsumi fainted and fell to the ground face first, where she lay motionless in her blood.

Wiping blood from his knife, Suetsugu next pointed it at the other women and children menacingly. "This is what you get when you embrace this useless faith. Christianity can bring you nothing good. You should recant this worthless faith before it brings you death!" The deputy then callously threw Hatsumi's nose on top of her limp body. "From this moment forward, you will all see an increase in the severity of our tortures. I promise, you will all break very soon."

Leaving the warehouse compound, Deputy Suetsugu commanded, "Put these dogs back in their cage."

As the doors slammed shut and several women rushed to aid Hatsumi, Etsuko stepped forward to address the group: "Do you remember Father Joaquim's sermon last month from the book of Matthew?"

"Which one?" Ayame asked, holding her two small children tightly.

"Father Joaquim said, 'Go to *Jesus* with your troubles.'"

"I am sorry, Etsuko. I am too distraught to remember anything from last month."

"Jesus said: 'Come unto me, all ye that labour and are heavy laden, and I will give you rest.'"

"Yes, I remember now."

"I have prayed for the Lord to give us rest," Etsuko stated softly. "I have prayed for our survival."

Forty-three

July 02, 1626
Chikuzen Province, Island of Kyushu

Shigemasa had pushed his men, and of course his recently re-captured prisoners, mercilessly on their return. Under most circumstances, the fastest route to reach the capital from the southern part of Kyushu took eleven days. But Shigemasa insisted on getting there faster, no doubt to impress the shogun and save his reputation. In their rapid push north, the prisoners and their captors had passed through Hizen province and were currently traversing Chikuzen, a beautiful territory in the north of Kyushu.

Following their recapture, Father Joaquim had heard Shigemasa send instructions to Omura Prison to collect the remainder of the male prisoners from the village and meet them in the north as quickly as possible. The designated meeting place was Kokura, one of the northernmost points on the island. From Kokura they would sail across the Sea of Japan to the country's mainland, Honshu.

★ ★ ★

As the recaptured escapees arrived in Kokura, Father Joaquim saw that all the men in his village were still alive, and for that he was grateful. The village men were clearly exhausted and in poor health, but they were pleased to see that Father Joaquim and the catechists had also survived.

"It warms my heart to see you all alive, Noburu-san. How are you, my friend?"

"Omura Prison is a living hell, but we are alive."

"Thank God for this."

"How did you escape, Father?"

"Our new friend, Master Watanabe, came to our aide. Twice he has shown us miracles."

Humbly, Master Watanabe bowed to Noburu and smiled, stating "You are very kind, Father, but all miracles are the work of our *Creator*. From the Bible, think on Isaiah 43.2."

Instinctively, Father Joaquim cited the passage in his mind: *When thou passest through the waters, I will be with thee; and through the rivers, they shall not overflow thee: when thou walkest through the fire, thou shalt not be burned; neither shall the flame kindle upon thee.*

As Father Joaquim reflected on its relevance, Miguel suddenly joined the conversation. Since they had been recaptured, they had spoken only a few words because of the horrible beatings inflicted on them for talking.

"I am sorry, Father—for everything."

"I know you are, Miguel, but you do not have to be."

"We could have escaped, but I ruined everything."

"Our village will survive. God has a plan for us. He will find another way."

"How? We have all been caught."

"I do not know, Miguel. God works in mysterious ways, but I know He will answer."

"Soon, we will be in the shogun's hands, and then it will be over for us."

"Remember, Miguel, keep your faith. These are tumultuous times, and your faith could very well save your life."

"I will try, Father."

"Do not try, Miguel. Faith is or it is not. You either have it or you do not. Set your resolve and be unfailing about it."

★ ★ ★

"Are the vessels ready?" Shigemasa asked, impatience evident in his question.

"We have one large ship, Lord," a retainer answered. "We could not locate any more."

"We are traveling to the capital to see the shogun, so fill the vessel with our most senior and experienced samurai and let us depart as soon as possible."

"Yes, Lord."

"How are our supplies? Do we have enough for the journey?"

"Yes, Lord. We raided several villages and took their food and water. Shall we load the Christian dogs onto the vessel, Lord?"

For a moment, Shigemasa contemplated the design and construction of a standard junk vessel of the time. Most junks in the region were built of soft wood with multiple internal compartments and bulkheads accessed by separate hatches and ladders. The purpose of these was to strengthen the ship and slow any flooding that might occur if the vessel suffered a hole or similar damage, the idea being that each compartment would be fully watertight. This meant partitioning the hull to add strength, which in turn also helped secure the vessel against foundering. This ingenious design had been developed by the Chinese, and Shigemasa had great respect for it.

"Yes, put them below deck."

"At the bottom of the vessel, Lord?"

"Yes, I do not want any of them trying to escape by jumping overboard." Nodding as he anticipated his reward, the daimyo added, "We need to keep these dogs alive. They are the shogun's property to slaughter now."

Forty-four

July 02, 1626
North Coast of Island of Kyushu

The lid opened again and the quartet of especially despised prisoners, in a separate compartment from the others, braced themselves for another repulsive shower. The samurai laughed as he relieved himself. Then, before closing the lid, he spat, the expectorate landing on Father Joaquim's shoulder.

The prisoners had no way of knowing the time of day—or night. They were crammed in one of the junk's utterly dark bulkheads with nothing but the hull itself between them and the open sea. Directly above them was the middle deck, where the samurai resided, so it was convenient—and despicably entertaining—for them to lift the lid to the bulkhead to deposit their wastes.

Despite the darkness, one thing the prisoners could sense was that they were in rough waters, and despite its solid build, the junk was pitching forcefully.

In the past, Father Joaquim had traveled over this portion of the waters before, from the north of Kyushu Island toward the capital city, albeit under more pleasant circumstances. The sea stretched 300 miles from northern Kyushu to Osaka, and was composed of five distinct basins linked together by channels. The beautiful sea had an irregular coastline dotted with hundreds of small islands. During the day, the waters of the Seto-Naikai were a beautiful emerald green color. To the west, the Inland Sea was connected to the Sea of Japan. To the east, three straits connected the Inland Sea to the Pacific Ocean.

In the opinion of many, the Inland Sea was one of the most beautiful parts of Japan, affording breathtaking views of coastal scenery, small fishing villages, and hundreds of small volcanic and granite islands.

But Father Joaquim suspected it was not the scenery that drew Shigemasa to travel via the Inland Sea to their off-load point at Osaka. It was the speed. He knew the daimyo was determined to travel the 300-mile distance as fast as possible. And while it was clear Shigemasa wished to keep the Christians alive until they arrived in Edo, he had no desire to treat them well.

"This is despicable," Tonia wailed as another samurai emptied his bladder on the quartet. "How can human beings treat each other like this?"

"I have no space to move. This is hell!" Miguel lamented. "Why did I not trust you, Master Watanabe? Why did I not cross through the fire?"

"I do not know, Miguel," Master Watanabe answered impartially. "People make choices."

"But why did I make such a bad choice?"

"Seldom are choices based on fear the highest choice."

"Then what is the highest choice?" Miguel asked.

"*Love*, Miguel. *Love*, and then you must trust."

"Why do you say this?"

"Fear contracts. Love expands. Fear resists and pulls backward. Love trusts and moves forward. The Source is love. When you love and trust, you move toward the Source. When you fear and resist, you move away from the Source."

"I believe Master Watanabe is right," Father Joaquim added. "No matter how challenging a situation, the Lord will be there for you, but you must trust. When you have trust, you move closer to the Lord, and He moves closer to you."

"Words are easy," Miguel answered, frustrated. "You disregard emotions in your advice. It is easy to talk about trust out of harm's way. It is another thing to live it and walk into an open fire."

"Precisely, Miguel," Father Joaquim replied. "It is when the fire is strongest that you need to trust the Lord the most. The Lord always walks alongside you, no matter what threatens you. You need only take the first step and trust that He walks with you and will save you."

"I do not need to be saved. Those damned samurai need to be killed!"

"Revenge has no place in Christianity," Father Joaquim answered gently as he helped Miguel clean himself. "Christ taught us to love one another unconditionally by showing love to our oppressors, even in return for the harm they have shown us."

"I do not know what to do, Father. I am just so angry."

"May I read a passage from my Bible, Miguel?"

Miguel was pleased that the padre had been able to retain his hidden Bible throughout these many trials. "Yes, Father," he said, curious to hear what the father would read.

Father Joaquim gently pulled out his small Bible from the secret compartment in his garment.

"First John 4:7 says, 'Beloved, let us love one another: for love is of God; and every one that loveth is born of God, and knoweth God.' Love our enemies, Miguel, for that is the only way to overcome them."

★ ★ ★

Katsuie Shigemasa was fast approaching the edge of Nagasaki. Pushing his horse to its physical limits through the dark, he was desperate to deliver his father's instructions to Deputy-Lieutenant Suetsugu as soon as possible. With cloudy skies and no moonlight, it was extremely dark outside and young Katsuie was unable to locate the correct path up the mountain. Impetuous and impatient, he decided not to wait until daylight, but instead to make his own path. He knew Nagasaki lay just on the opposite side.

"Why could I not find the damned path?" Katsuie swore as he pushed his horse up another steep portion of the mountain. "These damned Christians! We should just kill them all! Why stop at a few women and children? Why not kill all of them?" Katsuie's horse began to resist his forward commands, making the young man irritable and causing him additional frustration.

This journey is taking far too long, he reflected. *I should already be on my way to Edo by now. At least there I have money, rank, and respect. I should stop wasting my time with these Christians and just instruct the Governor to kill all the women and children …*

Again, Katsuie's horse resisted proceeding up a steep rock. "Get up there, you stupid beast!" Katsuie yelled. "Get up there!"

The horse attempted to turn around and reverse its direction.

With all his strength, Katsuie kicked the horse repeatedly in its side, forcing it up over the steep rock. As the bruised and bloodied horse and its rider reached the precipitous top, the steed lost its balance, and, along with Katsuie, fell onto the sharp rocks below. The horse died instantly. Katsuie, meanwhile, landed on top of the animal, bounced off, then smashed his head against more rocks. Unconscious, he lay hidden on the dark side of the mountain.

Forty-five

July 07, 1626
Port of Osaka, Osaka Prefecture

"Get up, dogs! Get out of here! Come on, get up and move, worthless beasts." As Father Joaquim forced his stiff muscles to move and reached over to give Master Watanabe a helping hand, he imagined the difficulty older villagers must be experiencing as they, too, sought to force their aching bodies to move.

"Do not make us wait! Get up and move, dogs!"

As the prisoners made their way to the top deck and into the morning sunlight for the first time in five days, Father Joaquim squinted as he gazed around, trying to verify that all the men of the village were still present and accounted for.

"We have landed at Osaka," a samurai declared brusquely. "Disembark from the vessel immediately."

"March them to the main town square and wait for me there," the daimyo commanded. "From the town square, we will prepare these dogs for their death march. Then we will depart."

Dozens of samurai began to tie up the Christians with ropes and shackles as Shigemasa strode triumphantly into the heart of the city, followed by his highest-ranking retainers. Then the march through the streets of Osaka toward the main town square began, punctuated by whippings and beatings.

Because Christianity had been outlawed more than a decade earlier, the residents of Osaka were shocked by the sight. Father Joaquim thought he saw empathy on the face of many. Most of the city's children had never seen a foreigner, and their surprise and curiosity were apparent. But some of the residents, either out of fear for their own safety or feigned disguise, threw waste at the Christians as they marched past.

When the Christians arrived in the main town square, they were quickly herded into a small circle and instructed to await the arrival of the daimyo, who was visiting Osaka's city hall.

Soon, carrying buckets of red paint, Shigemasa and his senior retainers arrived in the town square, accompanied by high-ranking Osaka officials.

"Stand these Christians up," Shigemasa bellowed as he sought a public audience.

As the Christians were yanked to their feet, Osaka's governor entered the square, surrounded by many high-ranking Bakufu officials.

"These captured Christians are criminals of the empire," Shigemasa shouted to the growing crowd. "I will escort them to Edo, but first they will be painted red so all Osaka and all Japan will see them as criminals of the empire."

Dozens of samurai grabbed large paint brushes and began to slop red paint onto the Christians, sometimes splashing it into their eyes, noses, ears, and mouths.

"I paint them red so all of Japan can see that death and torture await them in the capital," the daimyo roared.

"Let this be a warning to any Christians among you," Osaka's governor added as he stepped forward. "Recant your wretched faith before it is too late! Daimyo Matsukura Shigemasa will march these Christian dogs to Edo, where the shogun will torture and kill them. Who amongst you would like to join them?" The governor gazed intimidatingly at the gathered residents. "Who among you would like to have the belongings of the Christians in your midst? If you alert us of Christians, you may have their homes and all their belongings. The shogun will also pay in silver coins to those who inform us of hidden Christians. Who would like to become rich?"

Despite the mounting fear, no one spoke. Frustrated, the governor approached a poor resident. "You. Would you like to become wealthy?"

"Yes, Governor, I would," the old man replied. "But I do not know of any Christians in Osaka. It has been many years since I have heard of any."

"What about you?" the governor asked as he pointed to a woman standing nearby.

"No, Governor. All of the Christians are gone. If there are any left, they live in secret."

Father Joaquim watched as the governor walked back to face the daimyo.

"Let the death march to Edo commence," Shigemasa yelled as he signaled to his samurai. "Let this be the last day Osaka sees these dogs alive!"

Quickly, the daimyo's samurai grabbed the Christians by their ropes and dragged them down the street, causing some to fall down in the process.

"Get up," Shigemasa shouted. "You cannot stall your fate. You will all experience the vilest executions known to man, and nothing can stop it."

"What will they do to us in Edo, Father?" Miguel asked, visibly distressed.

"I do not know, Miguel. But worry not; the Lord walks with us."

"But why are we going through this?" Tonia asked as tears ran down her red-painted cheeks. "How can God allow this to happen?"

"Do not despair, Tonia. The Lord cautioned us that His

followers would face much suffering, and that our faith would be tested."

"But why must it be tested?"

"How else can you know if your faith is real?"

"What do you mean?"

"You cannot have faith only on sunny days, Tonia. You must also have faith during the storms. That is how you know if your faith is real."

"I just do not know if I can take it anymore." Tonia sighed as she struggled to get paint out of her eyes. "I feel broken. I can barely see."

"If your faith persists through the good *and* bad, God will *always* be there for you. That is His unbroken promise, and He always delivers."

"Yes, Father."

"Remember, nobody can take your faith away. Not the governors, not the daimyo, not even the shogun. Our faith is the only thing we have left, yet it is the most powerful thing we have ever had. In your most trying moments, I want you always to remember what Jesus said."

"What, Father?"

"He said, 'I am the light of the world: he that followeth me shall not walk in darkness, but shall have the light of life.'"

Forty-six

Leading the procession over the Tokaido, Shigemasa enjoyed showcasing his importance, as well as his procession of samurai and prisoners, past the myriad other travelers. From well-connected government officials to the poorest peasants, they lined the busy gateway to the grand capital city.

The assemblage soon arrived at the main *seki* on the city's outskirt. Seki checkpoints, strategically set up at key locations, were effectively barriers on the city's periphery, where guards stopped all travelers for interrogation to search for troublemakers and check for weapons. By law, the samurai or other high-placed individuals with special privileges were the only class allowed to carry weapons into the capital. As far as the shogun was concerned, however, the seki checkpoints existed primarily to ensure that no armed ronin entered the city.

In his own domain, Daimyo Shigemasa had a great deal of autonomy to govern his lands as he wished. However, once he entered the Kanto region—the area surrounding the capital of Edo—his activities were under the shogun's firm control.

As the procession approached the main seki, Shigemasa

215

moved to the front along with his flag-bearer. Shigemasa was proud of his family crest, his *mon*, so it was imperative that his flag-bearer remain by his side.

Noticing the flag and the arriving party, several guards left their post to greet them. "Daimyo Shigemasa, welcome to Edo," the senior guard said. "We have been expecting you for some time."

"We encountered some delays in our journey, but thank you. I have come to present these Christian criminals as a gift to the shogun. I hope he enjoys killing them."

The senior guard thoroughly inspected all the Christian prisoners, still painted red and standing in a long line. Following their arduous journey from Osaka, all looked haggard. Not surprisingly, the senior guard paid particular attention to Father Joaquim and his foreign catechists, who were indeed a rare sight. "One of our riders will speed word to the shogun about their arrival."

"And where shall we take these dogs?"

"Two guards will escort your procession to our prison, where we will incarcerate them."

"When does the shogun wish to view them?"

"Soon," the guard answered. "Perhaps you may wish to visit the pleasure quarters and enjoy some women while you wait, Daimyo?"

"I will indeed," Shigemasa replied with a smile.

The two promised seki guards walked the group through the checkpoint and toward the Tama River, which they would need to cross to reach the city. Not a particularly large river, the Tama flowed from the mountains in the west down into Edo Bay. However, as the river was too deep to cross on foot or horseback, it was necessary to take small ferries.

★ ★ ★

Already awaiting the procession's arrival were a half-dozen ferries, which would shuttle the group into the capital. On the ferries, finally, the Christian prisoners seized a moment to rest.

Father Joaquim marveled at the city's grandeur. As he observed his fellow prisoners, it was apparent they felt the same conflicted feelings: facing imminent death, they nonetheless could not help admiring the magnificent city. Father Joaquim and most of the prisoners knew that while Kyoto, home to Japan's imperial family, remained the nation's formal capital, Edo was the center of political and military power, and the seat of all decision making.

Stepping off the ferries and onto shore, the prisoners and their guards made their way past the jeers and insults of many citizens, including Buddhist monks in Ikegami Honmonji on Edo's southern limit. Slowly, the shogun's checkpoint guards led Shigemasa's procession toward the center of the city. All the while, the daimyo's samurai continued to insult and beat the prisoners.

Father Joaquim was troubled to see many houses of prostitution lining portions of the main road they traversed. Over time, many of the official lodgings along the road had turned into brothels, catering to government officials and other merchants during their long journeys.

As the group reached the *shitamachi* area of the city, Father Joaquim could see in the expressions of many of his fellow villagers awe at the sheer number of buildings and people.

Owing to the shogun's paranoia, myriad massive ramparts, moats, and other towering fortress walls surrounded the castle grounds. As they marched forward, Father Joaquim understood that the area surrounding the castle, known as the Yamanote, consisted largely of sizable mansions of the feudal daimyo, whose families were required to live in Edo as part of the *sankin kotai* system.

By explicit requirement of the shogun, the sankin kotai system mandated that all Japan's feudal daimyo make journeys to Edo annually. The purpose was to keep watch over the daimyo and prevent any of them plotting against the shogun. In addition, the sankin kotai system also required the daimyo's families to live in Edo year-round. Should any daimyo consider raising arms against the shogun, their families could be seized and taken as hostages.

Finally, after a lengthy and mortifying parade through the city, Father Joaquim and the group arrived in the eta district.

"Straight ahead," one of the guards yelled as he commanded the group to make their way down a filthy narrow street. "Do you see that dreadful building at the end?"

Exhausted, none of the Christians responded as they beheld the abominable, decrepit structure before them.

"That will be your last home before your execution."

Forty-seven

July 13, 1626
Shogun's Northeastern Prison, Edo

"I see the misery in your eyes," Father Joaquim exclaimed as he stood and looked around the prison chamber. "You think this is the end, do you not—all of you?"

It had been only an hour or so since Father Joaquim and the villagers had been shoved into the shogun's vile prison in the eta district. The prison chamber was filled with emaciated bodies, including half a dozen other Japanese Christians. Edo prison smelled rancid, even worse than the prison in Omura. Dead and near-dead bodies were strewn about, while healthier prisoners fought each other, often to the death, for food and more space.

But a few prisoners exhibited kindness amid the atrocities. One such, Akihiko, was a young man who lay nearly motionless on the floor. The shogun had recently amputated his ears and his feet. Yet, despite his extreme pain and loss, he often offered up his limited water and food to anyone who needed either, including Tonia, Miguel, and Master Watanabe, who sat beside him, giving him aid.

Only a few weak mumbles and groans answered Father Joaquim's trenchant question.

"Well, let me tell you," Father Joaquim continued. "You are wrong!"

Finally an old farmer from the village spoke up: "Why? Why are we wrong? What hope do we have now?"

"Let me remind you of a truth," Father Joaquim answered. "Man's frailty is God's opportunity."

"Your words are empty," an angry young man shouted. "Only death awaits us now. Every person in this prison will die!"

"Who are you?" Father Joaquim asked as he squinted, trying to see through the dark toward the back of the prison. "Why are you here?"

"My name is Susumu," answered the agitated young man. "I am a thief."

"Why do you steal?"

"To survive."

"Confess your sins, Susumu-san. Give your life to Jesus, and you will be saved."

"Do not waste your breath on me, foreign priest. I do not believe in your God."

"Do you feel death is on our doorstep and things cannot get worse?"

"Yes. Only death awaits me now."

"Then believe. Believe if only for one day that the Lord will save you."

"Are you insane, Priest? Do you have any idea where you are? You need to wake up. We are all on death row in the shogun's prison, and we *will* die!"

"Then believe," Father Joaquim repeated, hoping to rally his villagers. "Believe the Lord will help us, and see what happens."

"Why?"

"Because no harm can come of it; only good. And you risk nothing by believing."

"Why should I bother?"

"Because here in your darkest hour, you may find God—

the Light of the world. If your life is filled with darkness and you seek the light, seek God and He will reveal Himself."

Susumu grumbled an unintelligible response.

"Ask Him for help, Susumu-san, and He will answer you. Let me lead all of you in prayer." Father Joaquim withdrew his Bible from the secret compartment sewn into his garment, and began to read from the book of Psalms.

"*'I cried unto the Lord with my voice; with my voice unto the Lord did I make my supplication.*

I poured out my complaint before him; I shewed before him my trouble.

When my spirit was overwhelmed within me, then thou knewest my path. In the way wherein I walked have they privily laid a snare for me.

I looked on my right hand, and beheld, but there was no man that would know me: refuge failed me; no man cared for my soul.

I cried unto thee, O Lord: I said, Thou art my refuge and my portion in the land of the living.

Attend unto my cry; for I am brought very low: deliver me from my persecutors; for they are stronger than I.

Bring my soul out of prison, that I may praise thy name: the righteous shall compass me about; for thou shalt deal bountifully with me.'"

Father Joaquim closed his little Bible and placed it back in his secret compartment. "Now close your eyes, everyone. Seek the Lord first, and your troubles will go away."

With those last words, the prison sat in silence.

★ ★ ★

Inside the small meeting room, Shogun Iemitsu knelt atop a plush golden pillow as he awaited the daimyo. Owing to the formal nature of the meeting, the shogun was accompanied by his Go-Roju cabinet members, who sat in a short line perpendicular to him.

As Daimyo Shigemasa entered, the room became silent. Bowing deeply to the shogun, Shigemasa dropped to his knees and crawled to the center of the room, facing the shogun.

"We are pleased that you managed to arrive," the shogun declared, with no great conviction. "We have been expecting you for quite some time."

"Thank you, Lord. I know I should have arrived earlier."

"And why are you late, Daimyo?"

"I am sorry, Lord. We had a problem. The filthy priest escaped. It took us a short while to recapture him."

"You captured a priest on your fief and then you lost him days later?"

"I am sorry, Lord. He escaped from Omura Prison while I was collecting more gifts for you."

"That is very sloppy and negligent. Is this how you normally conduct your affairs?"

"No, Lord, no. We are very attentive to our duties in Arima. It will never happen again. I personally executed the negligent prison master."

"I am divided on this issue," the shogun declared, looking sternly at the daimyo.

"What do you mean, Lord Shogun?"

"On the one hand, I am very pleased that you have captured a hidden Christian village. I will enjoy executing them. On the other hand, Daimyo, I am very displeased that such a village still existed on your lands."

"Yes, Lord. I was very surprised myself."

"This makes me wonder whether you are fit to govern your lands, Daimyo."

"I am very sorry, Lord. It will never happen again."

"I will tell you what worries me, Daimyo."

"What, Lord?"

"If there is one hidden Christian village on your lands, there may be more."

"No, Lord. We do all we can to catch Christian dogs on my lands. I even starve families to death."

"It is not enough. Their cult still remains. You will not stay in Edo. You will return home to unearth more Christians!"

"But Lord, is it not customary for daimyo to spend time in Edo before returning home?"

"You have humiliated yourself, Daimyo Shigemasa. A rebuke is needed."

"I am sorry, Lord."

"When you return to your lands, I want you to consider one thing, Daimyo—whether you are fit to remain as daimyo of your domain. We are evaluating you more carefully now."

"Yes, Lord."

"Remember, Daimyo. I am not averse to giving your lands to someone else."

"That will not be necessary, Lord Shogun. I will annihilate Chrstianity from my lands."

"A vessel is awaiting you now, Daimyo. Return home immediately, and do not fail me again!"

Forty-eight

As Father Joaquim blinked open his eyes and sought to focus them, along with his sleep-addled brain, he saw Master Watanabe looking at him, clearly curious.

"You appear confused, Father, or perhaps unsure. What is it? Did you have a strange dream?"

"Indeed I did, my friend. And it was a powerful one," the Jesuit answered, still shaking his head and rubbing his eyes.

"What was it about, Father?"

Hesitating for a moment and scratching his head, he finally answered. "I dreamed that I am supposed to challenge the shogun."

"What kind of challenge?"

"I do not know." Father Joaquim shrugged his shoulders and shook his head again. "Perhaps it was just nonsense or fantasy."

"Do not disregard it, Father. Dreams are a way the Source speaks to us."

"You mean a way that *God* speaks to us."

"Yes, whatever you wish to call Him. I can call Him God if doing so helps our conversation."

"Thank you for that concession," Father Joaquim answered

224

as he looked around the cell at the other prisoners, most still asleep. "But what am I supposed to challenge the shogun about?"

"I do not know, Father. It is your dream. But God has spoken to you through it."

"Perhaps God wants me to challenge the shogun's closest Buddhist monks in order to refute their faith."

"I am not sure, Father, but the Creator does not favor one faith over another."

"That is a point about which we will have to disagree, my friend. Jesus told His followers that He was the only way to the Father. If I believed that all faiths are the same, I would have had no reason to bring my faith in Christ here."

"Hmm …" Master Watanabe leaned on his elbow, apparently pondering Father Joaquim's words. "One day we will have to discuss that thought in more detail. But for now, let us examine your dream and what you should do about it."

"What do you think I should do?"

"God has just given you a glimpse of a way out, but He wants you to be a part of His plan. You must now trust your own intuition on the matter."

"I wish He would be more clear."

"Trust your intuition as you would trust God. Your intuition—that still, small voice—is another way the Source speaks to you."

"But this is critically important, Master Watanabe. All our lives are at stake. An entire village is depending on me."

"It matters not. The principles are the same."

"What makes you so sure?"

"Did you not ask God for help, Father?"

"Yes."

"Well, I am helping you. And *you* are part of His plan."

"But I prayed that *God* would help us."

"I know you did, but you are a small part of God. In this situation, you will need to work in partnership with Him."

"Why?"

"To experience being part of Him."

Father Joaquim took a moment to consider. "And what about your role in this, my friend? I have seen your abilities, and they are incredible. Why can you not use your powers to free us?"

"I am here only as a guide, nothing more."

"A guide to what?"

"Consciousness, Father. I am here to help you raise your consciousness and remind you of who you really are."

"And who is that?"

"A small, but powerful part of Almighty God."

"Of what do you speak?"

"In the book of Genesis, does your Bible not say that God created man in his own image?"

"Yes, of course."

"Or elsewhere, does it not say, 'The Lord thy God in the midst of thee is mighty; He will save'?"

"Yes, that is Zephaniah 3:17."

"Then it is time for you to *know* that God resides in you, and that because of this, you have His powers as well."

The rhythmic thud of footfalls interrupted the men's conversation. Next, the sound of a key turning a lock was quickly followed by the opening of the prison door.

"The shogun wants to interrogate the priest, his foreign aides, and the ronin who helped them escape," a prison guard shouted. "Come out here immediately."

Father Joaquim emerged through the prison door, followed by Master Watanabe, Tonia, and Miguel.

"Prepare for the end," the prison guard declared. "You are about to meet the shogun."

Forty-nine

July 14, 1626
Shogun's Castle, Edo

"Strip the foreign dogs and scrub them down—and the ronin, too. Do not stop until the smell is gone," a senior retainer ordered several samurai.

"Including the woman?"

"She stinks too."

"I am sorry, Tonia," Father Joaquim called out as dozens of samurai descended on the father, the two catechists, and the ronin and began ripping their clothes from them. As soon as the three men were undressed they were made to stand a few feet apart from one another. The samurai who stripped Tonia took a bit longer, fondling her and laughing as they slowly moved her toward the three male prisoners.

As the samurai in front moved aside and the others shoved Tonia from behind, Father Joaquim and Master Watanabe quickly turned around to avoid seeing their female companion. Quickly, then, cold water was poured over each of the naked prisoners, who shook uncontrollably—all except Master Watanabe, who seemed unaffected by the icy water. Then, before the water could dry, servants used brooms to scrub the prisoners, from head to toe, before they were again splashed with water to rinse their bodies.

Each was then tossed a towel and their clothes. "Dry off quickly and prepare for your deaths. You are to meet the shogun."

After they were dressed, Father Joaquim and his companions were led to a guarded side-room next to the grand chamber—to wait. Silent, they sat on the floor as a half-dozen samurai stared at them, contempt visible in their eyes.

The order came soon enough. "Rise up, dogs. It is time."

Miguel and Tonia looked particularly nervous as they arose. Miguel's eyes shifted frantically over the room. But he had little time before they were shoved down a long hallway towards the main entrance of the grand chamber. As they approached, Father Joaquim heard the commotion of a large group on the other side of the door. At last, they were pushed inside.

"Bow, you dogs. Bow before my presence!" the shogun shouted as they entered the room. Before they could obey, the butt ends of samurai swords began to pound them from behind, forcing them to kneel.

Daring to peek upward, Father Joaquim gazed awestruck at the grandeur of the chamber, which was filled with high-ranking officials, samurai, retainers, and other prominent members of the shogun's regime.

"Place these dogs in the center of the room!" The shogun's command was quickly obeyed. "So you are the one has who caused all this trouble," the ruler observed, looking at Father Joaquim.

"I do not know of what you speak," Father Joaquim replied.

"The priest who escaped," the shogun sneered. "Your escape caused our Kyushu authorities great embarrassment."

Neither Father Joaquim nor the other prisoners responded.

"We will not make this long," the shogun avowed. "You are all criminals of the empire and will be tortured and executed for your crimes."

"Of what crimes do you speak?" Father Joaquim asked.

"Do not mock me, Priest. You Christians and your stupid beliefs were banished more than a decade ago. You have defied our laws by hiding here and spreading your filth. You can reduce your torture, however." The shogun stopped to glance at his Go-Roju cabinet members before resuming. "*If* you tell us the locations of other Christians and priests in hiding."

Again, no one in the group responded.

"You can also reduce your torture by telling us which factions of ronin helped you escape Omura prison."

"I think we have a difference of opinion about who is committing crimes in Japan," Father Joaquim interjected.

"Of what do you speak?" the shogun demanded.

"It is *you* who have committed a crime."

"*I* have committed a crime? Against whom?"

"Against God." Father Joaquim dared to look directly into the shogun's eyes as he answered. "*You* have deprived the people of Japan of His Word and the ministry of His servants."

"Enough, Christian dog, or I will cut off your tail and feed it to you!"

"You have denied the people freedom of choice and the freedom to know God. And you have done so for greater power, control, and self-glorification."

"How dare you speak out against me? I am the shogun of all Japan!" Iemitsu instructed his samurai to give Father Joaquim a thrashing. They quickly complied.

"Of all the Christians in my possession," the shogun declared when the samurai were done beating the priest, "*you* shall suffer the most. At the end of your torture, you will *beg* us to kill you."

"I have no fear," Father Joaquim replied as he wiped blood from his nose. "Actually, you should be more worried than I—"

"I should be worried?" the shogun roared, interrupting Father Joaquim. "Of what should I be worried?"

"Psalm 1:6 says, 'For the Lord knoweth the way of the righteous: but the way of the ungodly shall perish.' Your ungodly ways will perish."

"Do not preach your filth here, Christian Priest! This is *my* castle!"

"I am not afraid," Father Joaquim stated as he stood, defiant.

"Then why did you run away like a coward on Kyushu? Have you no backbone? Do you foreigners have no courage or honor?"

"You misunderstood our intentions. We will never leave Japan. By the hand of God, our mission *will* survive here."

"How dare you speak to me in such a tone? Give this priest another beating!"

With the butt ends of their weapons, samurai again pounded on Father Joaquim's head and chest. Lying on the floor, nearly unconscious from the beatings, Father Joaquim looked up at the ceiling and noticed the mon crest of the shogun's Tokugawa family, which hung beautifully from the rafters—inspiring a thought. "Your samurai have given me a great thrashing," Father Joaquim stated as he calmly wiped the blood from his face.

"I am proud of them."

"They can deliver a beating, but are they brave?"

"Tokugawa samurai are the bravest in all Japan. It is through battle that we gained the shogunate."

"Very good," Father Joaquim replied. "Then perhaps you will accept a challenge."

"What kind of challenge?"

Father Joaquim stood. "A martial challenge. A fighting contest."

At first only the shogun laughed, but soon all his cabinet members, dignitaries, and samurai were cackling along with him.

Father Joaquim interrupted the laughter: "Are you not interested in discovering the locations of more hidden Christians?"

"What?!"

"I hold the master list of all Christians in Japan, including all foreign priests and clergy."

With the chamber suddenly silent, the shogun asked, "What did you say?"

"I said I offer you the location of all hidden Christians."

"In exchange for what?"

"In exchange for our freedom. The four of us and all prisoners in Edo prison who declare themselves Christian."

"Why should I agree to such a contest? Now that I know you have this list, I can simply torture it out of you."

"I suspect you know by now that torture will not make me speak. And if I die in torture, the master list and your opportunity will die with me."

"Perhaps we will put your bravado to the test and re-evaluate once we start to dismember you."

"Do you have no confidence in your samurai?" Father Joaquim goaded.

"What did you ask, Priest?"

"Do you not have enough confidence that your samurai can defeat mere Christians?" Uncomfortable murmurs could be heard on the periphery of the grand chamber. Many samurai looked unsettled. "Are the samurai of the Tokugawa clan so weak that you must play games of hide and seek? Are they afraid?"

Raising his hand to quell the agitated samurai's grumbles, the shogun spoke. "Silence!"

Turning to face Father Joaquim, he declared, "You *will* die, Priest. No one challenges the Tokugawa clan and lives. But your master list of hidden Christians interests me."

Turning his back on Father Joaquim, the shogun consulted with members of his Go-Roju cabinet as the priest and his three companions waited.

★ ★ ★

"Shall we accept the challenge?" the shogun asked discreetly.

"I think we must, Lord," one of the Go-Roju members replied. "The priest challenged you in front of your men. I think you *must* accept the challenge for the honor of your samurai and for the Tokugawa name."

"I agree," another added. "The men will feel dishonored and shamed if we do not accept."

"But it is ludicrous," the shogun replied. "The foreign priest and his aides stand no chance."

"Why does he wish to fight?" another member asked. "He would challenge us only if he thinks he can win."

"Perhaps he believes the ronin will do the fighting for him. Perhaps the ronin is very skilled."

"Then we will not let the ronin fight. We control the rules of the contest. So shall we accept?" the shogun repeated.

"What could be greater than the master list, Lord?"

"And we could take it from him before he takes his last breath in battle," the shogun added.

One after the other, each Go-Roju cabinet member nodded in agreement.

The shogun turned to Father Joaquim: "It will be a pleasure to watch my samurai dismember your body—moments before you surrender the master list. Your challenge is accepted."

Throughout the chamber samurai roared their approval.

★ ★ ★

"If we win, how do I know you will keep your word? How do I know we will gain our freedom?" Father Joaquim asked, again looking directly into the shogun's eyes.

The shogun looked as if he would burst from anger. "Do not insult me, filthy priest. A samurai's word is stronger than metal."

"Then our contest is agreed," Father Joaquim answered.

"Consider this your death, Priest."

Father Joaquim nodded and bowed. "Daimyo Shigemasa took a valuable sword from us on Kyushu. We request the return of this sword for our contest."

"Do you really think that a sword can save you, Christian dog?"

"If your samurai can choose their weapons, so should we—"

"If you knew anything about budo, Priest, you would know that battles are won not by swords, but by the skill of the samurai who hold them."

"So you will not object?"

"Use your sword," the shogun scoffed dismissively. "It will not make a difference."

The shogun stood to address his retainers. "Prepare the Budokan immediately. These Christians will be slaughtered tonight!"

Fifty

"I am worried about this contest, Father," Miguel confessed as he sat alone in the corner of the room, mere feet from where the other three prisoners sat.

"Do not be, Miguel. The Lord has given us this challenge as an opportunity."

"What do you mean?"

"We prayed for freedom. Now this is our opportunity."

"But the shogun will bring his best warriors. Do you really think we can win, Father?"

Father Joaquim inched toward the nervous young man. "Look at me, Miguel. I do not *think* we can. I *know* we can."

"Why?" Miguel sighed. "Why are you so sure?"

"Because we were trained by the best, Miguel. Master Yamaguchi was one of the finest warriors in Japan, and he was a great teacher."

"But that was training. This is real life—life or death!"

"You are right. That was only training. But let us not forget the most important thing."

"What?"

"Faith that the Lord is with us." Father Joaquim sat down

next to Miguel. "We asked for His help, and He *will* answer. Just *believe*."

"I do believe, Father."

"If you believed, Miguel, you would not doubt the outcome. You would *know* He will answer."

"Listen to the noise coming from the hall next door. Others are being tortured and killed even as we sit here. The end is near."

"Do not let your fear prevent you from trusting God, Miguel. Have courage to trust Him."

"I will do my best, Father.

"When you feel weak or doubtful, do not try to rely on your own strength. Rely on God for your st—"

The door swung open and a dozen samurai entered the room. "Get up," the lead samurai shouted.

But as soon as they arose, the dozen samurai beat them to the ground with their fists and weapons. Then they pummeled the prisoners with vicious kicks. Finally, as the wounded prisoners lay on the floor, the warriors stomped first on their bodies, and then their hands and feet. "Now you are ready to meet the shogun's fighters," the lead samurai declared as he stood above them, smiling.

"Get up," the lead samurai shouted as before. "Do not worry. We are not going to beat you again. This time, the shogun's warriors will do it." Giving Father Joaquim one more kick to his back, the samurai repeated, "Get up, I said!"

But because of the tremendous beating, the prisoners were unable to rise quickly. Losing patience, the samurai yanked them to their feet.

"We must make you look pretty," said the lead samurai as he wiped blood from their faces. "We cannot have you look unsightly before you leave this world."

Wasting no time, the samurai shoved the prisoners toward the martial hall.

Father Joaquim looked at his young aides. "Are you okay, my friends?"

"My hand, Father," Miguel replied. "I think it is broken."

As the quartet was shoved into the main martial hall of the shogun's Budokan, the noise was thunderous as hundreds of Shogun Iemitsu's samurai stomped on floorboards and clapped their hands.

Up at the front of the Budokan was the shogun, his father, Hidetada, and his entire Go-Roju cabinet, sitting atop an elevated platform from which the shogun would run the contest. Adjacent to the front podium and running along both sides of the training mats were large spectator stands, holding hundreds of samurai, keen to witness the bloodshed.

As Father Joaquim gazed around the massive hall, his group was immediately yanked to the left side of the room, where they were forced to kneel as the shogun raised his right hand and the hall became silent.

"Welcome to the Budokan. This is where you will die," the shogun shouted from the front.

Instantly, the hall again erupted with cheers, yells, and loud rhythmic foot stomps.

"Silence," the shogun yelled. "I will now read the rules of the contest." The shogun smugly surveyed the hall before resting his eyes on Father Joaquim. "One: There will be three fights, one for each foreign Christian dog. Two: Each fight will be to the death, but in the priest's case, not until he has divulged the necessary information. Three: I choose the order and the adversaries for the fights. Four: The winning side of the overall contest will have at least two victories, although I doubt the foreign dogs will win even one."

Again, the hundreds of samurai cheered and stomped heavily.

"Give them their sword," the shogun instructed a retainer before turning his attention back to Father Joaquim. "After your deaths, your beautiful sword will look splendid in my collection. Now, prepare to be gutted!"

Again, hundreds of samurai began to stomp their feet enthusiastically on the floorboards and clap loudly.

"Fear not for the Lord is with us," Father Joaquim said, reassuring his young aides. "Believe in this and *know* that our freedom is at hand."

"Yes, Father," Tonia answered.

"Do you see this sword?" the padre asked. "This sword belonged to our teacher and dear friend, Master Yamaguchi. I want you to let this sword remind you of our training with Master Yamaguchi. When you use it, reflect on his teachings."

Tonia nodded. "Yes, Father."

"And remember the most important thing."

"What, Father?"

"Believe that the Lord stands with you, and *know* that you *will* be victorious."

Fifty-one

"The first death shall be your woman," the shogun roared from the podium.

Tonia spoke quietly to Father Joaquim, who stood beside her. "Any final advice, Father?"

"Remain calm and trust in God. Let Him inspire your movements. What technique do you see in your mind's eye, Tonia?"

"I see defense followed by a counter-attack."

"Good. There is wisdom in that. Follow your intuition. Your opponent will try to impress the Budokan and will come out strong. Focus on defense in the beginning, and protect yourself. When an opening comes, strike!"

"Yes, Father."

"Do not waste our time, woman," the shogun shouted. "Get on the mat!"

Gracefully, Father Joaquim extended Master Yamaguchi's sword to Tonia as she stepped onto the mat, where she respectfully bowed to receive it before jogging to the center of the mat to face the glare of hundreds of ruthless samurai.

"I call Akane-san," the shogun bellowed.

As the crowd roared and stomped, from the corner of the

Budokan emerged a large, barbaric figure. From a distance, Father Joaquim thought the samurai was a huge man, but as the figure moved closer he could see it was a woman—certainly the largest and most powerful woman he had ever seen. Father Joaquim could also see that Tonia was praying as she scrutinized her massive opponent.

"You will first bow to the shogun and then to each other," the official on the mat announced. "Then you will fight— until one of you is dead."

Without hesitation, Akane charged at Tonia, taking massive swings with her razor-sharp sword. Within seconds, Tonia was backed into the corner of the mat, defending frantically against the flurry of attacks. With each aggressive strike, Tonia raised her sword and blocked the attack, creating a fusillade of clacking sounds as the blades clashed.

Akane took another rumbling charge at Tonia, this time forcing her to the opposite side of the mat. Once more, Tonia barely eluded the series of strikes, two of which missed her throat by inches.

Surprised by Tonia's defense, Akane looked perplexed. Uneasily, she glanced at the shogun in bewilderment. The momentary lapse of attention was all Tonia needed. She slashed at Akane, cutting her deeply on her wrist and drawing a great deal of blood.

Akane shrieked as the pain tore through her arm. She nearly dropped her sword, and the Budokan went silent.

"Slaughter that mutt," the shogun yelled at Akane, as she quickly tried to re-focus. Akane raised her sword for yet a third round of strikes at Tonia, but her technique had been seriously weakened, along with her arm, and everyone in the Budokan could see it. As she tried to raise her sword again, Tonia deflected it and slashed open her right arm, causing the massive woman to drop her sword.

Akane screamed as blood spurted from her bicep. Seizing

the moment, Tonia raised her sword and slashed it through Akane's throat. The mountain of a woman teetered for a second before falling with a thud.

In the suddenly silent hall, the shocked shogun pounded his fist on the floor in frustration. "Get her body off the mat," he roared. "I have never seen such luck."

As Akane's bloodied body was dragged off the mat and thrown in a corner, the shogun yelled, "Young foreign boy, get on the mat! I promise you will not have such luck."

"What do I do, Father?" Miguel asked. "I cannot fight with a broken hand. What can I do?"

"Do you remember the sword removal technique Master Yamaguchi taught us?"

"I think so."

"You must remove his sword and then defeat him with your hands."

"Get on the mat boy," the shogun roared.

"But what about my hand, Father?" Paralyzed by fear, Miguel remained motionless, laden with uncertainty.

The shogun's samurai shoved him to the center of the mat.

"Suzuki-san," Shogun Iemitsu shouted.

Straightaway, a thick, dangerous-looking samurai emerged from the back of the Budokan and walked forward.

Instantly, the Budokan erupted again as all the samurai in attendance began to chant:

"Su-zu-ki! Su-zu-ki! Su-zu-ki!"

Among all the shogun's warriors and samurai, Suzuki was the most famed and talented, widely perceived as invincible.

Suzuki sped toward the mat with poise. As he arrived, he bowed twice to the shogun, who returned the gesture with a nod and a grin. Next, Suzuki turned and bowed to Miguel, whom he gazed at with a cold, dark stare.

Studying his form, Father Joaquim and Master Watanabe

240

knew immediately that Miguel was grossly outmatched. Talented fighters can quickly discern the skill of others by observing their general body movements and demeanor, and Suzuki looked like a master.

Miguel returned the bow, his nerves clearly on edge. Then, much to Father Joaquim's dismay, Miguel completely ignored his suggestions and charged wildly at Suzuki. Effortlessly, Suzuki defended the attacks as though he were playing with a child.

Miguel charged again, this time trying to strike his opponent with large, uncontrolled body blows, but to no avail. Suzuki's patience had worn out. As Miguel anxiously raised his sword again and thrust down, Suzuki moved out of the way and countered with a tremendous blow to Miguel's wrist, chopping off his hand.

Miguel screamed as his hand fell to the mat along with his sword, all the while blood spurting from his arm.

Grinning, Suzuki chased Miguel to the opposite side of the mat, where Miguel tried to retreat but was thrown back by a group of unsympathetic samurai. Trapped in the corner, Miguel was panic-stricken, with nowhere to go. Miguel frantically tried to locate his sword, but Suzuki struck him another vicious blow across his chest. Bleeding profusely, Miguel fled hysterically to the center of the mat, where he fell to his knees.

"Help me, Father," he cried as he reached out his remaining hand.

Suzuki stood behind Miguel. With a decisive nod from the shogun, the samurai raised his sword and brought it swiftly down on Miguel's neck, instantly decapitating him.

Straightaway, Tonia and Father Joaquim cried out in despair. But victory was not enough for Suzuki, who briskly walked over to Miguel's skull and kicked it off the mat in the direction of Father Joaquim, who could only stare, horrified at the shocking display of disrespect.

"Your head is next," the shogun shouted, laughing as he guzzled another shot of sake.

Several samurai quickly gathered Miguel's body parts— head, hand, and torso—and threw them into a garbage container.

Father Joaquim could no longer control himself. "The book of Psalms says, 'The Lord is known by the judgment which He executeth; and the wicked is snared in the work of their own hands.' The Lord has judged you, Shogun Iemitsu!"

"Shut your mouth, Priest, and get on the mat. Today your poisonous words die with you!"

Father Joaquim leapt onto the mat as he repeated a passage to himself. "Let my soul live, and it shall praise thee! Let thy judgments help me!"

"I again call Suzuki-san," the shogun shouted loudly.

"Su-zu-ki! Su-zu-ki! Su-zu-ki!" the crowd chanted again.

Interrupting their chant, however, the shogun raised his hand, and the Budokan quickly fell silent. "And … Daisuke-san!"

"Dai-su-ke! Dai-su-ke! Dai-su-ke!"

An enormous figure surfaced from the rear of the Budokan and slowly approached the mat. Standing almost seven feet tall, Daisuke was an ogre and easily the largest samurai within the shogun's forces. Master Watanabe jumped onto the mat in protest.

"Get off the mat, ronin," the shogun yelled. "This battle does not involve you!"

"You have called two fighters," Master Watanabe replied. "I am our second fighter."

"You will get off the mat or I will end the contest!"

"How is this fair? How can you send two fighters against one?"

"This is my Budokan and these are *my* rules! Get off the mat or I will have you both executed!"

Reluctantly, Master Watanabe stepped off the mat and Father Joaquim slowly approached the center of the mat to face his two adversaries.

Within a minute, all parties had bowed and the fight began.

Straightaway, both Suzuki and Daisuke charged at Father Joaquim, but the crafty priest managed to avoid them. From experience, the well-trained Jesuit knew it was far easier to contest one fighter than two, and he had learned how to use one attacker to block another.

In light of Daisuke's enormous size, Father Joaquim sought to use him to block the more skilled and dangerous Suzuki. And when the opportunity presented itself, the father deftly slashed Daisuke's enormous legs, drawing a copious amount of blood.

Then, with stealth-like speed, Father Joaquim strategically positioned himself between Suzuki and Daisuke for a moment as Daisuke angrily raised his sword in retaliation. But as soon as Daisuke began to cut down fiercely with his sword, the Jesuit swiftly slipped out of the way, and Daisuke's sword slashed down on the fast-approaching Suzuki, cutting his shoulder open in a devastating blow.

Shocked by Daisuke's mistake, the Budokan again fell silent. Never had any of them seen Suzuki suffer any kind of injury. But Father Joaquim had only just begun his offensive. Capitalizing on the confusion on the mat, he quickly slipped behind Daisuke and slashed open his ankles, causing him to crash to his knees.

As Daisuke fell, Father Joaquim also lowered himself, continuing to use Daisuke's enormous size as a shield. From his cover behind the giant samurai, Father Joaquim changed the grip on his sword and threw it over Daisuke's shoulder at Suzuki, piercing his stomach and nearly killing him.

Without pausing, the priest jumped out from behind Daisuke, ran to Suzuki, and kicked the sword deeper into his body, forcing the blade out through his back. Father Joaquim then grabbed Suzuki's own sword, raised it, and decapitated him with a devastating blow. Instantly, a shocked silence fell on the Budokan.

The end of the bout was nearly at hand. After removing his sword from Suzuki's lifeless body, the father approached the fallen Daisuke. Still on his knees, Daisuke roared loudly as he raised his sword high and tried to strike Father Joaquim over his skull. But the father was able to avoid the blow of the immobile giant before quickly and mercifully ending Daisuke's life by slicing through his jugular vein. Blood splattered across the room.

Fifty-two

The Budokan was silent as Shogun Iemitsu pounded his fists on the floor in fury. Three of his most venerated warriors were dead, and he'd lost the contest. Unsure how to respond, he turned to his Go-Roju cabinet members.

"We cannot let these dogs escape."

"I do not think we have a choice, Lord," the member closest to him replied. "You have already declared that your 'word is stronger than metal.'"

"I think you should honor the terms of the contest, Lord," a second member added. "But I would not worry. We can have our vengeance on this priest at a later time."

With veins protruding and pulsing in his forehead and neck, Iemitsu reluctantly agreed. "We will not tarnish our word, but I will have my vengeance on this priest and his flock!"

Turning to address Father Joaquim who was standing with Tonia and Master Watanabe, as together they mourned the loss of Miguel, the shogun spoke. "Filthy Priest, it seems you have done more than spread your poisonous cult in Japan. It appears you have also learned the way of our sword."

Father Joaquim stood silent.

"You and your band of Christians are free to leave."

Father Joaquim bowed in acknowledgement.

"Return to Europe or go to the Philippines. But do not stay here. If you stay in Japan, I will kill you!"

"We request the return of our friend's body so we may bury him."

His veins pulsing visibly again, the shogun replied, "Do not try my patience, Priest! His body will be incinerated, and not an ash of him will remain. Soon there will be no trace or memory of your kind in Japan!" As several samurai opened the doors, the shogun continued, "There is your door. The other prisoners will join you shortly."

★ ★ ★

"I command all Christians to stand up," the lead guard yelled.

Following his earlier angry outburst, Susumu had kept an eye on his new Christian cellmates. Their concern for one another seemed genuine. Quietly, unobtrusively, he'd listened to their discussions—and their prayers. While part of him wanted to hate them for their weakness, another part of him recognized that their weakness—their unwillingness to try to fight their way to dominance—was, ironically, their strength. He was impressed, although he was not ready to admit it.

So when the prison guards abruptly opened the door, startling all the prisoners who lay trapped inside and commanding the Christians to arise, Susumu wasn't sure how to respond.

Frightened, most of the prisoners were slow to move. Others were incapable of obeying, owing to their weakened state.

"Did you hear me?" the guard shouted. "I command all Christians to stand up!"

The Christians in the overcrowded jail began to rise, including everyone from the village.

"If you cannot stand, raise a hand or a limb," the guard yelled impatiently.

Slowly, a number of hands and feet started to rise, and the main prison guard began to make a count. "I count twenty-nine worthless dogs. Are there any others?"

Again he looked around the jail for any motion, but saw none.

"One more time," the main guard bellowed irritably. "Are there any more prisoners who believe in this Christ?"

One final prisoner rose in the far corner of the dark prison. It was Susumu.

★ ★ ★

Waiting for their friends to join them, Father Joaquim, Tonia, and Master Watanabe stood in a street next to the prison with their arms around each other, praying as they mourned Miguel. "We will miss you with all our hearts, Miguel," Tonia sobbed as tears poured from her eyes.

"Worry not, for he is re-united with God," Master Watanabe said. "He is now on the other side and lives on the spiritual plane with Master Yamaguchi. They have their arms around each other."

"He is in heaven," Father Joaquim said confidently. "Thank you, Lord, for preparing a place for him."

"Father," a young man from the village cried out as he ran down the street, "is it true? Are we really free?"

"We are free," Father Joaquim answered, smiling and nodding. "But we must leave Edo immediately. I do not trust the shogun."

As many of the villagers kissed the ground and praised God, Shinobu asked, "Where is Miguel, Father?"

"He was slain by one of the shogun's samurai. He is with God now."

"We will mourn him, Father, but rejoice that he is with the Lord."

"Where are the others?" Father Joaquim asked Shinobu.

"They are coming. The prison guard has released all Christians, but some are very ill or cannot walk."

"We must help them."

"In total, they have just released thirty Christians from the prison."

"Thirty? A new one?"

The words were no sooner out of his mouth than Father Joaquim spotted feisty Susumu coming down the path, helping to carry the crippled Akihiko.

★ ★ ★

Shogun's Private Chamber, Edo Castle

"I want them all slain, immediately!" the shogun shouted furiously.

"Yes, Lord," a Go-Roju cabinet member answered. "We will have them executed the moment they leave the city."

"Why not before?"

"Because Edo needs to know that you keep your word, Lord," the cabinet member replied.

"This is ridiculous. They are filthy exiled Christians! How can we possibly let them go?"

"This is a problem that *you* created," the shogun's father, Hidetada, commented. "Now you must hold your end of the agreement."

"But this is preposterous," the shogun yelled as he paced back and forth.

"Then you should not have accepted his ridiculous challenge," Hidetada interjected. "The Christian priest baited you."

"How was to I know the priest and the girl had mastered the art of *bushido*? Who could possibly know this?"

"It matters not," Hidetada replied. "It is now your responsibility to clean up the mess and maintain the honor of the Tokugawa name."

"This is one more reason why I abhor these foreigners," the shogun bellowed. "They deceive us. They come here under the guise of commercial trading, but they secretly learn our ways of battle, and then defeat us with it!"

"But how did they learn it?" a retainer asked. "Who would teach them?"

"Ronin," the shogun howled. "Dissenting ronin who roam the land and have nothing better to do than to plot against me. Could you imagine an invading Spanish army trained with such skills? They could teach our techniques throughout Europe and conquer us!"

"I agree, Lord," the retainer said. "It is a threat. Perhaps it would be wise to expel *all* foreigners from Japan, including all foreign traders and merchants as well."

"Perhaps we should seal off the country from the *entire* outside world. I will not tolerate any faction that could challenge my authority."

"Let us be careful," Hidetada interjected. "Your grandfather, great Shogun Ieyasu, believed international trade benefits Japan. I do not think we should rush to cut it off."

"I revere Grandfather Ieyasu, Father. He is our deity, but we must crush these Christians."

"Agreed. Their cult remains a threat and we must complete their annihilation."

"Let us decapitate this band of Christians and hang the priest's skull in my castle."

"How shall we proceed, Lord?" a retainer asked.

"We will place bands of samurai at all roads leaving Edo. Our spies will follow them through the streets. Once they have left the perimeter of Edo and are out of sight, we will massacre them."

"What shall we do with their corpses?"

"Burn their bodies and throw their ashes into the sea. But place their heads in a sack and bring the sack to me."

Fifty-three

July 14, 1626
Streets of Edo

"Well, my friend, you and Tonia have won our freedom," Master Watanabe stated as he and Father Joaquim gathered the villagers from the prison. "Now we must see if we can keep it. Can we escape the shogun's grip before he changes his mind?"

"You know it was God working through us who gained us our freedom. If He bought our freedom through the challenge, will He not secure it to the end?"

"Well said, Father." Master Watanabe nodded. "But I suspect we will have some testing experiences as He gets us there."

Adding to the immense task they faced was the appalling physical condition of many in the group. All were malnourished. Few had had a good night's sleep in weeks. Some had developed diseases, and many were victims of the shogun's brutality, having suffered the loss of body parts, including hands or feet. Among the worst was young Akihiko, who'd had both feet removed and had to be carried.

"What is our plan, Father?" Shinobu asked. "Shall we begin our walk toward the main seki to leave the city?"

"No, Shinobu." Father Joaquim. "That would be too risky."

"Why? I thought the shogun promised us freedom."

Responding to the question, the father answered bluntly. "The shogun is not to be trusted."

"Why?"

"Because Shogun Iemitsu lacks integrity and hates Christians and foreigners too much. I am sure he will not let us walk far."

"This is worrying," Shinobu replied. "What shall we do?"

"We will depart Edo straightaway, but not by foot."

"How then?"

"By boat. We need to get out of the shogun's reach as soon as possible, and it will be more difficult for the shogun's men to ambush us at sea."

"But where will we get a boat?"

Sighing, Father Joaquim looked first at Master Watanabe before answering Shinobu. "I do not know. We will need to pray for it."

Master Watanabe nodded affirmatively.

"Will we have time?"

"God will provide, Shinobu."

Master Watanabe nodded again as the two of them moved toward a small group of huddled men. Two of the men, Kenta and Jiro, finished re-wrapping Akihiko's stumps and were ready to carry him.

"I would like to thank you, Father," Akihiko said, looking up from the ground and cupping his hands at the sides of his head to funnel the voices, as his outer ears had done before the shogun's torturers removed them.

"For what?"

"For liberating us. For our freedom."

"Do not thank me, Akihiko-san. Thank our Lord."

"But I am told it was *you* who defeated two of the shogun's top samurai in battle."

"By myself, I can do nothing. The prophet Zephaniah said, 'The Lord thy God in the midst of thee is mighty; *He* will save.'"

"Yes, Father, but it was your hands that struck down the hands of evil. Surely, you have great skill to defeat such venerated warriors of the shogun. I did not know the Jesuits possessed such martial skills."

Father Joaquim shrugged and sat down next to Akihiko. "The founder and first superior general of the Jesuits, Saint Ignatius of Loyola, was a knight before leading his brothers."

"Then warfare is good?"

"No, it is not." Grimacing and shaking his head, Father Joaquim looked sympathetically at the young man who would never walk again. "The Society has evolved and is bound by a different set of vows now—vows of poverty, chastity, obedience, and love. We will never conquer by the sword, as that is not God's will."

"But this time the sword bought our freedom."

"Yes, Akihiko-san, but the sword must be a last resort. Our Lord Jesus told the apostle Peter that those who take up the sword will perish by the sword."

"I understand, Father." Akihiko looked briefly at his stumps, no doubt recalling the sharp, cruel saw that had removed his feet. "So what do we do now?"

"We make our way to Edo Harbor."

Several villagers joined the conversation. "Then what, Father?"

"We find a boat and set sail."

"Where will we go?"

"Nagasaki."

"Nagasaki?!"

"Yes—to rescue our women and children."

Seeing doubt and disbelief in the villagers' eyes, Father Joaquim stood and spoke up for all to hear: "I know many of you have many questions, and I regret I do not have all the answers. But God *does*, and nothing is impossible for Him."

"What shall we do, Father?"

"Pray everyone. *All* things are possible through prayer."

Fifty-four

"I invited you to join us, Governor, because I want you to be a witness as the first of these vile Christians breaks and recants," Deputy-Lieutenant Suetsugu stated as the contingent walked toward the deputy's warehouse.

"Hmm, what makes you so confident that today will be the day? You have had two weeks, with no results yet."

"They have been resilient, Governor, but when you see their broken state, you will be impressed." Suetsugu was almost giddy over his plans and his confidence.

"Good. The shogun expects results."

"I am sure we will see results this afternoon. You will tell the shogun I am painstakingly mutilating these Christians, will you not?"

"Yes, Deputy, I will."

"Thank you, Governor. I would love to be rewarded for my work here."

"I am sure you will be rewarded even more if you can get apostates," the governor replied as they reached the guarded perimeter of the warehouse.

To protect his warehouse from theft and damage, Suetsugu had built a fence along three sides of its perimeter. The open side faced the water of Nagasaki harbor, where trading ships could dock so that the deputy could load and unload his riches. To prevent escape, a dozen guards watched the perimeter throughout the nights.

As the deputy and governor arrived at the gate, the guards bowed deeply before admitting them. Then, as they approached the entrance, two more samurai guards slid open the large doors.

Inside, everyone remained still—not out of fear, but because none had the strength to move unnecessarily.

"I have allowed them *just* enough food to remain alive," Suetsugu chuckled. "Barely," he added as he opened the bag he carried and handed a piece of dried fish to each member of the contingent. "I love to eat in front of them as their empty bellies growl and their children whimper and cry." He swept his right hand fully, from left to right, as he continued. "Every one of them—except for that newborn, for which I have other plans— has been tortured in one way or another. I have no doubt they are at their breaking point," he added as he munched his dried fish.

"They look appalling," Governor Kawachi added. "You have done well, Deputy. Now let us see these recantations you promised."

"Bring them to the yard," Suetsugu shouted. "This afternoon someone is going to recant. I am tired of being merciful to you dogs." He turned to address the guards: "Is the water boiling yet?"

The guards nodded their affirmation.

"Who shall we pick to mutilate this afternoon?" Suetsugu asked as he gazed at the emaciated women and children.

All tried to avoid eye contact with the callous man as, slowly, he gazed at the women before making his choice. "You, young girl we have ignored you this week. Get over here."

The young woman, Hatsumi, broke down in tears and began shaking, unable to move.

254

"I remember this girl," Governor Kawachi interjected as he examined her. "Was she not the pretty one?"

"She was," Suetsugu chuckled. "When she had a nose. Bring her over here."

Several guards rushed over to Hatsumi and grabbed her.

"No more! No more!" Hatsumi cried as she was dragged toward the pot of boiling water.

"Young girl, I am not going to waste time," the deputy declared. "I ask you a simple question: Do you recant?"

Hatsumi only cried.

"Do you recant?"

The only response was her terrified sobs.

The deputy nodded to four guards, who dragged her toward the pot as she screamed hysterically. As two of the guards restrained her, the other two grabbed her arm and forced it into the boiling water. Despite Hatsumi's pitiful screams, the deputy's guards held her arm in the scorching pot.

After a minute or so, the guards withdrew Hatsumi's arm and threw her to the ground, where she cried and wailed, as did all the other women and children as they watched.

Suetsugu then approached Hatsumi and stood above her. "Do not test me, girl! Do you recant?"

Still in deep shock, Hatsumi did not respond.

"Let us boil her other arm."

Delirious, Hatsumi screamed, "I recant! I cannot take anymore. I recant!"

"Magnificent!" Suetsugu turned to the governor, smiling victoriously. "I told you someone would recant today."

"Very good, Deputy-Lieutenant. You are achieving results. The shogun will be pleased."

"The rest will recant within the next five days."

"How can you be so sure?"

"The first one is always the hardest. In five days, if the

remainder of them have not recanted through torture, I will start to kill them. I will start with their youngest and work my way to the oldest."

Hearing the conversation, the mother of the newborn cried out, holding her baby tightly.

"Very well, Deputy. I leave you in charge."

Suetsugu walked over to the new mother, snatched her baby from her, and held the infant up in the air with his fist around its neck. "Do you see this baby?" he shrieked. "If you have not *all* recanted within the next five days, you will all be responsible for this baby's death!"

Fifty-five

The sight of thirty emaciated, mangled, and crippled strangers walking—or being carried—through the streets of Edo in the early evening was unusual in itself. Add a tall European man and what appeared to be an old ronin leading them, and it was strange enough to attract an audience, much as would a parade.

"Where will we find a boat?" Tonia asked as she caught up with Father Joaquim.

First smiling and nodding to a young boy who had scampered away from his mother for a closer look at the bizarre congregation, Father Joaquim turned back to the young catechist and replied with a hint of a grimace. "I do not know, Tonia, but we had better find one soon."

"Why, Father?"

"Because I suspect the shogun will not allow us to live much longer."

"What kind of boat will we need?"

"One sufficiently large for all of us to travel in, and stout enough to navigate rough seas."

Tonia began to inspect the boats in the harbor. "I see only the shogun's red-seal ships, along with many small boats. I do not see anything in between."

"Neither do I, and clearly the shogun will not allow us the use of one of his red-seal ships."

"There is one boat that would serve us well," Master Watanabe commented as he approached the father and Tonia. The old ronin pointed to a mid-sized boat at the end of the harbor, below a small hill on which a Buddhist temple sat.

"Who do you think that ship belongs to?" Tonia asked.

"Almost certainly to the Buddhist monks of the temple."

"There must be others," Father Joaquim added, his frustration evident. "How could there be only one possible boat for us?"

"Because all the others are out at sea now, Father. Their owners are making a living. What is wrong with the monks' boat?" Master Watanabe asked, somehow keeping stride with the longer-legged padre yet looking utterly unhurried.

"It belongs to the Buddhists!"

"So?"

"Buddhist monks are our mortal enemies in Japan."

"You must resist *us-versus-them* concepts," Master Watanabe replied.

"Since the arrival of Christians in Japan, Buddhists have hated us. Our enmity has run for nearly a century. Why would they help us when they want us dead and gone?"

"Did you pray for a boat, Father?"

"Yes, of course."

"Well there is your boat."

"But the Lord would never send us a Buddhist boat."

"Have you not said *leave the how to God*?"

"Yes, I said this," Father Joaquim replied, feeling exasperated by the lack of options.

"Well, there you are. That is your boat. In the entire harbor, it is the only boat that fits your needs."

"I just find it difficult to believe God would have Buddhists help us."

"Do you believe God has greater wisdom than you?"

"Yes, of course."

"Then put away judgments that are clouding your mind. That is your boat."

"What shall we do, then?" Father Joaquim asked. "We have no money to offer."

"Go over and ask them for help."

"Perhaps it would be better if you ask. You are not a Christian priest. Perhaps they will be more receptive to you."

"You must not become overly dependent on me, Father." Master Watanabe stopped walking and turned his gaze from the Buddhist boat back to Father Joaquim. "I am only a guide to help show you the way." He placed his hands on the father's shoulders and gave him a reassuring smile. "*You* must do these things. I cannot do them for you."

The priest nodded. "Very well. I will do it."

"Are you sure, Master Watanabe?" Tonia asked, worry evident in her expression. "If you are wrong, they might turn Father Joaqim over to the shogun—or kill him. Most Buddhist monks are skilled warriors."

"Let us find out."

Fifty-six

Filled with trepidation, Father Joaquim still, somehow, sensed that Master Watanabe was right—he had to do this.

As he made his way up the seemingly endless stairs that ascended the steep hill, the Christian Father noticed a number of colorful flags along the way. Like most Japanese flags, they were long and vertical, affixed to long wooden poles and cemented into the ground. The flags displayed a variety of Buddhist phrases and bore the prayers used by the Amidist Buddhist sect in Japan. "*Namu Amida Butsu*" read the first flag, meaning "*I Iail to the Buddha Amida*". A little farther up the hill another flag read, "He who advances is sure of salvation, but he who retreats will go to hell." Reading the slogans, Father Joaquim paused and shook his head. "I must be out of my mind."

Over the years, the father had observed that Buddhist warrior monks placed far more emphasis on military matters and combat than on prayer. The phenomenon of the warrior monk had its origins in the introduction of Buddhism to Japan. He'd learned that Buddhism came to Japan through China, and when it reached Japan it complemented rather than threatened the existing religion, which was Shinto, known as "the way of the gods." Shinto involved the worship of thousands of *kami*, regarded by Buddhists as manifestations of Buddha himself. Hence, the creeds of Buddhism from China and Shintoism from Japan co-existed very well.

However, this was not the case with Christianity. Christian doctrine contrasted sharply with Buddhism, and conflicts always arose when the two religions came into contact.

Furthermore, Buddhism was aligned with the shogun, and the Bakufu regime practically enforced Buddhism as a matter of law. Given that Christianity had been banned from Japan, Father Joaquim couldn't conceive of the possibility that a warrior Buddhist monk would contradict the shogun's edict and help a Christian. Yet he had to try. And, in order to convey his peaceful intentions, he went alone and carried no weapon.

He was surprised to have reached the top of the stairs without being noticed and confronted. But that did not last long. "Halt where you are," a warrior monk bellowed in a threatening tone.

Father Joaquim raised his hands slowly, submissively. He was quickly surrounded by several warrior monks, all shouting and demanding to know who he was and why he had come. One monk ran over to a nearby structure and began ringing the temple bell to alert the remaining members of the community. Another ran to a lookout at the top of the hill to see if other trespassers were approaching. Grabbing their Buddhist prayer bead necklaces, many of the monks began cursing Father Joaquim for his presence in their community.

Within a few minutes of the bell ringing, dozens more warrior monks joined the crowd surrounding the intruder. All had shaved heads and wore beige kimonos and trousers, with lightweight black jackets. Underneath their robes, however, the Jesuit could detect lacquered plates of armor. Some also carried weapons, including knives, bows, spears, and swords.

Father Joaquim stood calmly before them with his hands

raised passively in the air. But the shouting intensified, and suddenly the priest found himself knocked to the ground, where many then pointed their intimidating *naginata* spears at him.

Surrounded by dozens of screaming and aggressive warrior monks, Father Joaquim could see little more than the sharp naginatas pointing at him from all directions. At a moment's notice, he could be speared and sliced into pieces.

"Who are you? A merchant? A trader?"

"I am a Christian priest."

"A Christian priest! Let us kill him," someone in the crowd yelled.

"No, let us collect a reward for him. His capture is worth money."

A quarrel broke out among the monks, who nonetheless continued to point their spears at Father Joaquim's head. The quarrel subsided when the temple's elder and head monk arrived and raised his hands.

"Quiet! Quiet, I said!" As the last of the younger monks stopped arguing, the elder continued. "What is the problem?"

"This gaijin is a Christian priest. We caught him on our grounds. He was approaching the temple."

"Is it true, stranger? Are you a Christian priest?"

"Yes, I am."

With that admission, the yelling and shouting flared up again. "We should kill him!"

"Quiet!" the elder monk ordered and raised his hands again. "Control yourselves. We will not have another outburst like this."

Looking again at the intruder lying passively on the ground, the elder asked, "Why are you here?"

"I am here to ask for help."

"He came to the wrong place," one of the monks replied as he jabbed Father Joaquim in his side with his pommel.

"Lower your weapons and be silent," the elder monk

ordered again. "*I* am conducting this interrogation." Looking down again at the priest, he continued, "It is strange that you are asking us for help, Christian Priest. We are a Buddhist community. Are you aware of this?"

Father Joaquim nodded. "Yes."

"Who needs help?"

"Our entire village. A farming village from Kyushu. Women, children, husbands, fathers, elders, everyone. Unless we can get a ship to Nagasaki, all will be slaughtered."

"The shogun wishes to annihilate you because your village is Christian and you are their patriarch?"

"Yes, he wishes to destroy us because we are Christian."

"The shogun is fierce," the elder monk added. "He crushes anyone he dislikes."

"He is a tyrant, nothing more."

"The priest is an enemy of the regime," interjected one of the younger monks. "Let us collect a reward for him!"

"Let us kill him!" another monk shouted.

"That is enough!" the elder monk scolded, turning his attention back to Father Joaquim. "You are very brave to come here alone. What inspired such boldness?"

"The thought of a massacred village." As he answered, memories of Master Yamaguchi's murder swept across the Jesuit's thoughts.

Reaching down to help the father up, the elder monk announced, "My name is Kansuke, and we will help you. We will take you to Nagasaki."

That was an announcement the other monks did not agree with, and they readily expressed their dissatisfaction. But again the elder quieted them.

"Thank you, Kansuke-san," the priest said. "I am Father Joaquim Martinez, and on behalf of our village, I thank you."

"Why should we help them?" another monk fumed. "Christians are our enemies."

"Enemies of yesterday can become friends of tomorrow," Kansuke answered calmly. "The teachings of the Buddha require compassion toward all beings, not just other Buddhists. Do you understand? Let us all appreciate this opportunity, as it is a chance to express that compassion. Remember, every situation allows us to express and experience a different part of ourselves."

Only partially convinced, a younger monk asked, "What shall we do, Kansuke-san?"

"Get the vessel ready. We depart at sunset."

Fifty-seven

Sneaking more than fifty people aboard a boat undetected was no small feat, especially when those people comprised two factions historically at odds with each other. The early-evening darkness aided their secrecy but, try as they might to be quiet, they were bound to make some noise. To aid their clandestine activities, in another part of the harbor, several of the monks staged a boisterous mock argument as a diversion.

Father Joaquim had traveled many times aboard junks and had learned quite a bit about them. He knew that *junk* was a generic term for Asian sailing vessels, and that the word was derived from the Portuguese word *junco*. While junks varied significantly in their size, one common feature among them was their fully battened sails. It was the structure and flexibility of these sails that made the vessels fast and easy to sail.

The sails included several horizontal members, called battens, which provided shape and strength. They could also be easily reefed and adjusted for fullness, to accommodate various wind strengths. The battens made them more durable than traditional sails, as tears would typically be limited to a single pane between battens. The Buddhist monks' junk possessed only three battens, considerably fewer than the sails on the much larger seagoing junks, which often had six or even seven full-length battens.

While the Buddhists' junk was just large enough to carry

all of them, it was far from massive. Father Joaquim guessed it to be about 300 tons, which meant it was much smaller than some of the enormous junks that approached 2,000 tons.

The boat looked old, and much of the wood was decaying, but the Buddhist community still used it to earn a marginal income. Like most traditional junks, the hull of the vessel had a horseshoe-shaped stern, supporting a high watch deck. Atop this deck flew a number of Buddhist flags, with the largest flag, of Amida Buddha, at the top. It was next to their flags that most of the Buddhists congregated on the ship as they boarded. The Christians moved to the bow.

Having quickly—and apparently without detection—boarded everyone, the monks swiftly set sail into Edo harbor, and then, with the benefit of a strong wind, out into the open ocean.

As Father Joaquim raised his head after a prayer of thanks, he spotted several of the monks glaring at him. Kansuke may have convinced his monks to cooperate, but it appeared he hadn't succeeded in convincing them of the rectitude of their actions.

★ ★ ★

Atop a beautiful velvet pillow on an elevated platform, the shogun spoke: "Approach," he commanded the four Buddhist warrior monks. The monks crawled, slowly, in deference to their great dictator. "We are told you have valuable information," the shogun said. "Communicate your tidings."

"We have information regarding a foreign Christian priest and a group of Christians."

"Speak at once," the shogun commanded.

"Our community was approached by a foreign priest seeking our assistance."

"Where is your community?"

"Edo harbor, Lord Shogun."

"What did the priest seek?"

"Use of our shipping vessel, Lord."

Flushed with fury, the shogun continued: "Where did he wish to go? The Philippines?"

"No, Lord. He asked to go to Nagasaki."

"And are they still at the temple?"

"No, Lord. Our elder temple leader agreed to take them."

"Why would your temple leader betray me and the laws I have commanded?"

"He said he would help them on grounds of compassion, but our individual loyalties lie with you, Lord Shogun. We only serve you and your regime."

"You are wise to serve me and to act as informants. In reward, you shall live and receive a small gift of silver. But your temple leader will not be so fortunate. He will die along with anyone else in league with him. Are you sure they went to Nagasaki?"

"Yes, Lord. It is what the foreign priest requested."

"Collect your silver as you leave my castle." The shogun snorted and huffed as he envisioned flaying the leader of the monks, this man who dared defy him.

"This priest is far too unruly," the shogun roared. "To save himself, he should retreat to the Philippines. But he has the audacity to return to southern Japan!"

"These Christians are an insolent group," a cabinet member responded. "They insult you with each act of defiance."

"But why return to Nagasaki?" the shogun pondered aloud. "Surely he knows they will face re-arrest."

"Their families are still in Nagasaki, Lord."

"You do not think they will try to rescue their families?"

"It is possible, Lord. These Christian criminals are renowned for their brazenness."

"Never!" The shogun stood and thundered. "They could never be so bold!"

"What would you like to do, Lord?"

"Prepare our greatest red-seal ships. We will destroy them at sea!"

"Yes, Lord. We will coordinate it immediately."

The red-seal ships were armed merchant sailing vessels bound for other Asian ports with a red-sealed patent issued by the shogunate. Such patents were valuable because they were limited in number and regime-authorized. Every red-seal ship was sanctioned by the shogun and protected from any would-be pirates at sea, as the shogun vowed to pursue any pirate or nation that dared to interfere with his authorized ships.

The shogun typically bestowed these coveted red-seal permits on his favorite daimyo and merchants in exchange for gifts, benefits, or other favors. It was for this reason the shogun was assured of assistance by those to whom they had been given.

★ ★ ★

Five minutes later, a senior administrator named Tadao was hurried into the grand chamber to speak with the shogun and his Go-Roju cabinet. The gray-haired man had been in the service of the regime since the time of Shogun Iemitsu's grandfather, Ieyasu.

Well-known in the shogun's administration, Tadao had administered more red-seal patents than anyone, and thus knew practically everything there was to know about vessels and the sea. Within the Bakufu regime, he was considered the foremost expert.

"We need to destroy a Buddhist ship," the shogun said. "The vessel is carrying a large group of runaway Christian criminals. We must catch them at once and destroy them."

"Yes, Lord Shogun."

"What do you advise, Tadao?"

"Send larger, faster vessels than the enemy's, Lord. Send more than one."

"Good. How many large ships do I have at my disposal?"

"There are currently five large red-seal ships in Edo Harbor, but you will not need five."

"Good, we will use all five."

"But, Lord, you will not need that many. I know the Buddhist vessel you seek. It is small and of no significance. You will need only two red-seal ships to firmly catch and destroy it."

"I will not take any chances. I want these Christian criminals dead!"

"But, Lord, some of these red-seal ships are already loaded with expensive goods and merchandise. There is no time to unload them for such an unexpected military mission."

"Then set sail with the goods aboard."

"But the goods and merchandise could be lost or damaged, Lord."

"I do not care about goods and merchandise. I care about exterminating Christians!"

"But what about the daimyo and head merchants, Lord? These vessels and cargo belong to them."

"I do not care about the daimyo or merchants. They all exist to serve me. Without me, they would not have their lands or red-seal patents!"

"Yes, Lord."

"Prepare the vessels immediately!"

"And what about men, Lord Shogun? How many men should we send?"

"How many can we load per ship?"

"About two hundred per vessel."

"Good, then put the maximum on each. We will send one

thousand men after them. And make sure all the cannons are fully loaded. I do not want any excuses."

"Are you sure we require such a large force to destroy such a small, decrepit Buddhist vessel, Lord?"

"I want to blow this ship to *hell*!"

Fifty-eight

July 15, 1626
Pacific Ocean

With only a couple monks awake, tending to the boat's navigation, Father Joaquim and Tonia sat toward the bow, gazing out over the portside, watching the sunrise. Filled with sorrow, tears welling up in her eyes, Tonia mourned the loss of Miguel as she and the Jesuit observed the contrast of orange, peach, and yellow colors emerging on the horizon.

Sensing Tonia's grief, Father Joaquim sought to bring her some comfort. "You miss him, Tonia?"

"I do Father, a great deal. He was not brave, but Miguel had a good heart."

"I know he did and that is why he is with the Lord now. Both he *and* Master Yamaguchi are with Him now."

"I hope so, Father."

"I *know* so, Tonia. They have the gift of eternal life."

Glancing now at the Buddhist monks on the opposite side of the vessel, Tonia changed the conversation. "To be honest Father, I am surprised *we have* made it this far."

"Oh? Why is that?"

"Because the shogun wants to destroy us, and the odds are greatly against us. I am very surprised we found a boat."

"I am surprised ... and not surprised," the priest answered, his hand rubbing his chin.

"What do you mean?"

"I am surprised the Buddhists are helping us, but I am not surprised the Lord has answered us."

"I just thought the odds were against us," Tonia's stomach grumbled as she replied. The monks had given the Christians some rice and a little dried fish, but they did not have much to spare.

"Jesus said, 'Ask, and it shall be given you; Seek, and ye shall find; Knock, and it shall be opened unto you. For every one that asketh receiveth; and he that seeketh findeth; and to him that knocketh it shall be opened.'"

"Thank you, Father. I like that passage."

"All prayers are answered Tonia, no matter how big or small."

"It is odd, but it almost seems as if we were *destined* to find this boat—as if this boat was waiting for us. Does it not seem like too much of a coincidence?" Tonia asked.

"I no longer believe in coincidences, but I *do* believe in God's providence. And I do believe He has a plan for us. Often the Lord answers even before we have asked."

"I agree, Father. I also believe He is looking out for us."

"Let us pray and thank God for this boat, and for His continued protection of us."

"Yes, Father."

For a few minutes, Father Joaquim and Tonia closed their eyes and sat quietly, facing the sun and praying.

"I saw you were awake," Kansuke stated as he approached the pair. "May I join you?"

"Of course, Kansuke-san," Father Joaquim answered as he made room for their benefactor. "Please, sit down with us."

"It is a beautiful morning, is it not?"

"Very beautiful," Father Joaquim and Tonia answered in unison as they all sat gazing at the sunrise.

"We would like to thank you again for your help, Kansuke-san," Father Joaquim added. "Without you, we would not have survived on Honshu. How can we ever repay you?"

"The survival of your village is more than enough."

"I am confused," Tonia stated. "Will the shogun and his regime not make you suffer for helping us?"

"Yes." As Kansuke replied, he smiled, revealing creases beside his eyes that reminded Father Joaquim of Master Yamaguchi. For a moment, he almost forgot to whom he was speaking.

Returning to the present, Father Joaquim asked, "Then why do you help us?"

"My son was killed by the shogun."

Father Joaquim's heart contracted with empathy. "I am sorry, Kansuke-san."

"He was killed for helping a homeless man in Edo, slain for offering him food while the shogun conducted one of his sword-swinging expeditions. The shogun despises the homeless, so he killed my son for helping the man."

"The shogun is evil."

"And that is why I stand up to him now. I should have confronted him then, but I did not, and I have regretted it ever since."

"Living under an oppressor is never easy," Father Joaquim replied.

"I believe the strong should protect the weak, not oppress them. The shogunate is a dictatorship and, eventually, all dictators will fall."

"You are brave to oppose him," Father Joaquim said.

"What about you, Father? Christianity was expelled from Japan over ten years ago. And yet you stay, at risk of losing your life."

"It is my mission. It is God's will that I am here."

"But it is dangerous for Christians. Why do you do it, Father? What do you want to accomplish?"

"Our Bible says, 'Go ye into all the world, and preach the gospel to every creature. He that believeth and is baptized shall be saved.'"

"And what does that mean?"

"I am but a servant in this world. In this life, I seek nothing more than to spread the Word of God and to save the souls of many."

"Even if it means your own life?"

"Our holy book assures us that even if we take on serpents or drink that which is deadly, it will not hurt us. Thus, I place all my faith in our Lord."

"And, like me, you defy the shogun."

"Then it looks as if we are both brave men." Father Joaquim chuckled a bit as he spoke.

Tonia suddenly jumped from her seat and pointed into the distance. "Look at that," she shouted as she ran to the edge of the boat to get a better view. "Do you see?"

Father Joaquim and Kansuke quickly followed her. Behind them, a gargantuan wall of gray-black clouds was quickly moving toward the coast.

Fifty-nine

July 15, 1626
Pacific Ocean

Commander Ogawa, commanding the fifth of the five red-seal ships, bringing up the rear as the flotilla traveled in single file, was enjoying a moment of calm on the relatively tranquil sea. With five masts, each bearing large, stout sails, the shogun's vessels, including Ogawa's, were surely gaining on the little Buddhist boat attempting to flee them—even in the fairly calm winds.

In addition to their cannons, each of the red-seal ships was armed with many European harquebuses, which would allow the samurai to pummel the Buddhists' boat when they got within about 150 meters. Their round bullets were made of lead and would cut right through the Buddhist ship.

Joined by some of his men, Commander Ogawa declared, "I feel sorry for those pathetic Christians. They do not stand a chance in hell."

"But why send so many of us?" one of the samurai asked. "It's as if we are going to war."

"Because the shogun despises them," Ogawa answered as he leaned against a railing.

"I heard a rumor that the Christians embarrassed the shogun with their fighting skills," another samurai added.

"That is not possible," Ogawa replied, almost laughing at the very idea.

"It is true. I was there," another samurai interjected. "The foreign priest and his female aide killed three of our samurai, including our great Suzuki-san and Daisuke-san. The priest and his aide were very skilled with the sword."

"It was luck," Ogawa huffed. "Only luck could allow them to accomplish such things. But I can guarantee they will not be so lucky at sea."

"It will be a pleasure to shoot holes through them," another samurai declared. "And then we can jump on their crumbling vessel and cut off their heads."

A shout from one of the samurai interrupted their conversation.

"What on earth is that?!" the man hollered.

The captain frowned, appearing confused as he observed a change in the tide.

"Look," the man yelled, panic etched on his face as he pointed. In the distance, a massive black cloud, obscuring the entire horizon, appeared to be fast approaching the flotilla.

A tremendous gust of wind, the leading edge of the storm, slammed the vessel, which began to gyrate on the rough waters.

"Where did that storm come from?" the samurai questioned.

Ogawa began barking out orders. "Lock down everything that can move. And guard the battens! Guard the sails!" Ogawa's hat flew off his head and into the sky as another powerful gust assailed them.

"How can this be?" the second mate shouted above the wind's fury. "How can a storm rise up out of nowhere?"

"I do not know," Ogawa yelled. "Watch that mast. It is bending!"

Another gust smashed into the ship, this one even stronger

than the last, and three unsuspecting samurai were blown off the deck into the water.

The waves spraying over the ship from below were met by torrential rain, both from above and horizontally, driven by the furious winds. As most of the men looked for a place to escape the winds and water, a massive wave rose up and struck the ship hard from the front, causing an enormous surge of water to crash down on the deck. A half dozen more men were swept off the boat.

Before anyone could recover from the last surge, a fourth blast hammered the vessel, breaking off the masts and sending a dozen more men into the raging seas.

"Look!" the second mate yelled.

Ogawa peered through the pounding rain. The black cloud, the force of the storm, hit the fleet ahead of them. A massive wave, unlike anything Ogawa had ever seen, rose from the sea beneath the black cloud and crashed down onto the lead vessel, smashing it into pieces and sending debris in all directions.

Seconds later, the next wave rose up and crashed down on the second ship, splitting it in two; each half quickly sank without trace.

Ogawa ran to the stairway leading below deck, but lost his balance as the vessel shifted under a huge wave. Falling to the level below, he quickly regained his footing and dashed into his office, where he grabbed a pencil and wrote one line on a tag. He seized a carrier pigeon out of a cage and quickly affixed the tag to its leg.

When Ogawa reached the deck again, pigeon in hand, the shogun's other two red-seal ships were nowhere to be seen. The full fury of the storm was now upon his own ship.

"Fly!" Ogawa shouted as he released the carrier pigeon into the air. As he did so, another squall threw him through the air, smashing him into the stern of the vessel and breaking his back. As he lay helpless, watching, a mountainous wave swelled above his ship, seeming to taunt him, before it crashed down, demolishing the last of the five red-seal ships and sending the remaining sailors and samurai to their deaths.

Sixty

July 15, 1626

Accompanied by three pre-adolescent boys, the shogun had been drinking heavily in his private chamber for several hours. As was typical, he had ordered that no adults enter his chamber and that he not be disturbed.

"Who would like to have a bath?" the drunk despot asked as he gulped another shot of sake before stumbling toward the boys.

"I already had a bath today," Eiji answered. "It is not necessary for me."

"Nonsense," the shogun slurred. "Having a bath is one of the best ways to relax."

"I do not know," Saburo, the youngest of the three, answered as he fidgeted.

The shogun walked back to the cabinet, where his sake awaited him. "You need to drink some sake. It will put you in the mood."

"But I do not drink sake, Lord," Saburo replied. "I do not like the taste."

"Nonsense. I started drinking sake at a young age, and you can too."

"But I do not want to, Lord," Saburo pleaded.

"Come, I will show you how to do it." Grabbing Saburo's

hand, Shogun Iemitsu yanked him over to an exotic Chinese cabinet on the opposite side of the room. Atop the cabinet sat a large collection of the finest sake available. He selected a flask, slammed it down on a nearby table, and filled a cup. "Take it," he ordered.

The frightened Saburo slowly lifted the cup.

"Now drink it."

Saburo hesitated and then obeyed, but coughed repeatedly upon finishing.

"There, your first cup of sake. Well done. The shogun is proud of you." Iemitsu turned to look at the other two boys. "Soon we will all be ready for a bath. Come, I command you. Come drink from this bottle."

Reluctantly, the other two boys walked to the shogun's sake cabinet, where he presented them with cups. Next, he lined up all the cups on the table and filled them quickly, spilling sake all over the table.

"Drink up. After this, we will remove our clothes and enjoy our bath."

A knock at the door interrupted the boys' first taste of sake. "What is that?" the intoxicated shogun rumbled.

"It is the door, Lord. Someone is knocking."

"I left orders that we are not to be disturbed!" The shogun stomped to the door and threw it open. Several petrified retainers stood before him.

"Do you wish to die?" the shogun screamed. "I told you not to disturb us!"

"We are sorry, Lord, but we have an urgent message—from a carrier pigeon."

"Who is it from?"

"From the commander of one of your red-seal ships. Here, Lord." The retainer handed the small tag to the shogun.

Hurricane and tsunami, fleet demolished.

The shogun turned to the boys. "Leave my quarters."

280

Within an hour, Shogun Iemitsu had convened his Go-Roju cabinet and a small group of his most senior retainers in one of his castle's meeting rooms.

"I simply do not understand how this priest can be so lucky!" the shogun bellowed, still drunk from his sake binge.

"I am confused by the message," one of the Go-Roju cabinet members commented. "Why would the commander write hurricane *and* tsunami?"

"What do you mean?"

"A hurricane is the result of violent wind, and a tsunami is the result of an earthquake. How could they be hit by both at the same time?"

"And why such a short message?" another asked. "Why only five words?"

"Maybe they did not have time for more."

"In my entire life, I have never heard anything like this," the eldest of the cabinet declared. "A storm of this magnitude would surely destroy our coastline, and Edo as well. And yet we have received no reports of this kind of damage."

"It is most unusual," several others agreed.

"It is *not* unusual," the shogun roared. "It is luck, pure luck! Well, his luck is about to run out. He and his followers will be annihilated!"

"What would you like to do, Lord?"

"This time, we will send *twenty-five* ships after them."

"But, Lord, there are no more red-seal ships left in Edo, and you will have to pay a fortune for the destroyed fleet and lost cargo."

"I do not have to pay anyone anything. I am the shogun of Japan, and this is *my* country! If any daimyo is not happy, let him *dare* come to me with his complaint!"

"We will need to make alternative arrangements, Lord," another cabinet member interjected.

"What do you mean?"

"The Christians have already traveled too far. Even if we manage to procure more vessels, we cannot catch them before they reach Nagasaki."

"How do we even know they are alive?" another member asked. "If our ships were destroyed, how would they have survived?"

"I do not care," the shogun bellowed. "We will assume they are alive and not stop until we have their skulls in a sack." The shogun slowly turned his head, looking at each cabinet member, signaling his demand for agreement. "Does everyone understand?"

"Yes, Lord," the cabinet members and retainers said in unison.

"Good. Now what is our plan?"

"We need to mobilize forces in the south, Lord."

"How do we do that?"

"Send carrier pigeons—"

"Wait," the eldest cabinet member interrupted. "I thought our activities were supposed to be covert. We need to be careful to protect the Tokugawa name. Remember, Lord, you gave the priest your word that his freedom was assured. You also said your word is stronger than metal."

"So what do you suggest?"

"We engage assassins and mercenaries," the elder answered. "Forces that are not official."

"Whom do we hire?" The shogun lifted his head, clearly interested.

"Tanaka-san. He is from the old province of Iga and is the most ruthless of all mercenaries."

"I do not know this man. Who is this Tanaka-san?"

"He is from before your time, Lord. Your grandfather, Ieyasu, was familiar with him," a cabinet member answered.

"He is an invincible assassin, Lord, and his entourage is made up of *shinobi* and other mercenaries," the elder member added. "They are discreet killers, but very expensive."

"Hire them and kill the Christians," the shogun nodded, his volume increasing. "I do not care how much it costs. Just bring me their skulls."

Sixty-one

While the waters had at times been rough, after four days at sea the monks' vessel and its unusual passengers were slowly approaching southern Kyushu and Nagasaki. In order to arrive undetected, Kansuke decided the vessel should not dock near Nagasaki but land in secret, some distance away in the brush.

Despite their time together, or perhaps because of it, the mutual distrust between the Buddhists and Christians continued. Unperturbed by any antagonisms, Father Joaquim was cleaning the wounds around Akihiko's ankles when Kansuke approached him. A short while before, one of the younger and more aggressive Buddhist warrior monks had lashed out at a Christian for eating the last of the food on board. The incident had led to some shouting and shoving, yet before Father Joaquim could intervene, Kansuke had diplomatically ended it.

"Do you have a moment, Father?" Kansuke asked.

"Of course, Kansuke-san. I always have time for you."

"I want to apologize on behalf of my young and impetuous monk."

"It is of no consequence." Father Joaquim looked up from his work on Akihiko's ankles and smiled at his rescuer. "Young men are … well, *young* men. After all, your apprentice was hungry too."

"Thank you for your understanding, Father."

"All is forgiven, Kansuke-san."

"I regret to say that some of my acolytes are quite self-centered." Kansuke sat down beside Father Joaquim and Akihiko. "I think some of them could benefit from a lesson in altruism."

"Indeed, a lesson we could all benefit from."

"I am reminded of a Buddhist idiom on which we meditate. It says, 'The source of all misery in this world lies in thinking of oneself. The source of all happiness lies in thinking of others.'"

"That is a delightful prayer," Father Joaquim replied. "We have similar passages in our Bible, such as 'Love thy neighbour as thyself' and 'Show mercy and compassion every man to his brother.'"

"Inspiring, Father. It appears we are not that different after all."

"Similarities bring us together. Differences set us apart," Master Watanabe added as he joined the conversation. "Do you really imagine there is more than one God?"

"What do you mean, Master Watanabe?" Father Joaquim asked.

"Is there a Christian God and a Buddhist God? No." The old ronin answered his own question, smiling: "There are not many Gods. There is only one God and one Creator— the Creator of us all. One way is not better than another way. They are just different ways."

Before Father Joaquim could respond, the men were distracted by a shout. "Look!" A monk pointed far off into the distance behind them.

"Let us hope it is a cargo vessel," Noburu, one of the villagers, said.

"It is not," Master Watanabe stated bluntly. "Its passengers have hostile intentions."

"How do you know?" Noburu asked.

"I can feel it."

★ ★ ★

As the ship approached, it became clear it was far larger and faster than the little junk, and had significant manpower.

"Look at the size of that craft," a Buddhist monk shouted from the observation deck. "It is enormous!"

"Who is it, Father?" Tonia asked again.

"It is Tanaka-san," Master Watanabe declared, "a very strong warrior from the old days. Now he is a mercenary who kills for money and glory."

"Can he be defeated?" Tonia asked, worry evident in her voice.

"Light always defeats darkness."

"How many are they?"

"I would guess about two hundred shinobi and other mercenaries," Master Watanabe answered.

"But we are only forty unarmed Christians," Noburu fretted. "And many of us are too ill and frail to fight."

"Perhaps they will not catch us." Tonia voiced her hope. "They are still quite far away."

"It is only a matter of time," Master Watanabe answered bluntly.

"Is there no way to avoid them?" Father Joaquim asked, trying to gauge the distance to land relative to the distance from their pursuers.

"Yes, there is a way. We land before they have a chance to take us at sea."

"Then let us land early," Father Joaquim responded decisively.

"But what about when *they* land?" Noburu asked, shaking visibly. "How will we evade them then? How can we defeat a force of two hundred mercenaries?"

"We will help you," Kansuke declared.

"We cannot ask you to risk your lives a second time, Kansuke-san," Father Joaquim replied, placing his hand on the old Buddhist's shoulder. "You have already done more for us than we could have hoped."

"Nonsense. We have not done enough."

"But they are a formidable force. You will be in great danger," Tonia said, tears forming in her eyes.

The old Buddhist smiled at her. "Perhaps, but we will *not* live in fear."

"Are you honestly prepared to die for us?"

"Compassion knows no boundaries, Father."

The Buddhist vessel changed course and approached shore in a thickly forested area. Trailing closely behind were their pursuers, quickly closing the gap.

"Look," a monk shouted. "There are so many of them, and they are heavily armed."

"This is not our fight, Kansuke-san," another monk asserted. "Why are we helping these Christians?"

"Agreed," another monk added. "They are our enemies; we should not help them."

"Do we have to go through this again?" Kansuke appeared to be losing his temper. "Will we be cowards and run away?" The old monk held up his hands, commanding attention. "Listen! Do you want to attain enlightenment? If so, you must abandon the thought of *us-versus-them*. Remember the Buddha's teachings: We are all *One*.'"

"I do not need to help Christians to achieve enlightenment," a young monk declared.

Looking first irritated then empathetic, Kansuke continued: "The aspiration to help others must be cultivated *before* the aspiration for enlightenment. This includes *all* others, not just other Buddhists. Beware! Spiritual pride is self-glorification in its lowest form. It raises a barrier to the light of wisdom and understanding. Let us not think of our way as a better way, just a different way. Remember, compassion is at the heart of our entire path. Compassion is the root of the Buddha's entire teachings. Thus, in the name of Buddha, I command all of you to treat our new companions as the dearest of brothers."

"Yes, Kansuke-san." Some of the monks appeared to have truly understood their master while others still struggled. But before anyone could reply, a thunderous boom jolted them, followed instantaneously by smoke and flying debris from the cannonball that had found its mark in the side of the junk.

Tonia screamed as a sharp piece of wood stabbed her in the stomach.

"Guns," one of the Buddhist monks shouted. "Ready your guns!"

"Prepare for landing," Kansuke hollered.

Manoeuvering their batten sails carefully, several of the warrior monks quickly steered the junk into shore.

Another cannonball slammed into the stern, instantly killing several monks as fire engulfed the rear of the craft.

The monks began firing their harquebuses at the enemy vessel closing on them.

"Retreat to the bow! Man the battens! Prepare for landing," Kansuke shouted.

Sixty-two

July 18, 1626
Outskirts of Nagasaki

Many of the more terrified Christian villagers jumped off the besieged boat and ran for the shore. Others tried to aid their sick and wounded brethren in the exodus from the targeted vessel. As Father Joaquim carried Akihiko from the boat he called out, "Are you sure you wish to fight, Kansuke-san? You can still flee."

"Go," Kansuke shouted back. "Escape to the forest. We will give you cover. Run!"

As Father Joaquim carried Akihiko up the shore, he glanced back just long enough to see a monk standing next to Kansuke fall, no doubt hit by a ball from a harquebus.

★ ★ ★

Volleys of shots pelted the Buddhists' vessel, and two more monks near Kansuke fell dead.

"Gather all the ammunition," the old monk shouted. "Disembark. Hurry!"

The heavily armed monks jumped into the shallow water and ran for shore as two more cannons fired from the enemy craft, obliterating the deck in two massive explosions. Volleys of gunshots continued to fly in, killing several more monks before they reached the forest's edge.

"Form a perimeter and fire as they disembark," Kansuke shouted as the warrior monks quickly re-grouped in the forest, readying their harquebuses.

Tanaka's boat was close to landing, but before the ship made it to shore it sent another round of cannonballs to pound the forest line, destroying trees, setting fires, and killing several more Buddhist monks on the periphery. It was obvious the ship would soon land and unleash a horde of bloodthirsty killers.

But the monks had taken the advantageous high ground, and as soon as the ship landed and Tanaka's mercenaries started to descend the long rope ladders from the huge vessel, Kansuke and his men began firing their harquebuses with great accuracy, killing scores of them. The remaining shinobi on board the ship lent support to their comrades by firing into the forest.

As a huge wave of mercenaries charged the forest, the monks displayed their shooting skills, dropping at least a dozen more of their pursuers.

"Retreat and reload!" Kansuke shouted as the monks ran deeper into the forest. Re-positioning themselves behind tree trunks to be shielded from return fire, the monks fired again.

Black smoke filled the forest as many on both sides succumbed to the barrage of lead balls. But the smoke also provided a cover, allowing the mercenaries to charge unseen. The monks fired their last remaining rounds into the smoke, hoping to kill a few more of their pursuers before they dropped their firearms and charged at the mercenaries with their deadly naginatas. The clash of metal and shrieks of the wounded and dying soon filled the forest.

★ ★ ★

Several miles inland, the Christians had stopped for a brief rest and to make sure they hadn't lost any stragglers. All were accounted for. So why, Noboru asked, did he—and then many others—hear someone approaching?

Father Joaquim set Akihiko on the ground and faced the forest behind them. Withdrawing Master Yamaguchi's sword from a brown canvas sack, he cautiously tracked back in the direction of the sounds. Many of the villagers huddled low as the Jesuit sought to defend them.

But they needed no protection—at least for the moment—as Kansuke emerged from the forest, setting everyone's fears at ease.

"Kansuke-san, thank God it is you. Are you alone?" Father Joaquim asked as he dropped the sword.

"Only a few remain," Kansuke answered as he approached, out of breath and bleeding from his shoulder.

"I am very sorry, Kansuke-san. We are forever indebted to you and your men. How can we possibly repay you?"

"Help a Buddhist one day, Father. That is all I ask."

"Without question, Kansuke-san. Without question."

"It is a pleasure to have your friendship, Father, but now I must return. My remaining brothers have suffered great injuries, and I must attend to them."

"Then why did you come to us, Kansuke-san? You should have stayed with them."

"I wanted to see you one last time and tell you that you are safe to continue your escape."

"You are a great friend, Kansuke-san. We will not forget you."

"We are forever brothers in spirit, Father."

"What about your men and Tanaka and his mercenaries?"

Nearly all dead … on both sides." Kansuke sighed.

"How can we help you, Kansuke-san?"

"Survive. You can help by surviving, Father. Save your village. Let the death of my brothers not be in vain."

"Yes, Kansuke-san. With your help, we will survive."

After embracing Father Joaquim, then Master Watanabe, Kansuke disappeared back into the forest.

★ ★ ★

"What now, Father?" Noburu asked. "Shall we continue?"

"Not yet. First we pray for our fallen Buddhist friends. Gather around, everyone. I will now read from the book of John. After I am done, please close your eyes and thank our fallen Buddhist friends for the great sacrifice they have made for us." He pulled out his little hidden Bible and began to read. "This is my commandment, That ye love one another, as I have loved you. Greater love hath no man than this, that a man lay down his life for his friends."

Sixty-three

July 18, 1626
Outskirts of Nagasaki Prefecture Forestland

About an hour into their march through the forest of massive *sugi* trees and various smaller deciduous trees and brush, Father Joaquim—who was periodically sharing with Master Watanabe the burden of carrying Akihiko—heard a commotion at the back of the procession. Looking behind him, he saw several of the villagers leaning over one who appeared to have collapsed. "What happened?" He yelled to be heard, for the slowest had fallen far behind.

"It is Tonia. She has fallen. Come quick!"

Gently, Father Joaquim laid Akihiko on the ground before running back to Tonia.

"She has lost a great deal of blood, Father," Noburu said, examining her condition.

"Why did someone not tell me about her wound?" Father Joaquim asked, frustrated.

"She kept it to herself," Noburu answered.

"Leave me, Father," Tonia moaned softly. "I cannot go on."

"You can, and you will," Father Joaquim declared as he knelt beside her, delicately brushing her black hair away from her bloodied face.

Kazuo, an old villager who had seen many wounds in his time, inspected Tonia closely.

293

Looking up at Father Joaquim, shaking his head, Kazuo declared, "I do not think she will survive, Father. Her wound is too great, and she continues to lose much blood."

"She will be all right," Father Joaquim insisted, tears stinging his eyes.

"I am sorry, Father," Tonia replied, shivering. "I have lost all my strength. I feel so cold now." Closing her eyes, she drifted into unconsciousness.

Master Watanabe stepped forward. "There is a way, Father."

"A way for what?"

"A way to save her. You could heal her."

The priest's heart skipped a beat, and he frowned. "What do you mean?"

"The healing power of God."

"Our Lord Jesus could heal through miracles, but I am not Him."

"But His power is also in you."

"I wish that were true, but *He* is the Lord; I am only His servant."

Master Watanabe smiled. "Give me your hand."

Quickly, Father Joaquim grabbed the man's hand.

"Now let us both place our hands on her wound. Close your eyes, Father."

Together, Father Joaquim and Master Watanabe closed their eyes as their hands rested gently on Tonia.

"Do you believe God can heal her, Father?"

"Yes, I do."

"Good. Now, I want you to *know* God *will* heal her."

"Yes, Master Watanabe. *I know He will.*"

"Good. Now I want you to *feel* that He has healed her. I want you to genuinely feel all the emotions, *knowing* that God has healed her."

"I feel them," Father Joaquim said fervently.

"Good. Now I want you to thank God for her healing. I

want you to thank God from the bottom of your heart for her healing."

"Yes, Master Watanabe. I am thanking Him now."

"Now, last, I want you to *feel* this thankfulness to God for His healing."

"I feel it!" Father Joaquim replied, tears of joy flowing uninhibited. "I genuinely feel thankful to God for her healing!"

"Now repeat after me. 'In the name of God our Creator, the Source of our Spirit, we pronounce Tonia to be healed, and so it is.'"

"And so it is," Father Joaquim repeated.

★ ★ ★

And so it was, although not as quickly as Father Joaquim might have hoped. As he, Master Watanabe, and the villagers huddled around the young catechist, she slept. Several of the villagers also took advantage of this time to take a much-needed nap. Two hours or so later, Tonia's eyes began to flicker. Father Joaquim, whose gaze had never moved from observing Tonia's face, noticed immediately. He touched his fingers to her cheek. "Tonia," he whispered. "Tonia, are you awake?"

Tonia lifted her hand and rubbed her eyes. Looking intently at Father Joaquim, she pronounced, "I am alive … and I feel …" She placed her other hand on her stomach. "I feel fine."

Looking more closely, she saw that the wound was healed—completely. Miraculously, not a sign of it remained.

Father Joaquim lifted Tonia and embraced her, repeating, "Thank You, Lord. Thank You, Lord."

Master Watanabe placed his hand on the priest's shoulder. "We need to move on now, Father. We are still being hunted."

Sixty-four

July 19, 1626
Outskirts of Nagasaki

After marching all night through the thick mountainous forest, the villagers were slowly, cautiously approaching the edge of Nagasaki.

"Look," Noburu, at the front of the procession, whispered to Akatsuki, pointing to a stream below where three men, appearing to be guards or officials of the regime, sat washing their feet. "Tell Father Joaquim."

★★★

"Did they see you?" Father Joaquim asked.

"No."

"Show me."

Moments later, hiding behind a boxwood shrub with Noburu, Father Joaquim peered down the mountainside, observing the three officials below. "What shall we do, Father? Shall we flee in another direction?"

"No. We will capture them."

"Capture them?" Noburu's wide eyes revealed his shock. "But what if more are down there, out of our sight? Or what if they escape? They could amass an army to pursue us!"

"They will not escape," Father Joaquim answered confidently. "We are meant to capture them. They are part of God's plan."

★★★

Minutes later, Father Joaquim and Tonia carried Akihiko down the mountain, toward the creek, creating much noise and making no effort at stealth. Not surprisingly, when the three villagers reached the spot where the officials had been washing their feet, the area was empty.

"Halt where you are," one of the officials shouted as he and his two companions burst from their cover.

Leaving Akihiko on the ground, Father Joaquim and Tonia fled up the side of the mountain, but not too fast.

"I said, do not move," one of the officials hollered as they ran after the pair of foreigners and hauled them back to the creek side, next to Akihiko, where they threw them to the ground. "You gaijins are under arrest. Wait until the governor sees what we have captured."

"Are you sure we are the ones who have been captured?" the father asked.

"What?" The guards spun around, scanning their surroundings, then spotted a dozen or so ragged-looking peasants running down the side of the creek towards them. They turned to flee in the opposite direction only to see another dozen peasants running towards them from the other side. Then from another direction several more ran towards them, all armed with thick branches, large rocks, and other makeshift weapons.

"Drop your swords," Father Joaquim instructed the guards.

Overwhelmed, the officials surrendered and were seized.

"What shall we do with them?" Noburu asked. "Do we kill them?"

"We will not lower ourselves to their level," Father Joaquim answered. "God creates life; He does not destroy it. *We* will follow the same principles."

"So we take them as prisoners?"

"Did you enjoy being a prisoner, Noburu-san?"

"Of course not."

"Then why would you subject them to captivity?"

"Because they would do it to us." Noburu looked agitated as he answered.

"No." Father Joaquim smiled, hoping to convey patience. "We do not seek to avenge anyone. We seek only our freedom. We give that which we wish to receive."

"What do you mean?" Now Noburu looked puzzled.

"We let them go."

"What? Why did we capture them just to let them go?"

"To deliver a message to the governor and the authorities." Father Joaquim scanned the villagers before speaking loud enough for all to hear, for by this point all were clearly curious. "We will give the authorities what they want—a final confrontation. We will unite all hidden Christians on the island of Kyushu and win back our freedom. I am tired of hiding. Do you not agree?"

"When and where?" Taro, one of the captured guards, asked as he stepped forward.

"In the fields of Arima, at dawn."

"I will deliver your message to the governor. Is that all?"

"Tell him Father Joaquim will unite a colossal force and will meet his army in Arima at dawn—if he has enough courage to come."

★ ★ ★

"Governor! Governor Kawachi!"

"What is all the commotion?" Governor Kawachi

answered. "Now is not a good time. I am meeting with the deputy-lieutenant this morning."

"But it is urgent, Governor," Taro insisted, breathless. "The Christians have challenged us to a war!"

"What?"

"We were captured by a foreign father and his band of Christians."

"You mean you captured them."

"No, Governor, they captured us. They were forty in number, and we were but three."

"How is it possible that forty Christians roam freely?" the governor asked, wide-eyed.

"I do not know, Governor, but I recognized some of them. I have seen them before."

"Where?"

"Here, Governor, in Nagasaki. You declared them guilty and instructed Daimyo Shigemasa to take them to Edo. It was that Father Joaquim, Governor."

"That is impossible."

"No, Governor, it was he; I spoke with him directly."

"How is that possible?" the governor repeated. "How in *hell* could that be possible?"

"Could it be that the priest has escaped a second time?" Deputy Suetsugu asked in shock.

"No one could be that lucky," the governor replied, seething. "How could anyone escape the shogun's grip?"

"It was definitely him, Governor," Taro affirmed. "And he challenges you to war."

"How can forty Christians wage war against the regime? It is ridiculous."

"He says he has amassed a colossal force against us, Governor. He says he has united all hidden Christians on Kyushu."

"Is it possible, Deputy? Could he accomplish such a thing?"

"Yes. If he unites all hidden Christians and ronin together, it is possible. There have always been whispers that a rebellion could arise one day."

"He said Christians are tired of hiding, Governor," Taro added. "He said it is time to re-claim their freedom. And he said he challenges your army to meet him in the fields of Arima at dawn—if you have enough courage to face him."

"If *I* have enough courage? *Me?* He has the audacity to challenge *me?* And question my courage? We will bury this priest."

"What shall we do, Governor?"

"We will employ every force available to us. In the blink of an eye, we will wipe them all from this earth! Call on every samurai and official capable of bearing arms." The governor turned again to his deputy-lieutenant. "Summon Daimyo Shigemasa immediately. This war will take place on his lands. Command Daimyo Shigemasa to bring every samurai he has—no exceptions. Then summon anyone in the regime who can bear arms—but not our prison guards. Those incarcerated must remain so."

"Is that it, Governor?"

"No. Make sure you communicate one thing to all our forces. *I* will be the one to cut off the priest's head in battle. *I* will finally put this dog to death!"

Sixty-five

July 19, 1626
Daimyo Matsukura Shigemasa's Castle, Arima Domain

"Is this a joke?" Shigemasa asked as he read the letter from Governor Kawachi.

"No, Lord, it is not," Taro responded sternly.

"How can this be? I have just returned from delivering this priest to the shogun."

"It is real, Daimyo Shigemasa, and you are ordered to make preparations immediately. Will you comply?"

"Of course I will comply. Like the shogun, I also despise these Christians." Shaking his head, still astonished at the news, Shigemasa added, "I shall mobilize my entire clan immediately. Every samurai under my command will present himself at dawn for battle. The Christians nearly cost me my son. I *will* see all of them dead."

"Good," Taro replied, nodding. "The governor and the deputy-lieutenant will join you on the battlefield."

Taro and the other two officials bowed and departed, leaving Shigemasa surrounded by his most senior retainers and samurai.

"How in hell could the Christian priest escape the shogun? And how could he get back to Nagasaki so quickly?" Shigemasa asked as he paced. "If this Christian army somehow managed to take control of even a part of Arima, the shogun would take *all* my lands."

He nodded his head, as if affirming his own words. "By dawn, I want my entire army on the battlefield, ready to obliterate these Christians once and for all. Tomorrow, this priest's luck finally runs out, and every Christian alongside him will perish!"

Sixty-six

The governor's entire legion had departed Nagasaki, and the city was eerily quiet. But the quiet was suddenly interrupted as men approached the warehouse, making no attempt at stealth. Several of the dozen men assigned to guard the warehouse ran to investigate and found three people attired in the governor's official uniforms.

"What are you still doing in Nagasaki?" Noburu, one of the men dressed as officials, asked the guards. "Do you not know war is about to begin?"

"We are guarding this warehouse, as the governor ordered us to do."

"What are you, cowards? Why are you not presenting yourself for battle in Arima?"

"We told you. The governor instructed us to watch over the warehouse."

"The governor ordered *twelve* men to look after a bunch of crippled women and children? What kind of men are you?"

"What is the purpose of your questioning?" asked the lead guard, tension visible in his face.

"The governor has ordered *us* to inspect the city for cowards who hide from battle. Where do you think the governor needs you most?" Noburu pressed. "On the battlefield facing the enemy or standing in front of a locked warehouse full of harmless women? Which action carries greater honor?"

"To fight in battle," one of the younger guards answered sheepishly.

"We cannot all go," one guard replied. "Some of us have to remain to watch the warehouse. Three of us will stay. The rest will go to battle."

"Good," Noburu answered. "The governor needs every man available."

"It must have been miscommunication regarding our numbers," the lead guard suggested. "We are not cowards."

"Show it with your actions. Show it on the battlefield." Noburu smiled triumphantly as he and the two other villagers turned and walked away.

***

"Halt," the senior of the three remaining guards yelled at the lone figure that had suddenly approached them. "Move and we will kill you."

"I have come to offer you a chance to live," Father Joaquim stated calmly.

"What?" the senior guard asked. "Wait. I know you. You are the gaijin priest who leads the rebellion."

"I repeat, I have come to offer you a chance to live."

"You offer the *three of us* a chance to live? *You* should be worried about *your life*, Priest."

"Do you see those men out there?" Father Joaquim asked. "They are the fathers and brothers of the women and children in that warehouse." In the dark, only faint outlines could be seen, enough to reveal many men, but not enough to reveal their emaciated conditions.

"They are Christians, outlawed by the regime," the senior guard declared. "They all deserve death and torture."

Ignoring the guard's rant, Father Joaquim continued. "The Lord has mercy for those who repent—and so do I."

"You were unwise to come here alone," the senior guard said as he withdrew his sword.

"Apologize and ask the Lord for forgiveness and you may live," Father Joaquim offered. "Do it not and your fate rests with the fathers and brothers on the hill."

"I am going to cut your head off, Priest."

Deftly, Father Joaquim produced a sword from behind his back. "Will you comply? Will you apologize and ask the Lord for forgiveness?"

"Die!" the senior guard shouted as he charged at Father Joaquim.

The Jesuit easily blocked the attack with his sword and sliced off the guard's head in one smooth blow. Stunned by the father's sword skills and the death of their senior guard, the two junior guards stepped back and froze, staring at the senior guard's lifeless head.

"I will extend our offer of mercy one more time. Do you apologize for your crimes against these innocent families and ask the Lord for forgiveness?"

"Yes, yes, we apologize!"

"Be on your way, young men, and may the Lord have mercy on your souls."

The junior guards dashed past the warehouse gates and ran down the street before the arrival of the village men.

★★★

"Hold on! We will get you out."

The lock was smashed open and the gate swung wide. After many hugs, the women and children were quickly ushered out of the dark confines of the warehouse. Father Joaquim counted the villagers and was pleased to know that not a soul was missing.

Smiling at the sight of baby Peter, whom he had baptized two months before, Father Joaquim gave thanks to God. "Before we depart, let us all thank our loving God. This joyous moment would not be possible without His divine intervention. Let me now read from our Bible before we thank God for this day, the day of our reunion with our loved ones against what appeared to be impossible odds."

For a moment, all closed their eyes and prayed in silence, giving thanks, before Father Joaquim spoke: "Let our joy here today also be heard far off and serve as inspiration to all Christians here in Japan and abroad."

"Amen," the crowd responded.

"Come, let us rise and go forward. The governor will soon learn of our escape. We are not yet out of the dark."

Sixty-seven

July 20, 1626
Fields of Arima

As morning light illumined a large plain in Arima, Governor Kawachi, Deputy-Lieutenant Suetsugu, and Daimyo Shigemasa happily surveyed their legions of samurai and other warriors in well-defined units, nearly 5,000 men in total. While Governor Kawachi was the symbolic authority figure and representative of the shogun's regime, Shigemasa was the most experienced in battle, so he would lead the forces in crushing the Christians and their ronin allies. The daimyo had dispersed his army evenly across the long field in twenty detachments of roughly 250 each. This was his battle plan.

First, the seven heavy cannons and five massive catapults wheeled in would unleash devastating carnage on the assembled Christians, no doubt sending them into panic. Then, on the front line of each detachment, stood *ashigaru* troops bearing harquebus-style rifles. Ashigaru were foot soldiers, whom the samurai class considered their social inferiors. Social class notwithstanding, the ashigaru were highly effective combatants, and their importance in the daimyo's battle plans could not be overstated.

Next, slightly behind the ashigaru troops, stood their

307

loaders who would prepare and load the next rounds of bullets into spare harquebuses as rounds were fired. The daimyo had also assembled a specialized class of expert bowmen who would fire on the enemy with unpredictable trajectories.

Following a devastating volley of lead and arrows, spearmen would advance to pierce through the Christians.

Yet, despite the overwhelming power of the daimyo's opening offensive, the real strength of his army was in his thousands of ruthless samurai forces, who would obliterate any remaining Christians with their razor-sharp swords in close hand-to-hand combat.

After his victory, Shigemasa pondered, would the shogun reward him with even more lands? The only other unanswered question was when the Christians would arrive. He had sent out multiple spies, but had not yet received word of the enemies' approach.

"Look," the deputy-lieutenant shouted at that very moment, as he pointed. "The spies."

A few minutes later, the informants arrived. "Have you spotted them?" Shigemasa asked.

"We have seen nothing, Lord. We inspected all the surrounding meadows and valleys," the spy replied and shrugged. "Nothing. No sign of them."

"They must be having difficulty coordinating their pathetic rebellion," the governor suggested.

"Perhaps it was a hoax," one of the spies stated.

"It is not a hoax," the governor replied. "The priest had gathered men and captured our guards."

"A Christian rebellion is overdue," Suetsugu added. "There have long been whispers of an uprising."

"Then where are they?" the daimyo growled.

The governor shook his head and huffed. "The stupid priest knows nothing of war preparation. He is probably overwhelmed."

"So what do we do, Lord?" one of the spies asked.

"Keep looking," Shigemasa replied as he spat on the ground from his elevated position in the saddle.

★ ★ ★

"What were you doing up there?" Tonia asked as Father Joaquim came down from an hour alone on the mountain.

"I was praying. Difficult decisions always require quiet contemplative prayer."

"And what have you decided?"

"We head to the mountains."

"I thought we were going to the fields of Arima?"

"No, I think the Holy Spirit is telling me we should head to the mountains."

"Are you sure, Father?" Noboru asked. "Many of our wounded are unable to climb and we could get trapped in the mountains."

"If your intuition tells you this, Father, you should follow it," Master Watanabe interjected. "This is how the Creator speaks to you—with that still, small voice."

"Will we hide in the mountains?" young Shiro asked.

"I do not know Shiro-kun," Father Joaquim answered softly. "I do not have all the answers yet."

"How will we escape, Father?" little Haruko asked.

"The Lord will show us the way, Haruko-chan. We need only to trust Him."

"Are you certain, Father?" Noboru asked. "The governor and deputy-lieutenant are very evil and strong in number."

Father Joaquim stopped and turned to face the villagers and former prisoners before opening his Bible. "Listen to this. Take it to heart." He began reading. "Have not I commanded thee? Be strong and of a good courage; be not afraid, neither be thou dismayed: for the Lord thy God is with thee whithersoever

309

thou goest." He closed the book. "That message God gave Joshua is for us as well."

"Yes, Father," Haruko answered. "I will try to be courageous."

"You need not try Haruko-chan." Father Joaquim smiled at her. "You already *are* very cour—."

Before he could complete the word, a woman near the father shrieked and grabbed her shoulder where an arrow had pierced it. Another arrow struck a tree beside Father Joaquim's head. "Protect the children," the father shouted. "Get them on the ground! Who has the rifles we seized from the guards?"

Having spotted the two horse-mounted samurai who had fired the arrows, three villagers fired the confiscated rifles, striking one of the riders. Quickly, the other samurai rode away, with the injured rider's horse following.

★ ★ ★

Back on the battlefield, two guards ran frantically past the daimyo's army, toward the official flag bearers, where they knew they would find the authorities. Moments later, the two officials arrived, nearly breathless.

"Why are you not watching my warehouse?" Suetsugu shouted.

"The Christian women and children …" The guard had to stop and catch his breath again. "… have escaped."

"What?" the governor shouted. "What happened?"

"We were ambushed by the priest and his companions, Governor."

"How is that possible?" the governor roared. "I instructed a dozen guards to stand watch!"

"All but three of us left the warehouse to join you in the fight, so when the Christians arrived, they outnumbered us, Governor. And the priest cut off the head of our senior guard."

"So it *was* a hoax," Shigemasa thundered. "We have been duped. This whole war challenge was meant as a diversion so the priest could carry out his rescue."

"Look," Suetsugu said as he pointed across the field. "More spies coming."

"Lord Shigemasa," the spy said, "we spotted the enemy on the edge of Nagasaki prefecture."

"Are they coming here?"

"No, Lord. Their direction is toward the mountains."

"How many men are they?"

"I do not know, Governor. Their force was hidden by the leaves."

"What happened to this samurai?" Shigemasa asked, nodding toward the obviously dead man hanging across his horse.

"They shot him."

"So they have weapons." Shigemasa said contemplatively, anticipating the final encounter.

"What do we do?" Suetsugu asked.

"We send our army into the mountains and finish this."

"Our entire army?"

"Yes. This ends today. It is time to kill this troublesome priest—and every last Christian with him."

Sixty-eight

July 20, 1626
Nagasaki Prefecture Mountains

Shigemasa had divided his forces into two units. The first unit, smaller and all on horseback, had by mid-day arrived at the location where the spies had spotted the fleeing Christians. The second unit was made up of all the samurai and ground troops, as well as those responsible for transporting the heavy cannons and catapults via oxen. But even the larger unit was moving fairly quickly.

"There they are," the spy leading the first unit shouted from atop a hill. Pausing, the horsemen scanned the Christians as they made slow progress across the narrow valley.

"Where are the rest of them?" one of the horseman asked. "I count fewer than fifty."

"That is it?" another said. "Maybe we should just take them."

"No. The daimyo specifically ordered that we only track, spot them, and report their location back to him immediately."

"Why stop there?"

"They could be a decoy, meant to lure us into a trap. We will not disobey the daimyo's orders."

★ ★ ★

"Look," Noburu said, pointing. "Samurai. We are moving too slowly. They are going to catch us."

"He is right, Father," Master Watanabe agreed. "We are moving too slowly."

"I know," Father Joaquim replied, carrying Akihiko on his shoulders. "But what can we do?"

"Leave me," Akihiko answered. "Leave me behind and save yourselves."

"We will *not* leave you." Father Joaquim shook his head, determined.

"I can take Akihiko-san," Master Watanabe offered. "I know of a small cave nearby. It has just enough space for the two of us to hide."

"I do not know, Master Watanabe." Father Joaquim was hesitant. "You have given us so much help on this journey. We need your help."

"No, you do not need me. Remember, Father, I am only a guide."

"But I cannot perform miracles like you do."

"Do you remember us healing Tonia together?"

The father nodded.

"I have a confession to make. I did nothing. I relied completely on the power of *your* prayer to heal her." Master Watanabe shrugged and grinned.

"What do you mean?"

"I merely guided and observed you, Father. It was *your* faith that healed her. You do not need me. The same Spirit that lives in Jesus also lives in you. You have the same powers." Master Watanabe paused. "Do you still have your Bible, Father?"

"Yes, of course."

"Read Mark 11:22–24."

Quickly, Father Joaquim pulled out his little Bible again and started to read. "'And Jesus answering saith unto them, Have faith in God. For verily I say unto you, That whosoever

313

shall say unto this mountain, Be thou removed, and be thou cast into the sea; and shall not doubt in his heart, but shall believe that those things which he saith shall come to pass; he shall have whatsoever he saith. Therefore I say unto you, What things soever ye desire, when ye pray, believe that ye receive them, and ye shall have them.'"

"The passage is clear, Father. Believe and *know* that you can move mountains, and you will."

"How do you know the Bible so well?" Father Joaquim asked, mystified.

Master Watanabe smiled, a special twinkle evident, but he did not answer. "It is time for you to bring these words to life."

"What do you mean?"

"The *living Word*."

"But surely there must be limits."

"The Creator has no limits. Praying for a grain of rice is the same as praying for the removal of a mountain."

"But one is tiny and the other is massive."

"Only to you, Father. To the Creator, it is all the same."

"I will reflect on this, Master Watanabe."

For a brief moment, there was silence as Father Joaquim and Master Watanabe acknowledged it was time to go their separate ways.

"Thank you, my friend, for everything you have done for us."

"You are most welcome, Father. I wish you well in the remainder of your journey."

"Thank you, Master Watanabe," Tonia added, her eyes brimming with tears. "We will miss you dearly."

All the refugees bowed to honor him. Then Master Watanabe picked up Akihiko, placed him over his shoulders, and walked away.

"We will meet again," Master Watanabe promised as he walked. "Now go, and remember the Creator walks with you."

Sixty-nine

With Akihiko and Master Watanabe hiding in the cave, the villagers were able to move more quickly. But their faster pace only served to bring them to a spot recognizable to many of them.

"I know these mountains." Noburu grew panicked as he studied the area. "There is no exit along this path. We have trapped ourselves."

"Should we go back, Father?" Tonia asked, wide-eyed.

"No." Father Joaquim shook his head then spoke resolutely. "We will *not* go back."

"Why not?" Noburu challenged the Jesuit. "The mountains are too steep ahead. We cannot get through."

"Because the Lord is telling me we must move forward."

"How do you know that?"

"Because my intuition is telling me so."

"If you are wrong, we will *all* die," Noburu declared, waving his hand toward the women and children.

Hisashi, an old villager, added to the fear: "Noburu is right. It is impossible. I know these mountains too."

"It is impossible," a growing crowd of dissenters cried out.

"*Nothing* is impossible for the Lord," Father Joaquim

315

roared, his uncharacteristic loudness quieting the crowd. Once they were all silent, the father jumped onto a rock in order to address them.

"Long ago a large group of God's people were captive to harsh, cruel overlords. Through many powerful miracles, God convinced those overlords to release His people. But soon the overlords and their armies chased after the fleeing people. Then the people came to the sea. They had nowhere to go. If they turned back they would encounter their pursuers. If they went forward they would drown. They protested to their leader, saying, 'Did you lead us into the wilderness just to die?' Does that sound familiar?"

"Yes, yes," Noburu answered. "It is the story of the children of Israel fleeing Egypt. But that is not the same as our problem."

"And how is it different?" Father Joaquim asked.

"*You* are not Moses." Noburu turned and looked at his fellow villagers, nodding his head, soliciting their agreement.

Father Joaquim spoke loudly again, so that all could hear. "You are correct, Noburu. I am not Moses. I am not fit to lace up Moses' sandals. But the same Spirit who spoke to Moses speaks to me. And He will speak to you, too, if you will truly listen."

"But how do we know for sure?" Noburu asked.

"Let me tell you another story, also from long ago." Father Joaquim saw he had all the villagers' attention. "A prophet had been bold enough to speak out against the evil king and queen. As a result, the queen swore to have the prophet killed. So this prophet escaped and ran into the wilderness and sat under a tree, waiting for death. When an angel came to him, he told the angel he was the only remaining servant of the one true God. Then the angel told him he was not alone, and to go up on the mountain, much like this mountain. And while he was on the mountain, a great wind passed by, but the Lord was not

316

in the wind. Then came an earthquake and a huge fire. But the Lord was not in the earthquake or the fire. But after the fire came a still, small voice that told the prophet what to do. He obeyed the still, small voice, and everything happened just as the still, small voice had told him. Do you know this story?"

Some villagers looked puzzled. Finally Tonia spoke up. "It is the story of the prophet Elijah fleeing from evil Queen Jezebel."

"That is right, Tonia. And how did the Lord speak to Elijah when his life was in danger?"

"Through the still, small voice," little Shiro shouted, smiling and clasping his hands excitedly.

Father Joaquim jumped down from the rock and lifted young Shiro in the air. "That is correct, Shiro-kun. And the still, small voice—my intuition—told me we must go on, just as it told Moses the Israelites must walk into the sea. God parted the sea for them. He will also make a way for us."

"Are you certain, Father?" Noburu asked.

"Nothing can ever be known for sure, Noburu. That is why faith is needed, so that you may trust the Lord."

"But are you sure this time, Father?" Hisashi looked for assurance. "In these mountains, there is no room for error. If your intuition is wrong, we will all be slaughtered."

"Going ahead, even though it does not make sense, shows we fully trust in God. Remember, where man is weak, God is strong. We were never meant to be alone and do everything on our own. Remember, man's extremity is God's greatest opportunity."

"Yes, Father," more villagers answered, as their morale started to build.

"Let us not fear. Nothing in this world can harm us with God to protect us and provide for us, if we ask Him." Father Joaquim opened his Bible. "I will now read from our good book. 'Yea, though I walk through the valley of the shadow of death, I will fear no evil: for thou art with me; thy rod and thy staff they comfort me.'"

Closing his Bible gently, Father Joaquim paused a moment. "Now close your eyes and let us all pray for the grace to trust God more fully."

★ ★ ★

Anxiously, but faithfully, the exhausted little band of Christians carried on toward the mountainous cul-de-sac. Before them was a small abandoned silver mine at the base of the mountain, but it was shallow and closed, deserted many years before. But, as Noburu and Hisashi had warned, beyond the silver mine the mountains were far too steep to climb. They were, as predicted, trapped at the bottom.

"Why are they not attacking?" Noburu asked as he pointed to the leading force of mounted pursuers.

"They are waiting," Father Joaquim answered straightforwardly.

"Waiting for what?"

"For their leaders."

"But why not charge? They have us cornered."

"The authorities want to execute us personally. They hope to gain political favor by it."

Noburu fidgeted anxiously. "What do we do?"

"We pray, and wait."

"Wait for what?"

"Their arrival."

"And then what?"

"Then it is up to God." Father Joaquim sat down on a large rock and everyone gathered around. "Our lives are in His hands now."

Seventy

Less than an hour later, Shigemasa, the governor, and the deputy-lieutenant arrived at the cul-de-sac, dismounted from their horses, and laughed as they approached the shabby little band of Christians huddled together at the bottom of the mountain.

"Stay here," Father Joaquim instructed as he briskly approached the three officials.

"So, we have finally caught the infamous Father Joaquim," Shigemasa gloated as they stood no more than a few feet apart. "You have caused us much trouble, filthy priest. You were fortunate to escape twice, but your luck has finally run out." Shigemasa looked at the governor and deputy-lieutenant and chuckled. "I think his head will look good hanging in the shogun's castle, do you not agree?"

"Where is your Christian army, Priest?" the governor asked. "Your message suggested thousands of hidden Christians."

"They are with us now," Father Joaquim answered.

"That pathetic group?" Shigemasa laughed again as he pointed at those behind the priest.

"Our greatest force is not visible to your eyes," Father Joaquim answered.

"What do you mean?" The governor looked perplexed.

"God. God is with us in these mountains."

"Your God does not exist," the governor answered. "And each of you will learn this today when you are beheaded."

"'For the Lord knoweth the way of the righteous: but the way of the ungodly shall perish,'" Father Joaquim stated.

"What?"

"It is from the Bible."

"You are a fool for believing in that," the deputy-lieutenant mocked. "The shogun is God in Japan."

"Have your men drop their swords and ask the Lord for forgiveness or I will pick up mine," Father Joaquim calmly warned them.

"Grab your sword, Priest," the daimyo shouted. "It is time to end this."

Father Joaquim turned and calmly walked back to his group at the base of the mountain.

"Now what?" Noburu asked.

"Now we thank God for protecting us."

"That is it?"

"No. Also have enough faith in Him to believe in a miracle. Now let us read from the book of Matthew." The father again opened his Bible. "'And Jesus said: 'If ye have faith as a grain of mustard seed, ye shall say unto this mountain, Remove hence to yonder place; and it shall remove; and nothing shall be impossible unto you.' Now let us hold hands, close our eyes, and have faith in the Lord."

Seconds later, Father Joaquim withdrew Master Yamaguchi's sword from a sack. Wielding it firmly, he walked into the middle of the cul-de-sac, alone, and stared at Shigemasa's army.

"What is that fool doing?" asked Shigemasa, who had smugly remounted his horse next to the governor and deputy-lieutenant. "Does he honestly think he has a chance against us?!"

Together, Shigemasa, the governor, and the deputy-lieutenant, laughed heartily at the Jesuit. Meanwhile, behind them, thousands of samurai were awestruck by the courage of the priest, who dared to challenge them alone with his sword in hand.

"Look unto me, and be ye saved," Father Joaquim shouted. "All the ends of the earth: for I am God, and there is none else!" Then, in one large masterful stroke, he raised Master Yamaguchi's sword high above his head and drove it into the rock beneath him.

Instantly, the ground shook and the trees swayed as men and horses clenched muscles, attempting to steady themselves against the suddenly shaking earth.

Leaving his sword firmly in the rock, Father Joaquim quickly walked back to the base of the mountain. "Into the silver mine," he shouted as he approached his people. "Get into the silver mine, quickly!"

Looking back as the earth continued to shift, this time even more powerfully, Father Joaquim saw Shigemasa's samurai stumbling and some falling to the ground.

"Get him," Shigemasa shouted. But as the samurai struggled to run across the shaking earth, the enormous vibrations intensified. Cracks formed below, and rocks and boulders crashed down from the mountain above.

And while the brave samurai struggled to cross the battlefield as ordered, their leaders fled on horseback, terrified, just before the worst of the divine avalanche buried the charging warriors below, crushing them all.

Seventy-one

July 20, 1626
Silver Mine, Tara Mountains

"Is everyone okay?" Father Joaquim called out. "Come now, everyone, please respond. Check your family members. Check your neighbors."

Gradually, chatter and commotion broke the silence in the dust-filled chamber, and after a few minutes, Hisashi called out, "We are all here. Everyone is accounted for."

"What was that horrible shaking, Father?" Haruko asked.

"God's answer to our prayers Haruko-chan."

"What a force," Shinobu exclaimed. "In all my many years, I have never felt such a powerful earthquake."

"But what do we do now, Father?" Tonia asked.

"Find a way out."

"It is not going to work, Father," Noburu declared. "The entrance is completely sealed shut. There is nothing but rock and earth."

"When the dust settles, we *will* find a way out. The Lord would not have led us into this mine to die. God has a plan for us. He has had a plan for us all along."

"But how do you know we are not meant to be buried in this mine?"

"Noburu, Christianity is meant to survive in Japan, and we are part of His plan."

"Father?"

"Yes, Tonia."

"I think I see something." Tonia carefully crawled toward a back wall. "I think I see a speck of light."

"That is impossible," Noburu remarked. "This mine has been closed for years, and the back leads into the core of the mountain."

"Check it, Tonia," Father Joaquim said. "But be careful."

Slowly, Tonia made her way through the narrow, debris-filled tunnel towards the back of the cavernous chamber. "It is light," Tonia shouted. "It is a small hole, but it is definitely light."

"Well, let us get started," Father Joaquim called out. "Let us follow the light."

With nearly forty people digging, it wasn't long before the rocks and debris were cleared away.

"Look!" Tonia pointed. "It looks like a tunnel."

"But how can that be?" Noburu spoke again. "That wall leads straight into the heart of the mountain."

"Anything is possible for the Lord," Father Joaquim answered resolutely.

"But how could He do all of this?"

"Leave the *how* to the Lord," Father Joaquim replied as he yanked away another large rock. "We need only pray, have faith, and thank the Lord. Come, everyone, let us move towards the light. In the light, we will find our freedom."

While the tunnel was uneven and imperfect, and took many hours to unearth, it nevertheless afforded an opportunity to reach the other side of the mountain, where everyone escaped the confines of the mine.

"We did it," Tonia exclaimed, jumping up and down excitedly. "This is incredible. We did it!"

"Every good gift and every perfect gift is from above, and cometh down from the Father of lights," Father Joaquim recited.

Tonia hugged Father Joaquim appreciatively and wept with joy as she was overwhelmed by emotions. As they hugged, however, a number of the most mangled women approached them.

"Father, we must confess a weight on our hearts," one of the women declared with tears in her eyes.

"What is it, dear?"

"Under the duress of torture, several of us recanted and apostatized in the deputy's warehouse."

"Have no cares, nor burdens," Father Joaquim replied. "The Lord knows your heart."

"What shall we do, Father?"

"Revoke your apostasy, and it shall be no more."

Quickly, a number of other women and children gathered around. "By the will of our hearts, we revoke our apostasy."

"And so it is," Father Joaquim exclaimed. "And let us not forget that *all* of this is possible because of God Almighty."

"Amen," the crowd praised.

"Now let us hear one more passage from our holy book before we close our eyes and thank the Lord for all we have received. John 15:16 says, 'Ye have not chosen me, but I have chosen you, and ordained you, that ye should go and bring forth fruit, and that your fruit should remain: that whatsoever ye shall ask of the Father in my name, He may give it you.'"

Seventy-two

July 23, 1626
Shogun's Castle, Edo

With a large crowd on hand to applaud his every move, Shogun Iemitsu practiced his archery skills in the large courtyard of his castle. His practice had paid off. He had indeed become quite skillful, and each time he hit the bull's-eye, the crowd responded with applause and cheers. And each time, in response, he raised his arms in triumph.

Amid one such display a senior retainer approached him. "Lord Shogun, you have a message from Nagasaki. It has just arrived via carrier pigeon."

"Give it to me." Snatching the note, the shogun quickly began to read, his temper rising until it turned into an uncontrollable fury. Crumpling the paper in anger, he threw it on the ground before grabbing his bow, which he then used to smash all the glassware atop a nearby table. Turning one way and another, looking for objects to help him vent his fury, he grabbed a handful of arrows and smashed them over his knee. He grabbed more arrows and was about to break them as well, but stopped and gazed around the courtyard, full of his samurai and scores of servants, each of whom sensed their vulnerability. Hell would be paid ...

Epilogue

July 24, 1626
Shimabara Village, Kyushu

As dawn broke, a lone peasant crossed a rice field toward a small village in Shimabara, on the island of Kyushu. In the center of the village, the peasants were preparing to have their only paltry meal of the day. As the stranger approached, a number of peasants arose to receive him.

"How may we be of assistance?" the village leader asked.

"I come to carry news to all the villages in Shimabara and Amakusa," the traveler answered.

"We are listening."

"I carry news of a Christian father who evaded the forces of the regime. Empowered by God, he has overcome the shogun, the governor, and the daimyo in one stroke. It is good news for all hidden Christians."

"But we are not Christian," the village leader replied, his voice shaking.

"I also come to recite a poem of Divine revelation," the visitor declared.

"Recite your poem," the village leader said.

"When five years shall have passed five times,
All the dead trees shall bloom;
Crimson clouds shall shine brightly in the Western sky,

And a boy of divine power shall make his appearance;
These things shall usher in a Christian revival in Japan."

"*Tachi-Aguru*," the village leader replied.

"*Tachi-Aguru* indeed," the messenger responded. "It is time for all Christians in Japan to rise up!"

IA

Laicheu

Tausem

XAN
TON.

COREA INSVLA.

Luicheu

NANQV:
IN.

Cory

Punta dos Ladrones

Ara
fod
Sich
Hivan

Nagato

Suchm.

Mechoza

Suouan

Chandequo
Sium

Anchee
Olepeyo

Nonpo
Liampo
Varella

Tiuncheu
Chapsi

Cumber
Timbaeun

Pancheo
Hiancheu

Crexma

Firando

P. Bon

Ogoto

Meacuun

S. Clara

Ilhas dos
ladrones

Dico

Hiuro

Cusa

Nagu
youm

BVEN

Fugen

Cheouge

B
G
Che

Fir
Cangu

Osu

Sacuma

Isla do
Fogo

Cumbo

Leques
grande

OCCIDENS.

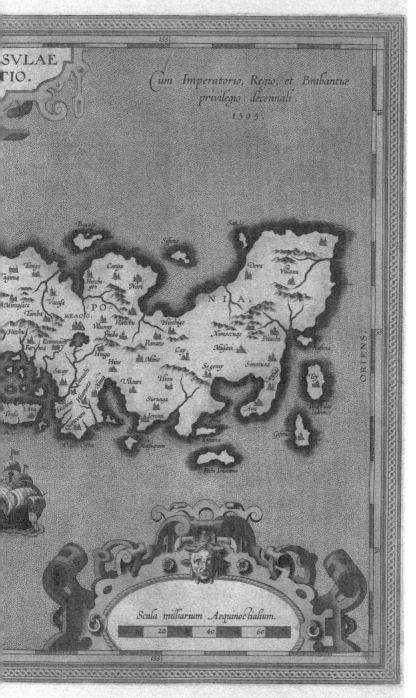

SVLAE
TIO.

Cum Imperatorio, Regio, et Brabantiæ
privilegio decennali.
1595.

Bacasa

Sifime

Sandc

Tango
Tagima

Canga

Deva
Villoxa

Hiechi
gen

Novi

N I A.

Mimajaca
Tamba

Vacasa

MEACO.

PO

Hitchu

Ecunoca

Viuomy
Finda

Hietchu

Hiechigo

Faraina

Hinga

Rinano

Cay

Nimocuqe
Musaxi

Pitachi

Nasinia

Sacay

Hixe

Mino

Segensy

Simotusa

Toy

Quicksise

Vlloari

Hiun

Tonsa

A.

Hizanu
Quincocura

Surunga
Iorumi

Axia

Gesima

Illa das
ladrones

Calda Costa

Sesto Ionecama

Scala milliarium Aequinoctialium.

10   20   40   60   70

107

The Author

For further information regarding S D L Curry,
visit his website at www.sdlcurry.com
or Facebook @TheHiddenTrilogy

The author also appreciates reviews and encourages readers
to share their thoughts on his website, Facebook page
or their favourite online bookstore.

If you enjoyed this book why not
browse our recent fiction titles at

www.bookguild.co.uk